Reinventing Herself

By

DJ Martin

Reinventing Herself
Copyright © 2021 by DJ Martin
Cover Art by Fiona Jayde Media

This is a work of fiction. Names, characters, places and incidents either are the product of the author's imagination or are used fictitiously, and any resemblance to actual persons, living or dead, events or locales is entirely coincidental.

ISBN: 978-1-7327027-5-2 (sc)
978-1-7327027-4-5 (e)

Published by The Herby Lady, LLC

The right of DJ Martin to be identified as author of this Work has been asserted by her in accordance with sections 77 and 78 of the Copyright, Designs and Patents Act 1988.

Without limiting the rights under copyright reserved above, no part of this publication may be reproduced, stored in or introduced into a retrieval system, or transmitted in any form, or by any means (electronic, mechanical, photocopying, recording, or otherwise), without the prior written permission of both the copyright owner and the above publisher of this book.

Some people talk to animals. Not many listen, though. That's the problem. ~A. A. Milne

"Now what do I do?" I braced my elbows on the kitchen table and held my head in my hands.

My daughter, Samantha, refilled my wine glass. "What do you *want* to do? Finish your degree? Learn something completely new? Get a job? Your choices are wide open."

"I don't know, and that's the problem," I whined.

My husband of thirty years, Thomas, had died – at his desk – of a massive heart attack two weeks previous. While I mourned Thomas, I was glad the funeral was over, the out-of-town guests had left, and the condolence calls were slowing down. We'd just returned home from the lawyer's office where he had me sign all sorts of papers to start the probate process. It wouldn't be *that* complicated, I was told, because Thomas had had the foresight to put all our assets in both our names; and the business partnership agreement ensured his share went equally to his two partners without me having to do anything. But because he had more than the clothes on his back, the courts had to be involved.

"Mom, you don't have to make any decisions right now," my son, Jason, told me, a gentle look in his eyes. "And honestly, I wouldn't even think about the future right now. It's not a good time."

I side-eyed him. "But I can't just sit here and wallow. You know that."

I knew I needed something to do to keep myself busy. For thirty years, I had devoted myself to my children and my husband. As Thomas climbed the corporate ladder then started his own company, I divided my time between being a mother and being a socialite wife. After the kids graduated and left for college, my calendar had changed from PTA meetings, baseball practice and games, and ballet practice and recitals, to charity board meetings and their subsequent fundraisers, tea or coffee with people who could further those charities' aims, and parties hosted either by us or Thomas' work colleagues.

Now? I still had the charity work if I wanted, but there would be no more parties for quite some time. Honestly? I was looking forward to not having to interact with blueblood wives for a *long* time. I grew up solidly middle-class in a small town in northeastern Iowa and was never comfortable around women who seemed to vie for who had the most plastic surgery or Botox injections and who spoke like stereotypical blondes – even if their hair was brunette. Maybe. Only their hairstylists knew the true color of their hair. Of course, I wasn't one to talk. My grays were covered, too.

Later, I watched from the deck as our dog, Cooper, gamboled around the back yard, carefully avoiding the flower beds while keeping an eye on the squirrels who sat on tree branches just out of his reach and chattered at him. Thomas had wanted everything to look perfect all the time, so Coop wore a collar with a small box on it which would shock him if he got close to the electric fence buried at the bed edges. He had learned his lesson early on, but Thomas refused to take the box off, telling me the dog would just dig in the beds if there was nothing to deter him. I thought Coop was smarter than that. On a whim, I called him to me and took the box off. He went back to watching the squirrels and never went near the beds.

I had designed our yard but had not been allowed to keep it up – not even the rose bed. Oh sure, I went out with a pair of secateurs to deadhead or take cuttings for a floral arrangement in the house, but I never stuck my hands in the soil and ruined my manicure. Thomas didn't want a wife with dirt under her fingernails. It would have made me look common, he said, which would have ruined his carefully cultivated image. This from a man who grew up dirt poor in the mountains of western North Carolina and hadn't been back to see his relatives since graduating high school.

Thomas was no longer around to complain about dirty fingernails, and the gardeners weren't due for another two days, so I left the deck and, with Coop's supervision from a careful distance, started pulling weeds from the flowerbeds. I suppose me working in the dirt was an oddity for him. So was the pile of weeds I made, which he sniffed at before rolling in it. I laughed at his antics, which felt good. Then groaned as my knees complained when I stood. Getting older sucks.

That night, I curled up in bed with Cooper at my side but, as usual since Thomas died, I had a hard time falling asleep. Even with a one-hundred-pound dog next to me, the king-size bed felt entirely too large. It shouldn't have. One of the reasons we had such a huge bed in the first place was Thomas needed his space to sleep. He hadn't been a cuddler. I got up, padded into one of the guest rooms, Cooper following, and fell into a much smaller queen-size bed. It felt better, and I slept.

The next afternoon after saying goodbye to my son, I was in the study, paying the weekly bills. Coop was quietly snoring in his bed in the corner of the room. Sam stuck her head in the door. "Mom, can I talk to you for a minute?"

I nodded as I clicked, "Pay These Bills" on the screen, printed out a copy of the confirmation and closed the bill pay screen. "Of course, honey. What's on your mind?"

She sat on the guest chair, pulling her knees up to her chin. "I didn't want to say anything while Jay was here because I know he worshipped Dad. But as much as I will miss him, I think his death is a *good* thing for you."

I almost choked. "What?"

"Hear me out. For thirty years, you have put Dad and us first, to your own detriment. I know it kills you not to be working in the garden. I can see it in your eyes every time the gardeners are here – you watch them like a hawk. Yet, because he wanted the perfect socialite wife, you haven't gotten your hands dirty in years.

"Even after I moved to New York, you never went back to finish your degree or do anything else *you* wanted to do. You just added more charity stuff and more networking parties. Networking for *Dad*, not you.

"Dad's gone; Jay and I are gone, too. You have a chance to be *you*, whatever you think that might be. Don't let your past be your future. I want you to be *happy*."

"And you think I'm not?" I asked, incredulous. "I don't regret anything I've done. Honest. You and Jay are my pride and joy. Your father's success made all this (I waved to encompass our mansion of a house) and your degrees at private colleges possible. I like the work I've done with the charities – especially the women's shelter."

"I know, Mom, I really do. But, if what you've told me is correct, you had always envisioned either being a gardener or designing them. That's why you were going after a degree in horticulture before meeting Dad and the 'oops' that was Jay. Yet in all that time, you've designed exactly one garden – this one."

She was correct…sort of. I *had* wanted to design gardens and play in the dirt as much as possible. Yet, I'd met Thomas in my sophomore year of college, fallen in love, and Jay's conception pre-dated our marriage by three months. Mother was thankful I fit into my wedding dress with nary a bump in sight. After, I put my plans on hold. Life was all about being a mother to my kids and doing what it took to move Thomas up the ladder. I hadn't minded. At all.

"I'll tell you what I've been thinking about," I started. "While I believe in the charities I've been working with, I really don't want to deal with the other women. Not now, and probably not in the future. I think I'd rather just write them checks.

"Also, now that you two have your own places and I don't have to host endless parties and out-of-town guests for your dad,

I want a smaller house. *Much* smaller. One that doesn't require an army to keep up with it. Would it bother you if I sold your childhood home?"

Sam laughed. "Mom, we didn't move here until I was ten. I remember the house in Smyrna, all four of us sharing a bathroom and having to keep the doors to my bedroom closed if I wanted any privacy. Otherwise, Jay just used it as a shortcut from his bedroom to the kitchen. No, it wouldn't bother me at all. I don't think Jay would have a problem, either. Even if he does, so what? This is *your* life we're talking about."

"Okay, then." I heaved a sigh of relief. "Do you remember the cottage in the mountains we rented for vacation about ten years ago? The one in the woods?" Sam nodded.

"I want to sell this place and move to something like that. Something small enough I can clean it on my own, a few acres of trees so I don't have to interact with neighbors if I don't want to, and enough clear space I can have a garden to play with."

"That sounds *perfect* for you!" Sam's face erupted in a grin. "Then what?"

"I haven't gotten that far," I said sheepishly. "Getting out of this monstrosity was my first thought. It was too big for just your dad and me when we didn't have guests, and now? I feel like everything I do creates an echo."

The following afternoon, my daughter had left to go back to her own life. I sat alone on the deck with my five o'clock glass of wine and looked at the perfection surrounding me. It was *too* perfect. Nature didn't artistically arrange flowers in swirls of color, nor did it like lawns of manicured Bermuda grass sprayed with chemicals so there wasn't a single dandelion to mar the smooth, green carpet.

"I can't wait to leave this place," I said to Coop, who was now my only companion. "I want something that's not *perfect*, just nice. Quiet would be good, too. I'm tired of the sound of cars and golf carts whizzing by, occasionally drowned out by the drone of lawn mowers and electric hedge clippers."

"*A larger place to run and chase squirrels would be nice,*" I heard.

I looked around and saw no one besides me and Coop. Was I going crazy in my solitude? Since when did I start hallucinating on only a half glass of wine?

I looked down at Coop, who was curled up next to my chair. "Did you say something?"

Coop raised his head and looked at me. "*Yes. I said a larger place to run and chase squirrels would be nice.*"

I *was* going crazy. I was hearing my dog speak. "You're *talking* to me?"

"*I could always speak to you. You just weren't listening.*" Same man's baritone-range voice coming from nowhere I could tell, just in my head. I looked at him incredulously.

A sigh echoed in my head. "*Some humans can hear other species. You're one of them.*"

I drained my wine glass in one gulp and went inside for a refill. Coop followed, his nails clicking loudly on the hardwood floor. "I need to take you to get your nails clipped," I muttered.

"*Can you request the female groomer with glasses? She's gentler than the others. She smells good, too.*"

God. This was going to take some getting used to. "Why now?"

"*I don't know the answer to that. I think you should ask your mother. Or that other female in your line. They could probably explain it.*"

I looked down at my dog. "You're telling me Mom and Aunt Beth can hear you?"

My dog bobbed his head up and down in a very human nod. "*We had lovely conversations when they were here after your mate died.*"

I grabbed the phone and dialed Florida.

"El, what a lovely surprise!" Mom said even before "hello." "How are you holding up?"

"I called because I'm going crazy," I said. "I can hear Coop in my head."

"Oh." the chagrin in her voice was almost palpable. "I probably should have told you after the funeral, but it didn't seem the right time."

"Well, it's the right time now. What the hell is happening to me?"

"Sit down. It's a lot to take in. I'd prefer to do this in person and had planned on it at Christmas, but that's now too late."

Pouring myself another glass of wine, I migrated to my favorite chair in front of the fireplace in the family room. Coop curled up on the rug at my feet. "Okay, I'm sat. Tell me!"

She sighed. "All the women in our family can hear other species. Not *all* other species, though. I think that would truly drive us over the edge. But what they call higher orders. Mammals, birds, reptiles, I think, although the geckos around here don't talk to me.

"I'll tell you, the communication on our end only happens when you speak aloud." I sighed with relief. My thoughts couldn't be read. "But you'll hear everything else in your head.

"The ability usually manifests with menopause, but I don't think you're there yet."

"I'm not. Just perimenopausal." I abhorred the hot flushes, the mood swings were horrible, and the fact that my period was no longer regular was irritating.

"I figured as much. But you've had a huge shock with Thomas' early death, which has probably thrown your hormones all out of whack. That's probably what precipitated it."

"So you've been talking to my pets for what? Fifteen years?"

"Or so, yes. Cooper is more forthcoming with what happens in your house than Thumper was."

(Thumper was our previous dog. He was so-named because if you scratched his back in just the right spot, he thumped his rear leg.)

"That's almost disgusting. You're gossiping with *pets* instead of asking me."

She laughed. "Hey, they're more honest than you are at times. You have a tendency to avoid talking about feelings.

"But there's more."

"I can hardly wait." I grimaced into my wine glass.

"Along with the ability to speak to other species also comes the ability to see other species for what they are. Ones you wouldn't notice if you didn't have these gifts."

"What do you mean?"

"All those stories about vampires, were-beings, fairies, dwarves, gnomes, and others? Those species exist, too. But unless you have magic of some kind in your blood, you can't see them as their true selves."

"So you're telling me I'm a witch or something?"

"I don't know if I'd call us that. I can't do spells, neither can Beth, and I doubt you can, either. Although, I guess there's a first time for everything. No, our gift is communication. Knowing whether and where an animal is hurting, things like that.

"And knowing about the other humanoid species and how to deal with them. For example, now that you can see a vampire, you'll know not to let them near your veins or arteries. You know the disease pernicious anemia?"

"Yeah, I've heard of it."

"I don't have any statistics, but I'd be willing to bet maybe half of those cases are due to vampire bites."

"Wouldn't a doctor notice the marks on the neck?"

She laughed. "Of course, the carotid or jugular are nice spots. They're easily accessible. But the femoral artery is preferred, I'm told, because it's easier to hide. Think about it. How many times have you read in a romance novel where the man *nips* her thigh on the way up to…? One swipe of their tongue and the saliva stops the bleeding. She just thinks she cut herself shaving her legs or bikini line."

I blushed crimson with no one but Coop to see. My mother discussing sex was embarrassing.

"So other than gossiping with my dogs and avoiding vampires, what else do you do with this *gift*?"

"Not a lot. If I find an injured animal or one comes to me, I'll help if I can, or tell the wildlife rescue people what's wrong. They think I'm weird but have come to trust what I tell them. By the way, you might want to make a list of those folks near you. I have a feeling once word gets out, you'll have some unexpected visitors."

"What do you mean, *word gets out*?"

"*Once you start acknowledging you can hear other animals, like those irritating squirrels, they'll tell others, who will tell others. Soon, everyone in the area will know you can talk to them, and if they have a problem, they'll come to you,*" Coop told me.

"Once you…" Mom said.

"I know. Coop just told me. I'm not sure I like this *gift*, as you put it."

"Too bad, so sorry," Mom piped in a perfect imitation of Sam. "You can't give it back or get rid of it, so use it."

"I don't suppose there's a book I can read?"

"Not that I'm aware of. Your grandmother told me and Beth what to expect before she died. Not that either of us believed her until it actually happened. Her mother told her, and so on. There's always been at least one female in every generation as far back as I've gone, which is only about six generations. You'll have to keep track of your own experiences so you know what to tell Sam when the time comes."

"Can't I tell her now?"

"And would she believe you? Would you have believed me if, when you were her age, I told you, 'By the way, when you hit menopause your life is going to turn upside down?'"

I thought back to me at twenty-five. Probably not. I was too busy with my family to think about something in the "far future."

But my daughter wasn't a mother yet, and her life revolved around her job and girlfriends, with the occasional male thrown in for good measure. She *might* believe it. Maybe. More likely, maybe not.

"I have a lot to think about," I told Mom. "Can I call you again with questions?"

"Of course, darling girl. I may or may not have answers, but I'll certainly try. I'll let Beth know you've transitioned, too, so if I'm busy, you can call her."

We talked a few more minutes about what was happening in my life (not much) and hers (a lot more), then rang off. Although another glass of wine sounded wonderful, I knew I needed to eat something so went into the kitchen and pulled out the ingredients for shrimp scampi, which was fairly quick to make.

"*May I have a piece of shrimp?*" Coop asked as I put a pot of water on to boil for the linguine and turned the oven on.

"No, bud, sorry. The garlic always gives you gas, and as long as you're sleeping on the bed, I'm not breathing your farts."

"*Then a piece before you put the sauce on it?*" He made big puppy eyes at me.

"I'll cook *two* shrimp separately for you, okay?"

He head-butted my leg, nearly knocking me over. "*You're the best.*"

After I ate, I took another glass of wine out to the deck and pondered my new "gift." Hearing all sorts of animals speak wasn't something I was truly comfortable with. Especially given the number of squirrels and other animals hit by cars in our area.

Then there was the issue of other humanoid species. How would I know what I was looking at? I mean, if fairies were the Tinkerbell type then yeah, I'd know. Did dwarves and gnomes look like they were portrayed in books and movies? Did vampires have permanently-elongated canines? Were were-beings always overly hairy? Inquiring minds wanted to know.

"Have you ever seen another humanoid species?" I asked Coop.

"Yes. The man living in the house with the big tree in the front yard is a were-rat."

I knew exactly which house he was talking about. Our subdivision was only about twenty years old, and there were few trees older than that – they had razed most of a forest in order to build the houses and streets, the clubhouse, the golf course, and other amenities. As a consequence, most of the trees had been planted after construction and were still fairly small.

Coop was talking about Jeff Smalley, a single man in his late thirties who lived five doors down and across the street. He'd moved in about five years earlier. *He* wasn't all that hairy, but his face was narrow, and he had a long nose. He wore his stick-straight hair slicked back from his high forehead, making his nose look even more prominent. It wasn't difficult to imagine whiskers sticking out from that schnozzle.

"Wait," I said. "You don't go out of the yard. How did you meet him?"

"He roams the neighborhood at night in were-form. He came into the yard some time ago while I was out doing my business."

"How do you know which house he lives in?"

"The night I caught him — and yes, I caught him before I got a good whiff of him — I chased him out of our space and saw which house he went to. He's tried coming into our yard again a few times, but each time I barked, you let me out of the house, and I was able to convince him not to come here anymore."

"So what? You're saying he spies on the neighbors?"

"I suppose. Each time I saw him, he was at the base of or on the stairs coming up here. Probably to look through the door."

That was creepy! We weren't the only house in the subdivision with a dog. Some had a cat or two, but many, many more had no pets at all because they required attention, and that interfered with a busy (or wealthy, carefree) lifestyle. But it explained why Jeff was the neighborhood gossip.

"Any others?"

Coop cocked his head just as humans do when they're thinking. *"I don't think so."*

That was a relief! But if Jeff was any indication, I might be able to pick out were-beings based on their appearance.

I had another question for my dog. "Can *you* hear all other species?"

"No. Only my own and those related to me like coyotes, and…what did your mother call it…those with magic in their blood."

"Besides Jeff, my mother, and my aunt, has anyone else spoken with you?"

"Yes. There's a female who comes to your gatherings. She's not very nice. I was told to keep my fur away from her clothing."

"Can you be more specific? A lot of women come to our parties."

Coop cocked his head again. *"She smells like roses and coffee. She is larger than you and has long, light-colored hair."*

Dogs are color-blind, at least according to human standards, so the "light-colored hair" could be anything from light brown to blonde to gray. No one I knew, except Mom and Aunt Beth, had obviously gray hair. But that and "larger than me" still left a long list. I also didn't go around sniffing anyone, so her scent meant nothing, either. I tabled that for another day.

"This is so much to take in," I said. "I have a feeling it's going to be a good long while before I'm comfortable with all of it."

Coop head-butted my leg again. *"I will be here for you and will help identify other beings. My sense of smell is better than yours."*

I patted his head. "I know, bud. But I can't take you *everywhere* I go, so there will be a lot I will have to figure out on my own."

"Places that do not allow dogs should be forbidden. We should be able to go everywhere humans do."

"Not every dog is as well-behaved as you are," I told him. "Not to mention you shed fur. There are humans who wouldn't appreciate finding dog fur in their food in restaurants."

"We can't help that."

"I know, but those are the facts of life."

I finished my wine and even though it was just before nine, thought it was time for bed. Since moving to the bed in the guest room, I had been sleeping more than usual, although I was told that was normal after the loss of a loved one. There was also the problem of night sweats, oftentimes necessitating a change of nightgown and/or linens. Interrupted sleep meant I needed more, either going to bed earlier or sleeping in later.

"I want to go to bed. If you need to, please go relieve yourself before I go in." I had to admit that being able to converse with Coop made things easier. I didn't have to coax him out the door with a "Come on, boy. Time to do your business!" that I now knew he understood. He ran down the stairs to the back of the yard, peed, and bounded back up.

"*I am ready,*" he told me.

We went back inside. I put my wineglass in the dishwasher, fixed a pot of coffee, and set the timer. Wearily, I climbed the stairs, and in minutes, my head hit the pillow. As soon as Coop settled himself next to me, I drifted off.

My dreams were filled with talking dogs, birds, snakes, and spiders who all came to me asking me to heal this wound or that. Vampires with deathly-white skin and fangs stalked me, and in one, I ran from a man on the street in downtown Alpharetta when he turned into the proverbial werewolf before my eyes.

That last had me sitting straight up in bed, wide awake, with my heart pounding a staccato rhythm. Coop only stirred next to me.

The clock told me it was nearly six. I knew after that adrenaline rush I wouldn't get back to sleep so got out of bed. *That* woke Coop.

"*It's still dark. Why are you getting up?*"

"Because I had a bad dream and know I won't sleep again."

Coop got up, too, and waited for me to put on my robe before trotting down the stairs in front of me to the kitchen. I flipped the coffeepot switch from "auto" to "on" and waited impatiently for at least a cup to brew. While I paced in front of the counter, Coop lapped at his water then asked to go out.

"If you can wait a couple more minutes, I'll go out with you," I told him.

Coop whined. "*I can't.*"

So I let him out then returned to my pacing. *Finally,* the pot had enough coffee in it for a cup. I poured one and headed for my favorite chair on the deck. Coop was sniffing the perimeter of the back yard. I watched him with amusement. He did this every morning. As if the scents would change all that much in a day's time. Then I thought, perhaps they might. I knew coyotes roamed our area, and there was the fact that plants were starting their fall sleep. Those probably changed in scent, too. As a human with a severely limited olfactory system, I'd never know.

I drank a couple more cups of coffee, just enjoying the relative peace. When I heard the neighbors' cars drive down the street, I knew the day was starting. *They* had something to do that day. I saw another day ahead of reading or staring at the boob tube. Or napping. The only thing I knew that would break up the monotony was the housekeepers would be arriving in an hour, and for four hours, I'd hear others quietly talking or the sound of a vacuum cleaner.

After my shower, I went into the study and opened my laptop to check email and social networking. My Facebook feed showed socialite acquaintances at various parties, and a couple of high school friends posted pics of their children and grandchildren. Was I really that interested in all that? Not really. I thought about closing that account completely,, but then again, Jay and Sam occasionally posted what they were doing, and it was nice to see it at the time, rather than wait for our weekly call.

It really didn't take long to make the decision I'd mentioned to Sam – I resigned my position on the four charity boards. I just couldn't face the comments about my widowhood ("I know a *lovely* man" was said with alarming frequency) or the catty remarks about others anymore. It was time to do what *I* wanted, whatever that was, without the hen party.

I had always talked to myself, and even my college roommate had asked what I was saying to her a few times when my muttering was louder than I'd thought. Thomas had done the same until I learned to say his name if I was addressing him directly. Having someone actually respond to what I said when thinking out loud took some getting used to. Cooper had stayed very close to me after Thomas' death, was always within earshot, and commented on nearly everything I said out loud. Even when he didn't understand the subject matter. Nine times of ten, I was startled when there was a coherent reply.

I was reviewing meeting minutes prior to my final board meeting and muttered something under my breath, I thought, about the futility of one of their fundraising ideas that would, in my estimation, cost more than it would bring in.

"They should sell dog food," he replied. *"That would bring in a lot of money!"*

Then there was the time I was going through the refrigerator, making up my weekly shopping list. I had a hankering for spinach-and-artichoke dip with tortilla chips, and I announced the ingredients to myself as I wrote them on the list.

"Cheese? Make enough for me, too!"

I jumped, then laughed and scratched his head as I told him, "I'll give you a bit of cheese when I'm making it, but you can't have the finished dip. It has spinach in it, which isn't good for you."

Over time, I began to appreciate being able to hold a conversation with my dog. It made the house seem a little less large.

A little more than a month after meeting with the lawyer, my computer dinged with an incoming email from him. *Finally,* everything, including the house, was in my name alone. He told me he'd be forwarding the legal documents and to watch the mail for them. There would also be new titles for the cars coming from the state. As soon as those arrived, I could sell one of the two cars. Or I could sell both and buy something new. I'd think about that when the time came.

With the name change on all the documents complete, I had something to do! I grabbed my phone and popped a quick text to the kids, telling them I was now officially house-hunting. Both sent a "thumbs-up" in return.

The housekeepers never went out on the deck (except to wash the windows twice a year), and it was a nice day, so I took the laptop, a pen, and paper out there. I found more than a dozen websites listing real estate for sale but started with one. I made a note of the URL so I wouldn't duplicate my efforts.

In order to search, I had to put in criteria. What did I want? First, I knew I wanted hills and trees, just like that cabin we had rented. I didn't want to be *that* far from a major airport so it wouldn't be onerous to visit Mom or the kids. Or maybe even go on a vacation somewhere. I opened a new tab to look at a map of the United States. I didn't want hard winters either, so it looked like I was going to stay in the southeastern US. Parts of the Appalachians in Tennessee, Georgia, and North Carolina were all within reasonable driving distance of the Atlanta airport. Zooming in on that area of the map, I made notes of the county names in each state.

Then, the house itself. At least two acres, I thought. That would give me enough room for a garden with plenty left undisturbed. Did I want two or three bedrooms? Three. One could be a study with a pull-out couch if both kids visited at the same time. I also wanted a ranch – no stairs. There were days my knees hated the stairs in this house, and I knew they'd just get worse over time. I put all that into their search engine, starting with the southeastern counties in Tennessee. *Four hundred* listings came up. This was going to take a while!

I was cross-eyed by the time I finished with that state, writing down the MLS number for ten that looked promising. I'd narrow it all down later. It was lunch time.

My phone pinged with a text from Sam. **Any luck?** she asked.

Too many. I replied. **This will take some time.**

Chin up. You'll find the perfect place, I know!

A sandwich later, I was back at it. Four counties in North Carolina yielded more than five hundred listings. I nixed all but five. Most were in fancy golf communities or other developments that had at least a clubhouse and pool. I already lived in one of those and didn't want the restrictions the homeowners' association piled on.

The sun was going down when I finally decided to call it quits for the day.

The next morning, I pulled up the same website and input my criteria for Georgia. Eight counties yielded nearly a thousand results. It took me all day to whittle my choices down to an even dozen. I spent another two hours getting the street addresses off another website (I wasn't ready to work with a realtor yet) and mapping them out. It looked like it would take me three days to look at the outside of all of them in person. If none looked promising, I'd look at other websites to see if I had missed anything.

"You up for a road trip, bud?" I asked Coop.

"*Car ride? Yes!*" he replied eagerly.

After dinner, I booked two nights in a pet-friendly hotel in western North Carolina that was centrally located to the area I wanted to search. I also packed an overnight bag and threw that in the car, along with food and dishes for Coop. For the first time in what seemed forever, I was excited about the next day and had a difficult time getting to sleep.

I was up with the sun the next day which, at that time of year, wasn't really all that early. After inhaling two cups of coffee, I showered, poured the rest of my caffeine into a travel mug, and we climbed into the car. Coop complained about his harness.

"Sorry, bud, but it's for your own safety," I told him. "If something bad happens, I don't want you thrown around like a rag doll. You could get hurt!"

"*But I can't go between front and back!*" he whined.

"You've never been able to before. I've always clipped you in your harness before we go anywhere."

"*Yes, but now you know how I feel.*"

"Too bad. If you want car rides, you have to be clipped into the harness. I could leave you home and ask the lady next door to let you out and feed you."

"*No, no, I want to go with.*" Coop, as a Newfie mix, completely covered the back seat of my BMW 430i when lying down, and he did so now, looking pitiful all the while. I chuckled as I pulled out of the driveway. I knew as soon as I hit the road and he could put his head out into a brisk breeze, the complaining would stop.

Our first stop was the rest area at the Georgia-Tennessee border so Coop could do his business in the designated pet area. It gave me a chance to stretch my legs, too. I hadn't driven farther than the grocery store in a couple of months, and my butt was already sore. An hour after that, we were off the expressway and onto a two-lane scenic highway. There were three possible houses in this section of Tennessee, but one glance at their steep driveways, and I wasn't interested in what the houses might look like. My knees complained just thinking about walking back up that incline after checking the mailbox!

I wound my way through the hills, north, east, then south again. Although the pictures in the online listings of all the houses looked nice, in person, none made me feel as if I wanted to look inside.

I was *very* tired of driving when I checked into the hotel in Murphy, North Carolina, which was only fifteen minutes from the Tennessee border. The clerk offered to watch Coop for me if I wanted to visit the casino that evening, but I declined. All I wanted was a decent meal that wasn't drive-through food and bed. I was told there was a good restaurant only a couple of blocks away, and since they had tables outside, I could take my dog with me.

Fed, watered, and walked for the night, we hit the rock-hard hotel bed. I never understood why anyone needed a mattress that stiff. Just sleep on the floor, already! But I was so tired, I barely noticed and dropped off quickly. I wasn't comfortable enough to sleep soundly, however, and tossed and turned all night.

I had made one error when booking my hotel room. They didn't have in-room coffee, which meant I had to get dressed and go downstairs to get my caffeine fix. I cheated and took two Styrofoam cups back to my room to drink while I checked email on my phone.

Thinking about what I still had to look at and where it was located, I thought perhaps I could squeeze all seventeen houses into one day, and after I'd showered, I checked out of the hotel. Honestly? I didn't want to sleep on that bed another night. The clerk was surprised that I wasn't staying the second night but didn't give me any grief.

"*I like the smells here,*" Coop told me, his head hanging out one of the back windows. "*It smells much better than home.*"

"Although there are still a lot of cars up here, there isn't as much air pollution. That's probably why," I replied.

It took three hours to find and drive by the five houses in North Carolina. Again, none of them looked like *home*. I headed south into Georgia, driving by three before I hit a Wendy's for lunch for both of us. Hamburger patties were a rare treat for Coop, and he almost inhaled his two.

Another seven houses later, I was beginning to despair that I'd find a place I really liked. Everything thus far had either a too-steep driveway, too much lawn, or just didn't trip my trigger. I stopped at a scenic overlook for Coop's convenience and was considering just giving up and going back to my monstrosity of a house. But there were only two left, and I still had an hour or so of daylight so decided to soldier on.

Of course, it would be the last house I looked at. I wound my way down a two-lane country road to a gently-sloping, tree-lined driveway. As I crested the rise and rounded a curve, I saw a house with log siding nestled in a clearing in a dense forest. I got out of the car, let Coop out his door, and walked around as he investigated on his own.

Looking around, I saw pines, oaks, maples, and holly. Whoever owned this house loved the place…there was little underbrush and, surprisingly in an area like this, not a single dead tree.

I felt a peace such as I'd never known. It was *quiet* with only the breeze ruffling the remaining tree leaves, and an occasional bird call. Looking around, I determined that the utilities must be buried because I couldn't see a power pole or line anywhere. I was in love…so far.

At least the outside of the house was what I'd envisioned. It had a covered front porch with a deck off the back looking out to where I could put a garden. There was no lawn, *per se,* but there were grasses that would need to be torn up before I put beds in. Beyond that clear space was nothing but trees. I pulled up the listing on my phone and saw that it was bordered by US Forestry Service land. I hit the button on the website to contact a realtor. I wanted to see the inside of this one!

"Come on, Coop. Let's go home," I called. While I waited for him to return, I snapped a couple of pictures and texted them to the kids. I was clipping Coop back into his harness when I heard a faint "*Help!*" echoing in my head. The voice was high and child-like, yet like no voice I'd heard before.

I hastily unclipped Coop. "Can you find the source?"

"*Of what?*" he asked. I told him what I was hearing.

"*Something small, then,*" he said before taking off. He ran around, sniffing both the ground and the air, while I heard the call over and over. I followed him slowly, using my puny human eyes to find the source of the cry, too. "*Here!*" he said, standing under a window on the deck.

I ran to where he was sitting, looking up. A small bird, a wren, I thought, had its talons stuck in the screen. He was fluttering his wings wildly, trying to get free.

"Leave the deck, Coop," I said. "You probably scare him just as much as I do." Coop did as I asked, and I slowly moved toward the window.

"Calm, little guy. Let me get you loose," I said in a quiet voice. I folded my hand around him to keep him steady, then gently worked his talons free of the screen with my other hand.

"Are you okay now?" I asked as I placed him on the deck railing.

The wren looked up at me in wonder. *"You heard me? I thank you muchly for your assistance. Yes, I believe I am quite well. May I repay you somehow?"*

"I'm fine, little one. I would suggest you avoid this place in the future, though. Those screens can be hazardous to little talons such as yours."

"I will. Thank you again!" he called as he flew off. Having done my good deed for the day, Coop and I returned to the car and headed for home. My thoughts were on the wren, and finally, I felt a little gratitude for this odd gift I had been given.

My phone rang halfway home. It was the realtor. She was all hopped up to show the house that night, but I declined. Not only did I not want to make a U-turn and drive an hour back, I wanted to see it in daylight, anyway, so we made an appointment for the next afternoon.

I didn't feel like cooking, so when I got home, I ordered a pizza. That would serve for dinner for a couple nights. After eating, I let Coop out, then fell into bed. All that driving had exhausted me.

I slept in the next morning, barely getting up in time to inhale some coffee, shower, then hit the road for the mountains again.

Pulling into the driveway of the house once again felt like coming home. The realtor was already there, eagerly awaiting me.

"Good afternoon, Ms. Mackay!" she said as I climbed out of the car. "This house is a marvel, and I'm sure you'll really like it."

"Let's reserve that judgement, shall we?" I replied as I unbuckled Coop. "Stay outside, please," I quietly told him, hoping the realtor couldn't hear me. "I don't want your fur there."

Coop hung his head. *"But I want to see inside, too. Perhaps I won't like it."*

"Nonetheless, the current owners may not have dogs, and if I don't like it, future buyers might not want to see your fur."

Kay, the realtor, unlocked the door, and we stepped inside. It felt crowded. Whoever owned this house had tried to pack in as much furniture as possible. I tried to imagine it with about half of what was there, and that helped.

"May I ask why it's being sold?"

Kay's face drooped. "The husband passed away last year, and the current owner doesn't feel she can keep up with the acreage. She has moved back to the city to be closer to her daughter."

I kind of wondered about the "keeping up with the acreage" comment. The vast majority of it was wooded. But it wasn't my place to say anything.

I wandered through the rooms. The house was a warren. Whoever had designed it had no sense whatsoever. There was no central living room but two rooms with an arch between. One bedroom opened up into another. The half bath was a closet I wasn't certain Jason could fit in, directly across from the front door. The kitchen was adequate, but the appliances were old. I liked the master suite. Kay was extremely enthusiastic about a closet off the kitchen which housed a stacked washer and dryer. For one person, that was okay, but I certainly wouldn't gush over it.

I also wasn't thrilled about the knotty pine paneling throughout. It made the place darker than it needed to be. That could be taken down, drywalled, and painted, I knew.

"Have there been any serious lookers?" I asked.

"Not that I'm aware of. The two couples I've shown it to didn't like the isolation."

I snapped a bunch of pictures of the interior and texted them to Jason. **I love the property but hate the house. Can anything be done with this?**

My talented son had followed in his father's footsteps. After graduating *magna cum laude* from Cornell with a degree in architecture just like Thomas, he'd snared a job with one of the top architectural firms in Los Angeles. Unbeknownst to Jason, Thomas had made a few phone calls on his behalf. After five years, without his dad's help, he'd made a name for himself in commercial construction, been found by a headhunter, and taken a job with a real estate development firm. Jay was responsible for new shopping centers and had been hired because with his degree and work experience, he knew when architecture and construction firms were cutting corners *or* being too extravagant with building costs.

"I *may* be interested," I told Kay. "The house would need quite a bit of work to bring it up to my standards. I'll get back to you after I've spoken with my son, who is an architect."

Kay looked crestfallen. Perhaps she thought I'd be an easy sell. "Of course," she said. "You have my number."

After she left, Coop and I wandered the property again, this time going a little farther into the woods.

"*You didn't like the house*," he said.

"Not particularly," I replied. "But Jason may have some ideas to make it better."

"*I* like *this place*," he said. "*There are all sorts of good smells, and plenty of squirrels to chase.*"

I sat down with my back to a large oak tree at the edge of the clearing to ponder. I stared at the house. I knew if I sold the monstrosity, I could afford almost any property within reason. But having been through the trials and tribulations of the construction of one house, did I want to go through another? Also, did I want to wait? I wanted *out* of Thomas' tribute to his success.

My phone pinged with a reply from Jason. **I think so, but I need to see it. I'm on the redeye out of LA, arriving at 6 AM tomorrow. Can you pick me up?**

Gads. That meant I'd have to leave the house at five to pick him up. But, **Yes, of course.**

I called Kay. "My son wants to see the house. Can we come back in the morning?"

"I can meet you at noon, if that would be convenient," she said.

"That would be fine. See you tomorrow." I rang off and went back to my pondering.

"*Yoooooouuuu woouulld beee a goooooddddd neighbooorrr,*" a deep bass rumbled in my head. It took me a beat to interpret what it said. The voice was deep and so slow my human brain had a difficult time understanding.

"Huh? Who's that?"

The tree behind me rustled its leaves. There was no breeze this day. "*IIII sppeeaakkk for the treeees.*"

Oh. The *gift*. But trees? Mom hadn't mentioned that. I stood, turned, and faced the oak. Not knowing if it would help, I put my palm on its bark. "Why do you think I would make a good neighbor?"

"Beeecause of the birrrrddd."

So the tree had seen me yesterday. *"Yoooouuu have maaagic. Yooooouuu caaannn heeearr us. That is gooooddd."*

I put my hands on its bark. "I'm not sure I'm going to move here," I told it.

"Yoooouuu willll."

Trees were prescient? Who knew? But I *really* hoped Jay could figure out how to fix the house. I wanted the property.

"Come on, Coop," I called. "I have to get up at dark-thirty to get Jason from the airport, so I want to go home."

He bounded out from the woods. *"Car ride again? Let's go!"*

I moaned as I crawled out of bed at four. I hadn't gotten up this early in…ever (discounting sick children, of course). I thanked all the gods for coffeepots with timers as I felt my way downstairs in the dark. Not wanting to face bright light, I eschewed the overhead fluorescents, but still squinted in the dim illumination provided by the fixture over the sink.

A half-cup of coffee later, my phone pinged. Who would be texting me at this gawd-awful hour? I pulled it from my bathrobe pocket and peered at the text from Jason.

Engine trouble, it said. **Diverted to DFW. ETA 8:30**

Understood, I replied before putting the cup on the counter, turning off the light, and stumbling back upstairs. I could get another hour-plus of shuteye. It would take longer to get to the airport in rush hour traffic, but I still wouldn't have to leave the house until seven.

Coop was mad that I was leaving him at home, even after I explained we'd be going somewhere I'd have to leave him in the car. Having allowed an hour and a half to get to the airport, I was still late by twenty minutes. There had, naturally, been a wreck on the expressway. But I needn't have worried. Jay was just walking out the airport door when I pulled up to the curb.

"Hi, Mom!" he said as he folded himself into the passenger seat after throwing his overnight and laptop bags into the back. "So you like this place, huh?"

"The property, yes. The house? Not so much. We have time before meeting the realtor. You hungry?"

"You know I'll always eat, so yeah."

I drove us to a small café on the square in Marietta. It was only open for breakfast and lunch but had the best omelets around. Jason and I chatted about the property while eating.

"It's almost six acres and probably five and a half is woods," I told him. "It's so peaceful, yet only a fifteen-minute drive into town."

"Lots of room for Coop, then," he said around a mouthful of omelet.

"You're damned near thirty and still talk with your mouth full," I admonished him. "I taught you better than that."

He swallowed. "Sorry. But will you want to put an invisible fence up? That's a lot of perimeter to cover."

Thinking back to my new *gift*, I said, "No. Coop's smart enough that if I show him the boundaries, he won't leave the property."

"If you say so," he said doubtfully.

I looked at my watch. "We need to go. It's about an hour from here."

Jason stuffed the rest of his omelet into his mouth, chewed and swallowed quickly, then, wiping his mouth, said, "I'm ready."

His jaw dropped when I pulled up to the house. "This is *awesome*," he exclaimed. "The pictures you texted didn't do it justice."

Kay walked up to me, shook my hand, then turned to Jason. "Hi, I'm Kay. I presume you're the architect son Ms. Mackay mentioned?"

"Jason Mackay, at your service," he grinned. "Let's see the house."

He pulled a small notebook from his back pocket, a pen from another, and made notes as he wandered around both inside and out, occasionally tapping walls or opening windows. Kay and I trailed after him, curious.

He stood in the kitchen, reviewing his notes and muttering to himself. He looked up, seemingly surprised to see both of us waiting expectantly.

"Can I talk to Mom alone, please?" he asked Kay.

"Sure. I'll be out on the front porch if you need me."

When we heard the front door close, he turned to me. "It's doable, but…"

"But what?"

"It's not in the best shape, but it has good bones. The kitchen is way outdated, that knotty pine paneling *has* to go, the windows need replacing, and the deck flooring needs to be replaced, too. That's not taking into account dealing with those two so-called bedrooms and the joke of a half bath. What are they asking for it?"

"Three twenty-five," I replied. "I knew the appliances would have to be replaced at minimum, and the deck floor is rather obvious with the warping."

"Hmmm. If you can get it for three hundred, go for it. Another fifty or so and you'll have a nice house. Want me to take measurements and make some preliminary sketches?"

"Please. I *really* like the property. *And* I don't want to start shopping for dirt and going through the hassle of building from the ground up. Been there, done that. Don't want to do it again."

"You got it!" We both walked out. While I told Kay I wanted to make an offer, Jason walked to my car, dug in his overnight bag, and pulled out a big tape measure. As I filled out the paperwork, offering two seventy-five to start, Jason went inside to start taking measurements.

"I doubt she'll take this offer," Kay cautioned.

"The windows and deck flooring need to be replaced, at minimum. That's at least fifteen thousand right there. She's selling *old* appliances that are likely to fail in the first year or so. That's another five thousand. The rest is personal changes that I wouldn't knock off for." I shrugged. "She can counteroffer or reject it outright. But this house has been on the market for nearly six months. If she wants to sell, she'll negotiate."

"Okay," Kay replied. "I'll let you know what she says."

As soon as Jason was finished inside, she locked up and left. We were right behind her. I stopped at a drive-thru for a late lunch and almost immediately regretted my decision. In the years since he'd left home, Jason hadn't changed his habits, and I knew I would have to vacuum the passenger seat and floorboards after he left.

When we walked in the door, Coop almost knocked Jason over with his enthusiasm. *"Play!"* he said. Of course, Jason couldn't understand him but knew what he wanted. He gave the dog a good head scratch then said, "Sorry, Coop. I have work to do," and walked up to his room, bags in hand.

"Play!" Coop turned his attention to me.

"Hang on a minute," I told him. I poured the last of the coffee into a mug and heated that in the microwave before heading to the deck. From there, I threw a much-chewed tennis ball into the yard. Coop galloped down the stairs to retrieve it then got distracted by squirrels. I didn't want to ask them directly, but I had a sneaking suspicion the squirrels tormented my dog on purpose.

On a whim, I grabbed my laptop and opened our – my investment portfolio. Thomas had made sure we didn't have a mortgage on the monstrosity, and I was of a similar mind. Then I emailed the CPA, asking her to run projections on selling some asset or other to cover all the costs of the new house versus getting a mortgage for a few months until the palace sold.

About ten minutes later, my email pinged. Thinking how unusual it was to get a reply that quickly from the accountant, I was surprised to find a counteroffer from the owner. She came down ten grand. So I completed the online form to increase my offer by ten grand. I could do this all day – figuratively speaking, of course. If she *really* wanted to sell, she couldn't.

Jason joined me on the deck, leaning down to kiss my cheek. "What's for dinner?"

"You and your stomach. DoorDash or UberEats are for dinner. Pick one and order me grilled fish of some kind and a salad." I handed him my phone, which already had the credit card information stored in the apps.

Coop saw Jason on the deck, picked up his ball, and brought it to him. *"Play!"* he said. Jason threw the ball, and Coop thundered down the stairs to retrieve it. They did this several times before Coop got tired and flopped at our feet.

"Any news on the house?" he asked me.

"She countered at three fifteen. I upped mine to two eighty-five. We'll see."

After dinner, we stayed at the kitchen table. Jason had a blank pad of paper and a pencil. I had a sudden twinge as I remembered other evenings at a table in the house in Smyrna, Thomas sketching his ideas for his latest project. I blinked back tears and tried to concentrate on my son.

Quickly, he sketched something on two separate sheets. "This is what's there now," he said, pointing to one of them. "This is what I'm proposing," pointing to the other.

First, he'd moved a couple walls and added closets and doors to make the two bedrooms smaller but separate. Then, he had opened up the wall between the kitchen and "living room" and deleted the arch which served no purpose. He added a breakfast bar between the two spaces with cupboards underneath. The half bath was now a coat closet, and he took part of the kitchen to convert the closet with washer and dryer to a half-bath that did double duty.

The "eat-in" part of the kitchen had been transformed by taking out the single door and adding a French door and floor-to-ceiling windows. One of the windows included a doggie door large enough for Coop.

"Once we get rid of the paneling, this will make it very light and airy," he told me.

Without thinking, I said, "Hey Coop, you're going to get your own door to the outside!"

Coop bounded from his bed in the corner to my side, tail wagging so hard I thought it might fly off. "*Really? I can go out without asking?*"

"Yes! If I get that house, that is. I'm not doing it here."

His tail drooped, then started wagging again. "*Then I want you to get that house. To be able to go outside and sniff around and chase squirrels without having you open the door would be great!*"

Jason watched me with wide eyes. "Are you *having a conversation* with the dog?"

Oops. "Um, yes?"

"Since when do you talk to the dog?"

"Well, talking *to* him, always. Actually conversing? A couple of months?"

"I think you should explain."

So I told him what had happened to me and what my mother had said. I told him about the bird and the tree at the house in the mountains. His jaw dropped a little farther with every statement.

"I know Gran is a straight-shooter and wouldn't lie to you," he told me. "But this is so far-fetched. Are you sure you're not hallucinating or something after Dad's death?"

"If Gran and Aunt Beth experience this, too, then I don't think I'm crazy," I replied. "Also, although I might hallucinate the tree conversation, how do you explain the bird…or Coop, for that matter?"

"Wow."

"That's a mild version of what I said."

"Does Sam know?"

I shook my head. "Gran said she wouldn't believe me if I told her. But now that you know, I suppose I'll have to talk to her."

Coop followed our conversation like watching a tennis match. I knew he could understand me but wasn't sure about anyone else.

"Can you understand Jason, too?" I asked him.

"*No. I just know his usual words like 'play' and 'outside.'*"

"That's a relief. I think," I replied.

"Can he understand what I say?" Jason asked. I shook my head.

"I agree with Gran that Sam wouldn't believe you…unless she saw and heard what I just did. I won't say anything if you don't.

"This just boggles my mind. I haven't gotten a lot of sleep the last couple of nights so I'm going to bed. I'm going to assume you're getting that place, so I'll start on the plans for the house in the morning."

He kissed me goodnight, and I was left with my thoughts. I was still uncomfortable with my new *gift*, and my son, I was sure, was even more so. It was a truly awkward situation. But there was nothing I could do about it. I poured another glass of wine and curled up in my favorite chair with a book until I got sleepy.

The next morning, I assumed Jason would sleep late. His body was three hours behind. He surprised me by coming into the kitchen just an hour after I got up.

"I thought you'd sleep in," I said as he reached into a cupboard for a coffee mug.

"I set an alarm. That's the only way I can stay on Eastern Time while I'm here. Then, on Tuesday, I'll probably be awake at dark-thirty, and it'll take a few days to readjust to Pacific Time. It's okay. I'm used to it."

I knew he flew coast-to-coast on a regular basis for his job. I thought it was good he was young because it took me over a week to get back on a normal schedule after visiting him or worse, going to Europe.

"So you're working on house plans today?" I asked.

"Unless you have something else you'd rather I do, yes."

I mused. "If I get this place, I'll have to find a contractor. I don't know anyone who would drive that far."

My son laughed, then patted me on the back. "Ahead of you, Mom. I know a residential developer in Chattanooga. On the off chance we would need it, I emailed him and got three names of folks he trusts in that general area. Once you get the house and I get the plans finalized, I'll contact and negotiate with them on your behalf."

Gads, I loved my kid. "You're such a good son," I told him after I'd kissed him on the cheek.

"I know!" he laughed. "But seriously, I do this all the time, just on a commercial basis instead of residential. It's no big deal.

"That said, you'll have to be the one to actually work with the general contractor and check in on the progress in person from time to time. I know you can sort of read plans, having lived with Dad's job for so many years. I'll get a set printed and sent to you so you know what to look for.

"While I sit here and draw on the computer, you should probably start thinking about what furniture and other stuff you want to keep and what you're going to do with the rest of it."

I had been avoiding that particular chore ever since I made the decision to move. There was *so much!* I knew it had to be done, though.

Jason looked up from his laptop and saw the bewildered look on my face. "Have you thought of an estate sale company? They do more than just clear out a house like when a parent dies.

Not sure about around here, but in LA, a lot of them will help you choose what to take, what to sell, and what to donate."

Now *there* was an idea. I grabbed my laptop and started searching. It took quite a while to figure out the proper keywords, but I found the National Association of Senior Move Managers. Okay, I wasn't a senior – not yet – but I thought the rest of my issues qualified for help of the kind they could provide. Searching their database for Atlanta members, I found three. Hallelujah! I filled out contact forms and sat back to wait.

Just as I was about to close the lid, my email pinged again. It wasn't another counteroffer from the seller; it was an acceptance of mine! I whooped with joy. I'd gotten it for less than Jason said the maximum should be.

"I'm taking *you* to dinner tonight to celebrate," Jason said as he hugged me. "Where do you want to go?"

I had a favorite restaurant about a mile away and told him. They didn't take reservations, which meant we might have to wait a bit since it was a Saturday, but I didn't mind.

I spent the rest of the day wandering the house, envisioning what furniture pieces I wanted to take with me. Honestly, it wasn't all that difficult once I put my mind to it. I found the family room the most comfortable and wouldn't need anything from the formal dining room. However, Coop had decisions to make.

"You have seven beds in this house," I told him, "but you can only take two with you when we move. You'll have to decide which two."

I quietly laughed as he raced around the house, lying in each bed several times and moaning. His whine was audible in the kitchen even when he was upstairs or down.

"You're torturing the poor guy," Jason said with a chuckle. "I don't think dogs are wired to make decisions like that. And if you couldn't converse with him, you'd be making the decision, anyway."

"If he can't decide, I will," I replied. "But they're all different, so I thought I'd give him a choice."

By noon the next day, Jason had the plans for the house drawn up, including the renderings. The only drawings left, he told me, were the trade plans, which would let the plumbers and electricians know what had to be changed.

"There are a couple decisions for you to make," he said. "I'd like to put in new cabinets throughout, do a rock face on the fireplace and, this is the big one, change the siding from wood to plastic."

"But I like the log siding!" I protested.

"I don't mean vinyl siding like what this house has. They make plastic log siding that will look just as it does now but means you'll never have to stain or paint again. We can use the same material to rebuild the deck and front porch. It's even eco-friendly because they use recycled plastic to make it. It's expensive to begin with, but if you stay in the house thirty years, it'll pay for itself."

Since I had no plans to move ever again, that sounded wonderful.

"Okay. Do that. And I agree about putting in new cabinets and the rock on the fireplace. What else?"

"That's it for now. Eventually the general contractor will ask you about the new tile needed for the half bath and kitchen, countertops, plumbing fixtures, and paint colors. I'm leaving the lighting as is, but once things get rolling, you might want to change those, too."

Construction. I hated it. Thomas may have designed our house, but I was the one who made the rest of the decisions. "Décor is up to the wife," he said.

Jason took a Lyft to the airport Monday morning, and I was once again left with just Coop for company in the cavernous house. However, I had plenty to keep me busy until construction actually started at the new house. The accountant said to take out a mortgage and a home equity loan instead of paying cash for the new place, so I had several exchanges with the banker.

Then I had appointments with the downsizing/relocation people. I chose one and signed a contract. It took several meetings for us to decide what was going to the new house, what would be sold at auction, and what would be donated. There were a lot of things that would simply go in the trash because she thought they had no value. I sighed at that but agreed. After that, it was a question of waiting for moving day.

Jason emailed me the contract with the general contractor he'd chosen, which I signed and returned to someone named John Carpenter (how appropriate) in Blue Ridge, the town closest to the new house. Construction would start a week after closing, which was scheduled for the end of October, and was estimated to take a month. That was just for the interior changes. The exterior wouldn't happen until the following spring. I'd have to put up with the banging of hammers and the whine of circular saws for a week then.

I crossed my fingers, hoping I'd be able to celebrate the big five-oh in the new house. *That* would be a lovely birthday present! However, it was not to be. My kids and mother all called with gushing good wishes for making it a half century, sorry they couldn't make the trip for such a huge occasion. I toasted myself several times and wished wine bottles were smaller the following morning.

No surprise, construction took longer than estimated. I was finally able to move the week before Christmas. As the movers were unloading the last of the furniture and boxes, it started to snow. My first night in the new house was postcard-perfect: snow lightly blanketing the outside and a roaring fire inside. Naturally, the white melted with the next morning's sun, but for a few hours, I reveled in the sight.

Coop was enjoying his new-found freedom. I rarely saw him in the house, but after a long conversation about boundaries and more than one trek around the perimeter, I knew he wouldn't leave my property, regardless of where a particular scent might take him.

The one thing he *didn't* like about being able to come and go as he pleased was the increase in the number of baths he was required to take.

"I thought you like water?" I asked. "You're always jumping into ponds or even mud puddles."

"*For playing, yes! But not with all the soap. And besides, I do not smell bad,*" he complained.

"To a human nose, you do, especially after you roll in scat. *That* stinks!"

"*I think it smells lovely. Rolling in it allows me to keep the scent with me for a while.*"

"You may like it, but I do not. Deal with the baths, or stay in the house."

I had a crowded house for Christmas. Both kids and Mom descended upon me, wanting to see the new place. Thankfully, I had decided to buy a brand-new sofabed for the living room, which Jason slept on without complaint, despite the fact that Mom and I were both early risers, and even though we tried to be quiet, we woke him every morning.

I was grateful, however, that it was Jason and not Samantha sleeping in the living room. Mom and I discussed my progress with the gift almost every morning…something we didn't want to do where Sam could hear. I argued I should just tell her, but even Jason said not to.

Mom was flabbergasted that I was able to speak to trees. Neither she nor my aunt could. "Maybe you'll be able to speak to the plants in the garden, too," she exclaimed. "Wouldn't it be wonderful to know *exactly* what they needed?"

I wasn't so sure about that one. If I could hear the plants in the garden, what would be next? The grasses and other groundcover I squashed every time I walked? Or hearing the basil's cry as I harvested it? No, thank you!

I was sitting in my chair by a roaring fire on a late January morning, contemplating my future, when I heard a car pull up and shortly, a knock at the door. When I opened it, a man in a forestry service uniform stood on my porch.

"Mornin', ma'am," he said in a thick drawl, doffing his hat. "I'm Caleb Doyle." He flashed his identification. "May I come inside? I'd like to talk with you about a problem we're having."

There was something off about this man, although I couldn't put my finger on it. He was young, perhaps in his mid-twenties, tall and rangy, with carrot-red hair and the corresponding pale skin and freckles. There was nothing unusual in that, but I still felt apprehensive about him.

However, he was a Forestry Service officer, and since my land backed up to theirs, it wouldn't do to antagonize my neighbors. Wondering what the problem could be, I invited him in (he pointedly wiped his feet on the mat) and offered him a cup of coffee before indicating he should sit. Coop, who had been outside, barreled inside, and with a sniff, sat beside my chair and eyed the ranger.

"On a cold morning such as this, a cup of hot coffee would be most welcome," he told me. Then, turning his attention to Coop, without moving in his chair, he held out his fisted hand, palm down. "Hi, fella."

Coop didn't move. Ranger Doyle withdrew his hand and sat back. "He's protective of you."

"Yes, he is," I replied. Once I'd gotten his coffee, refilled mine, and sat back down, I asked, "What's the problem?"

"You know your property backs up to USFS land, right?" I nodded. "There are many hiking trails to the west and north of here, and they're popular, even in winter. One runs only a hundred yards beyond your back property line. We've been getting complaints of items being stolen from campsites and attacks by unknown creatures while on the trail.

"I was wondering if you'd seen or heard anything unusual in the last, oh, two weeks or so."

"I haven't really been outside in that time. It's been too wet and cold for me," I told him. "Nor have I heard any unusual noises, either during the day or at night. Coop would have barked if he'd heard a strange sound, and he hasn't.

"What sort of attacks are you talking about?"

The ranger slurped his coffee. "The claims are being tripped when there is no rock or root in sight, and one man said a tree branch came out of nowhere and beat him about the legs. I wouldn't have believed him except I saw the bruises on his shins and calves, and they weren't the kind you get from plowing through undergrowth.

"No one has been seriously hurt, but that could change."

That sounded scary. I wasn't the hiking type, but I knew a lot of people were. If news of this got out, it would deter hiking in the area, and tourism was the most important revenue stream for the county.

"I don't know anything to help you at this time but if you give me a number, I'll be sure to call," I told him.

He nodded, finished his coffee, and rose. From his shirt pocket, he pulled a business card. "If you can help *at all*, my cell number is the one below the office number. I'd appreciate a call."

Once I'd seen him to the door, I turned to Coop. "What was that about? You're normally a lot more friendly than that."

"*He is strange. He smells odd — not completely human, even. You are alone here. I will protect you.*"

I ruffled his fur and thought maybe my dog was just a little *too* overprotective. "Thanks. But this one is someone we should be nice to. If he returns, be a little more friendly, huh? Now, about his visit."

I reiterated what Ranger Doyle had said. "Have you smelled or heard anything unusual?"

"*No, but the squirrels are afraid. They are slinking around with tails between legs and rarely come down from the trees so I can chase them.*"

Not that I blamed the squirrels for that, but it *was* weird. I needed to investigate.

As I pulled on boots and a jacket, I asked Cooper to show me where I might find a squirrel or three to talk to.

Before heading deeper into the woods, I paused at the old oak. I had learned the trees saw *everything* and communicated with each other through their underground network of roots. I had spoken with it several times before, during, and after construction to build up a rapport — and to better understand the deep, slow speech. Putting my hand on its bark to get its attention, I asked about what the ranger had said.

"*There is a disturbance in the forest,*" it rumbled. "*We do not know what it is, but it walks on two legs,*" it continued.

I thanked it and walked a little farther into the woods, watching Coop, who had his nose alternately to the ground then the air. "*Squirrels up there,*" he said, nose pointed up a large maple.

I saw only branches, but trusting a dog's nose better than my eyes, I called, "Hello up the tree. May I ask you some questions?"

One squirrel poked its head from a hole in the trunk higher than I could see from my position on the ground and peered down at me. "*You* speak *to us?*" it squeaked.

"I can, yes," I replied. "May I ask some questions?"

The squirrel eyed Coop. "*You will not chase us such as that creature does?*"

"No. You can stay where you are if it makes you feel better."

The head disappeared for a moment, then reappeared. "*We agree. Ask your questions.*"

I told it what the ranger and tree had said, then asked if they had seen anything. The head disappeared again, then another one, a little more brown in its fur than the first, looked down.

"*We see nothing. But we hear something moving through the trees, crunching leaves and such. It smells like old dirt, what is deeper in the earth than we usually dig,*" it squeaked, but this voice creaked a little, too, as if it were older than the first.

"*Our neighbors say they have heard the cries of two-legs such as you but do not know why. But if two-legs cry, we wonder if something will happen to us, so we stay in our nests, only leaving when necessary. You should stay in your nest, too.*"

I thanked them for the information and headed back to the house, perturbed. I really hadn't learned anything new, just that there was a problem in the forest. But without specifics, there wasn't much I could do. I resolved to put it on the back burner until and unless I saw or heard something myself.

Early February saw a rare heavy snow. Cooper was beside himself with joy as he bounded through the drifts. I was less joyful when the power went out for three days. Without the sounds of modern living like the compressor on the refrigerator, it was *really* quiet, and the blanket of snow seemed to hush things even further. Although the fire kept the living room warm and I could cook on the gas stovetop, I missed the creature comforts of electric lights, forced air heat, and…running water! I had been told about wells and well pumps so had put aside gallons of water for flushing toilets and cooking, but my first shower after the power came back on was nothing short of heavenly.

As the weather slowly warmed, I spent more time outside. The first item on my to-do list was to plot out a garden. I had learned from the general contractor I had a septic system and needed to leave the back yard clear of deep roots so the pipes would drain properly. That explained why there were no trees closer to the house and also explained the odd plastic lid protruding from the ground about twenty feet from the house – that was the access to the septic tank, so I couldn't cover it up.

With abject apologies to the grasses, I covered them with weed block rather than try to dig it all out. Then I started building raised beds over the drain field. It was a small garden, but only one person was maintaining it, not the team of gardeners I had in Atlanta.

After the new car titles had arrived, I had traded my BMW and Thomas' Mercedes sedan in for an SUV, which was much more practical for living in the country. There were times during that first spring I had to leave Coop at home so I could use the entire cargo area for hauling – first stone blocks and cement for building the bed walls, then dirt to fill the beds.

Coop was *not* happy to be left at home, then even more unhappy when I asked him to *not* dig in the beds. It went against his nature, he told me. "Get over it," I retorted. "If you don't, I'll get one of those electric fences again, and you'll get a shock every time you go near the garden." A whimper signified his acquiescence.

For almost two months, I labored every day it wasn't raining, falling into bed exhausted beyond belief every night. The first week, I had to force myself out of bed in the morning. I wasn't used to physical labor and hurt where I didn't know I had muscles. I practically lived on ibuprofen, hot baths, and arnica cream. But it got easier over time, and soon I was the gardener I had always wanted to be.

I had just finished filling the garden beds when the contractor showed up to re-side the house and rebuild the deck and porch. He chided me for doing all the garden labor myself, telling me he'd have been happy to send along a couple of his men to do the hard work. He was surprised when I told him I enjoyed it. I didn't tell him I was also happy I was losing some of the extra pounds I had started to acquire with a fairly sedentary lifestyle.

For an entire week, I was grateful I was used to getting up just before sunrise. I only had time to inhale a cup of coffee and get into my outside clothes before the workmen arrived. As predicted, all I could hear was the thump of nail guns and whine of circular saws from sunup to sundown. In order to keep working in the garden, I had to dodge their vehicles and equipment as I hauled bags of gravel for the paths between the beds. Coop disappeared into the woods each day to get away from noise that hurt his ears, not reappearing until the last of their trucks left the driveway.

After the final construction was done, it was back to the quiet life for me. I was in my chair by the fire one late March evening, musing on what I wanted to do with the rest of my life. The garden, once planted, wouldn't take but a few hours a week, and there were many more hours to be filled. Unlike my previous life where I sat at a table, either in a board meeting, or a coffeehouse or a banquet to schmooze donors, I wanted to be active in whatever I did. I knew I didn't want to go back to school to finish my degree. I was content with my own garden to worry about and no one else's. I had no idea what to do.

That evening's Skype call with the kids was interesting. After I'd caught up on Sam and Jason's week, I told them of my dilemma.

"Have you looked at the specialty shops in town to see what they sell?" Sam asked.

"I've been in them but only glanced at their wares. I wasn't shopping for anything specific, just wanted to familiarize myself with my new town. Why?"

"Look on the internet for craft ideas. Then go back into town to see what they sell. Is there anything you can make that would be different or better?" My daughter, the marketing expert, was thinking in a business-like fashion.

Jason chimed in. "Isn't there an arts association in town, too? Maybe they offer classes that might interest you."

He had a point. I knew the arts association had taken over the historic courthouse when the new one was built. I assumed they offered classes but would have to look.

We hung up, and I went back to musing. In a way, I missed the charity work. It was *something* to do. But after six months, I didn't miss the politicking that came with it.

Following my daughter's advice, I started searching for "craft projects." Good heavens, there were *thousands* of websites with *thousands* of ideas. Nixing that search because I didn't want crossed eyes, I went to the arts association website. They did, indeed, offer classes in activities like painting, pottery, jewelry, and the like. But nothing looked interesting.

When I went to sleep that night, my dreams were filled with images of various types of crafts, and my feeling was one of despair.

Cooper woke me with a bark and a face-nuzzle early the next morning. It was still dark, but the clock read six-thirty. So not too early.

"What is it?" I mumbled.

"*We have a problem*," he said.

"What sort of problem?" I asked as I turned on the beside lamp, blearily grabbed my robe, and fumbled for my slippers.

"*There is a body at the edge of the woods. It smells dead,*" he said.

"*Excuse me?* A body? A *human* body?" I was awake in an instant.

"*Yes. Come see.*"

It was still cool in the mornings, so after turning the coffeepot on, I put a jacket on over my bathrobe and grabbed a flashlight before following Cooper outside.

He led me in a straight line off the deck, through the garden, and to the edge of the woods. Sure enough, I could see a dark lump lying on the ground. I played the light over it, noting the lump appeared to be a man lying on his stomach with his head turned to the side, and he also appeared to not be breathing. Even in that little light, I could see the clothing was slashed and dark splotches covered his back.

Utilizing expletives that weren't normally in my vocabulary, I made a beeline for the house and the phone.

"9-1-1, what's your emergency?" A calm female voice asked.

"My dog found a body at the back of my property," I said, voice and yes, whole body shaking. "I think he's dead."

"Is your address 21356 Highway 2?" she asked.

"Yes," I confirmed.

"I'll dispatch an officer right away. Please stay inside until he arrives."

My hand shook as I turned on lights and made my way to the kitchen for coffee. I think I got more coffee on the counter than I did in the cup but finally managed a full pour.

By the time I'd gotten my coffee poured and cleaned off the counter, a car pulled into the drive, gravel crunching under the tires as it skidded to a stop. I had the door open before the officer even made it to the porch.

"Good morning, ma'am," he said as he approached. "I understand you think you've found a dead body?"

Cooper nosed his way around me and stood at attention on the porch. "Cooper, go back inside," I admonished. "This man poses no threat."

"*He is a stranger,*" Coop woofed.

I couldn't reply to that without being thought crazy, so I moved around to put Cooper behind me.

"Yes, sir," I said. "It's at the back of the property. I can show you…"

"No, ma'am. Please just tell me where it is and stay in the house."

I gave him directions and watched as he slowly walked around the house, his flashlight moving this way and that along his path.

"Stay inside with me," I told Cooper. "You don't need to be getting in his way."

I shut the door and we, the dog and I, went to the back of the house where I could watch the officer while still following the instructions to stay indoors. It only took him a few minutes to inspect the lump before heading back my way, cell phone to his ear. He saw me watching him and headed for the deck.

"You're right, the man is dead," he said as I opened the deck door. "The coroner and the watch commander are on their way. May I ask you some questions?"

"Of course," I said. Then, remembering my manners, "Would you like a cup of coffee, Officer…?"

"Deputy Johnson and no, thank you. I'm at the end of my shift and don't need any more caffeine."

"Then please, sit and ask your questions." I motioned him toward the living room.

We arranged ourselves by the fireplace, Cooper sitting attentively at my side. The officer pulled out a notebook. "First, your full name, then how you came upon the body in the dark."

"Ellen Bixler Mackay is my full name. Most people just call me El. My dog woke me barking about twenty minutes ago. As you can see (I pointed to the doggy door), he has full access to the outside. He obviously wanted me to follow, so I did. As soon as I saw what he wanted me to see, I came back to the house and called you."

"Did you touch anything?"

I made a face. "No. Ick. I just shined my flashlight on him to see what the lump was. It was a man, obviously, and he wasn't moving at all."

"Since you saw it was a man, did you recognize him?"

"No. I haven't lived here long, only about three months, and don't know many people at all."

He'd just finished noting that comment when two more cars pulled into the drive. It was getting light enough to see at this point, and in addition to the SUV Deputy Johnson had driven, I saw a pickup truck and a car that looked like a hearse.

"That will be the watch commander and the coroner," Deputy Johnson said. "May I let them in the house?"

"Of course," I said as I stood, ready to meet the new arrivals.

Two men followed the deputy into the living room. One was about my age, wearing a uniform. He had a kindly expression on his face, and I could tell his blue eyes would twinkle if he laughed. He wasn't laughing at the moment.

The other was perhaps in his sixties with a long-suffering expression on his face. He was dressed in civilian clothes.

The man in uniform held out his hand. "Sergeant Anderson, ma'am," his smooth baritone voice intoned as I shook the outstretched hand. He didn't speak with the thick southern drawl I had become accustomed to hearing from mountain natives. "I'm sorry for your trouble. This is Deputy Coroner Larkin. We'll try to get this resolved and be out of your hair as quickly as possible."

He turned to Deputy Johnson. "So where's the body?"

The three men trooped out the deck door and back to the lump that, in full light, had now resolved itself. The man appeared to be wearing jeans and a barn jacket, and even from the house, I could see the blood clearly. My hands started shaking again so I put my cup on the table. I didn't want to drop it and spill coffee all over the living room.

"*This is not good,*" Cooper said as he pressed against my legs.

"No, it's not," I replied. "Did you hear anything at all last night?"

"*No, just someone walking out of the woods, and a thump, which is what woke me. I went to investigate and came to get you as soon as I saw and smelled him.*"

The three men had been crouching over the body. Sergeant Anderson and Deputy Johnson stood while the coroner continued his examination. Deputy Johnson started walking at a right angle to the house while the Sergeant came back my way, slipping his phone into his pocket.

I opened the door as he approached. "We won't be out of your hair as soon as I'd thought," he told me when I let him back in the house. "The man hasn't been dead long; he's still warm. And it looks like something happened farther back in the woods because there's a trail of blood leading that way.

"We'll have to get more men to scour the area looking for clues. And we need CID here."

"CID?" I asked.

"Criminal Investigation Division," he told me. "They're the ones who take care of problems like this. We're just the uniform division, or the street cops, if you will. I'll stay long enough to introduce you to the investigator when he arrives, then I'll leave it in their hands."

More expletives I didn't normally use passed my lips. "May I at least get dressed?" I asked. I wasn't thrilled to be greeting so many strangers in my PJs.

He smiled. "Of course." Then, eyeing my cup on the table, "May I bother you for a cup of coffee? I was just about to leave for my shift, got the call at home, and came straight here without my travel mug."

I smiled back. "Help yourself. Mugs are in the cupboard above the pot. Sugar's on the counter. I'm afraid I don't have any creamer, but there's milk in the fridge if you want that."

"I like mine black as night so don't need any additions. Thanks."

While he poured himself a cup of caffeine, I went into the bedroom and hastily pulled on the jeans and sweatshirt I'd worn the day before. I ran a brush through my hair and reemerged, feeling a little better about meeting newcomers.

Sergeant Anderson stood at the deck door, sipping his coffee while watching the coroner. He turned as yet another car parked behind the hearse. I was beginning to think it was good I had a long driveway. Then I wondered what the grass would look like when they all tried to leave. There was only a small section in front that was graveled for me to turn around in when I backed the car from the garage.

A man in a suit emerged from the new vehicle. Unlike the deputy and sergeant, this one looked all business. The expression on his face was forbidding as he surveyed the house from the drive, then strode to the porch with purpose.

I opened the door as soon as I heard him on the steps, Sergeant Anderson right behind me, coffee cup still in hand. He reached around me and shook the new man's hand.

"Hey, Will," he said. "This is Ms. Mackay. Her dog found the body about six-thirty, right?" This last was directed at me, so I nodded.

He turned back to the man in the suit. "Jack is already back there, and I'm guessing he'll use Johnson to put the body on the gurney when he's ready. After that, I need Johnson back so I can send him home."

Turning to me again, he said, "Ms. Mackay, this is Inspector Woods. He'll be taking it from here, but if you have any questions or concerns, you're always welcome to call me at the Sheriff's Department." He handed me the now-empty cup. "Thanks for the coffee. I really needed it." He walked off the porch, got into his truck, and backing onto the grass (I sighed), made his way around the hearse and the inspector's sedan back onto the drive and left.

Inspector Woods shook my hand. "I'm sorry this has happened on your property. Let me get up to speed with the deputy and coroner. Then I'll come back and tell you what more will happen."

As he made his way around the house, Cooper sidled up to me. *"I suppose I have to stay in the house today."*

"That would probably be a good idea. At least until they tell me they're done here. Anything you did in the woods might mess up a clue they need."

"But I could help!" he said. *"I have a better nose than they do."*

"Yes, you have a point," I replied. "But how would I tell them if you found something? 'My dog told me' won't cut it, you know."

He sighed. *"I know. But it's frustrating."*

50

We went back in the house, and I poured myself another cup of coffee. Logic told me I should eat breakfast, but my stomach wasn't up for it. So I took up my post at the back door and watched Inspector Woods talk to the coroner and Deputy Johnson, who had returned from his sojourn in the woods. All three turned to look at the house and caught me watching them.

Inspector Woods smiled and came back to the house, the coroner and Deputy Johnson on his heels. As the Inspector came up the deck, the other two veered off toward the front of the house, presumably to get the gurney.

"Ms. Mackay," Inspector Woods said as I opened the door for him. "Is your dog good at scenting?"

"Yes, he is," I replied. "He's Newfoundland mixed with Retriever, we think. Those are good scenting dogs. Why?"

"We need to follow a trail. Our K-9 units are currently over in Rabun County helping with a search-and-rescue, and it will take time to get one team back here. The forecast is for rain in a couple of hours, and I'd rather not lose any evidence if I don't have to. Can you get him to follow the blood trail?"

I looked at Cooper, who was looking at me expectantly. "I think so," I said. "Let me put a jacket on and get his leash. Wait. Do I have to see the body again?"

"No, Jack and Marty will be putting it in the wagon in a couple of minutes. As soon as they're gone, we can start."

By the time I'd put on outside shoes and a jacket and grabbed Cooper's leash from the garage (I only used it when we went to the vet, where it was required), both the hearse and Sheriff's Department car were leaving the driveway. I was sure I was going to have to do some patching on the front yard.

"Come on, Coop," I said as I hooked the leash to his collar. "We have some searching to do."

"*I* knew *I could help*!" he said. We followed the inspector back to where the body had been.

The inspector crouched down, picked up a leaf covered in dried blood, and handed it to me. "I need him to follow this back to where whatever happened, happened," he said.

I took the leaf from him and held it to Cooper's nose. "Can you follow this scent?"

Cooper quivered, eager to prove he could help. "*Yes!*" he said, tugging hard on the leash.

"Slowly," I admonished, holding him back. "I can't run as well as I used to!"

Cooper dutifully slowed his pace, nose to the ground. He walked in almost a straight line to the woods near the old oak. Even I could see the splotches of blood dotting the dead leaves and grass here and there. Inspector Woods was right behind us, noting every minute turn Cooper took.

Past the oak and farther into the woods, my human eyes lost the trail, but Cooper's nose didn't. We walked a few more paces south, then turned west. The trail zig-zagged, as if the man had staggered. Which he probably did. I certainly would have if I'd been hurt that badly.

Cooper continued to walk, sniffing as he went. The path took us around large trees and small, and even directly through a briar patch. I felt the thorns snag my jeans and wondered about the inspector's dress pants.

Finally, Cooper stopped at the edge of a small clearing. In front of us was a tent that was partly down. I knew one of the hiking trails lay just past it. The victim, whoever he had been, had taken a roundabout path to my house. I knew if I turned east and squinted, I'd be able to make it out through the trees.

"Please don't move any closer to the tent," the inspector admonished. "And hold your dog in place."

"Stay," I told Cooper, shortening my grip on his leash so the inspector would know I understood.

As we stood nearly immobile, the inspector walked carefully to the tent, watching where he put his foot with each step. When he got to the front of the tent, he paused and pulled a pair of latex gloves from his pocket to cover his hands before he lifted the flap.

He closed the flap quickly, pulled out his cell phone, and grimaced. "No signal here. We'll have to go back to your house so I can call more men."

"It's this way," I told him, turning east. "If you look carefully, you can see the house from here."

We made our way back, the inspector muttering under his breath. There were times I wished Cooper, with his keener hearing, could understand him – I would have liked to know what he was saying.

Once we got back to the yard, Inspector Woods stopped, once again pulled his cell out, and with a sigh, punched a button. As I continued toward the house, I heard him say, "Jack? Need you back at the Mackay's. There's another body."

My Wednesday was completely ruined. (Not that I had any great plans but…) Within an hour, there were five cars in my yard: the coroner's hearse, two sheriff's SUVs, a Forestry Service SUV, and finally, a big box truck with a Georgia Bureau of Investigation emblem on the side. Six men and two women, all in official-looking uniforms, tromped back and forth through my yard which, apparently, was the fastest access to the campsite. I sighed in frustration. The rain had arrived as predicted, and now not only the front yard would have to be smoothed and re-seeded, but the side and back as well.

I couldn't do much but sit at the table and watch the goings-on, Cooper at my side following the action with interest. I did manage to collect myself enough to text Mom and the kids to tell them what had happened, but as far as I knew, I was in no danger, and apart from being scared when I found the body, was fine. Naturally, everyone was concerned but would wait for further updates.

Shortly after noon, I was surprised by a knock at the front door. I opened it to find a young man, perhaps my daughter's age, with an eager look on his face.

"Good afternoon," he said with a smile. "I'm Mark Upton, a reporter for the *Fannin News-Observer*. May I ask you some questions?"

I supposed it was just a matter of time before the press got wind of this. "I don't know anything," I told him. "My dog found a body, I called the cops, end of story. You'll have to ask them for more information."

"But," he managed to get out before I quietly but firmly shut the door on him. Having my name in the newspaper was *not* the introduction to the neighborhood I wanted! I was, however, thankful that my house was isolated and not visible from the road. Otherwise, I probably would have had a passel of gawkers on the lawn, too.

It was almost full dark before the authorities finally left my property. Inspector Woods stopped at the house on the way to his car to give me what information he could. He stood on the porch, water dripping off his plastic raincoat.

"This is all *very* preliminary until the coroner issues his report," he started. "We have the man found in your back yard and a woman found in the tent. Both were badly cut up. Neither had identification on them. We're not sure if it was a random attack or premeditated.

"I would ask you to avoid the campsite for the next few days. Stay close to home and keep your phone on you at all times.

"I know you can't prevent your dog from going in the back yard or woods, but could you keep him on a leash until our investigation is complete? I don't want him messing up any evidence."

"He doesn't leave my property," I said, rather indignantly. "The campsite is a good two hundred feet away from my property line, so I don't think you have to worry."

"Nonetheless, in case he decides to chase a squirrel…"

"I will do what I can," was my reply. It was all I could think of without telling an outright lie. I wouldn't have to confine Cooper, just tell him where he couldn't go. "Now, are you going to be using my yard as a staging area again, or can I start fixing the damage done by your vehicles and people?"

"I'm really sorry about that. And no, we won't need to come through again. Now that the main investigation site is the clearing, we can use ATVs along the trail."

I thanked him, and he finally left, leaving me to wonder just what I'd gotten myself into by moving to such a remote location. I admonished Cooper to stay within the property boundaries until given leave to do otherwise. After I explained what the investigator had said, he sadly agreed.

The rain had stopped overnight, but the clouds remained, and it was damp and chilly the next morning. After watching the news, I made a list of seeds and plants I wanted for the garden then, taking a deep breath, walked outside to see what damage had been done to the soft ground. The front was an absolute mess with ruts and tire tracks, made worse by the rain which had been heavy enough to soften the ground. I would have to hire help to get it all fixed. The side and back weren't too bad, although those had only seen foot traffic. The more I thought about it, the less I wanted to plant grass. That would just need to be mowed.

I was musing what sort of ground cover I wanted when a Sheriff's Department SUV pulled into the drive. I sighed, wondering what they wanted now.

I was surprised to see Sergeant Anderson emerge. I'd thought his involvement in the case was over!

"Good morning, Mrs. Mackay," he called.

"Good morning, Sergeant. What can I do for you?"

He looked around at the yard, just as I'd been doing before his arrival.

"I think it's more what can *I* do for *you*?" he said. "I caught up with Will – Inspector Woods – last night, and he told me everything that happened yesterday. Including your complaint about the damage to your yard.

"My nephew runs a landscaping service. I was wondering if he might be of assistance to you."

"Sergeant, you might be my favorite person right now. I was just contemplating how I was going to get this fixed. As I told your deputy yesterday, I've only lived here three months and don't know many people. Among those I don't know are landscaping people! What's his name and phone number?"

He chuckled. "I remembered you're new. And on the off chance you *didn't* know anyone who could help, I've already called him." A truck rumbled up the drive. He twisted his head to look over his shoulder. "That's him now."

A man in his thirties jumped out of a Ford F-350 Super Duty truck. He was a couple inches shorter than the sergeant, but his coloring and facial features were similar. He walked up to Sergeant Anderson, shook his hand, and said, "Hi, Uncle Dave." Then walked up to me, extending his hand.

"I'm John Anderson, and I understand you need some help after yesterday," he said as I shook his hand.

"I'm El Mackay, and you're a godsend. I was just contemplating what to do when your uncle pulled up."

He surveyed the damage. "It's not as bad as it looks. You only have maybe a foot of soil until you hit rock in these parts unless it's already been disturbed for septic systems and such. A little grading, a little seeding, and in a month and a half, you won't know there was a car rally here."

Sergeant Anderson had joined us on the porch. He eyed my coffee cup with interest and chuckled as I caught him. "Would you two like some coffee?"

"You know I won't say no," the sergeant said as his nephew said, "Oh, that would be great!"

"Then let's go in. I hadn't planned on standing here this long without a jacket."

We trooped into the house, and once again, Cooper barreled through the doggy door to inspect the new arrivals. Honestly, I was surprised he hadn't come around to the porch when the first vehicle pulled up. I wondered where he'd been and what had caught his interest so intently.

"They smell okay. Not like the others. I like this one," Cooper said as he sniffed at Sergeant Anderson's outstretched hand. Then he

turned to the younger man. *"This one smells like dirt and grass. I like him, too."*

"I believe you've met with Cooper's approval, which is more than I can say for Ranger Doyle." I smiled at the men. "Now, coffee, then what are we going to do about my yard? And by the way, Sergeant, aren't you supposed to be on duty?"

"I am. My men are out patrolling, and I have my squawk-box here," he said, pointing to his shoulder. "So far, it's been a quiet morning, and I thought I'd take a moment to see how you were doing after the goings-on yesterday.

"Now, what was that about Caleb? He was here? Why?"

John took the mug I handed him and shook his head when I gestured toward the sugar. "No, thanks. Black as night, just like my dad and Uncle Dave."

"I'm naturally a little shaken up," I said as we sat at the table. "But all things considered, I'm more pissed about the extra work that'll need doing. I had only planned on the garden this year.

"As for Ranger Doyle, he was here sometime in late January, although I don't remember the exact date. Seems there'd been some attacks along the hiking trail, and he wanted to know if I'd seen or heard anything. I hadn't and haven't seen him since."

Sergeant Anderson excused himself, pulled out his cell phone, and went out onto the deck to make a call in private. I turned my attention to his nephew.

"So, John, I was thinking about planting something like sedge rather than grass. I'd like to not have to mow. I'd thought about it for next year's main project but since it needs doing now..."

He thought for a moment, then said, "That might work but you're still going to have a grass problem, regardless. All the wild grasses easily seed themselves, and sedge will take a couple of years to crowd them out. Even then, you'll have strays cropping up unless you start using chemicals."

"No chemicals," I said firmly. "I had enough of that crap at the house in Atlanta."

John stared out the back windows. "I'm not sure of the sun path here, but I think in five years or so, that part of the back is going to be mostly moss," he said, pointing to the southern edge of the clearing. "Especially if you don't trim any of the trees and allow them to hang naturally over your drain field.

"That would eliminate mowing about twenty-five percent of your cleared area. In five years. As for the rest? How about clover?"

Sergeant Anderson had returned from the deck and interjected, "If you plant clover, you'll be overrun with rabbits and deer in a month. They'll progress into your garden faster than a cat runs to catnip."

I'd already thought about the rabbits and deer and had made plans to stay up a few nights to talk with them when I got the garden planted. I couldn't tell the men that, though.

"No," I said. "Sedge is the way to go. Can you do that, John?"

"I can," he replied. "May I ask? How do you know so much about landscaping?"

I laughed. "I was going for a degree in horticulture before I got married. Ground cover was one of the first modules. Then I read up on what grows in the mountains before I moved, knowing I didn't want a *lawn*. Now, how much is this going to cost me?"

"Nothing," John replied.

"The Sheriff's Office will cover the cost," Sergeant Anderson added.

"What?" I was aghast. "No way. That's not in any police budget I've ever heard of."

"Normally, no. But I spoke with the sheriff this morning. He wasn't happy when he found out from Inspector Woods about all the vehicles parked in your yard. They should have used ATVs along the trail as soon as the campsite was discovered. Which, by the way, we also have to thank you – and your dog – for since our K-9s were otherwise engaged."

"Sheriff Danforth called me after Uncle Dave did," John said. "He'll cover the cost of the grading, and I'll throw in the seed. You shouldn't have to bear the cost of repairing the damage this soon into your residency in the county."

Wow. Small town living at its finest, I thought. "Okay. I'll take that. But in exchange for the seed, John, do you have someone who can do the mowing for me? My knees will only handle the garden. I know the yard is too uneven for me to comfortably walk behind a mower for two hours, and I was thinking about getting a lawn service anyways."

"I do. How does a hundred thirty every two weeks sound?" He thought a moment, again. "I can schedule you in on Wednesdays, late morning."

"I can live with that," I told him. Given that I'd paid twice that every two weeks just for mowing our postage-stamp sized yard in Atlanta, I thought it was a bargain but wasn't going to tell him so.

He stood. "You have yourself a deal," he said. "One of my guys will be here on Monday to grade and seed. It should take him a half a day. Unless it rains this weekend. Then we'll have to wait a couple of days until it dries out a bit. My wife, who does my books, will be in touch about billing."

I shook his hand. "Thank you. For everything."

He left, but Sergeant Anderson hung behind. "Something, Sergeant?" I asked.

He cleared his throat. "This is going to sound really forward and totally unprofessional. But may I take you to lunch tomorrow?"

I choked. "Ummm, what?"

"I like you, Mrs. Mackay. May I call you El? You didn't panic yesterday. You didn't even get the vapors, as my mother used to say. And here you are, the day after discovering a body, more angry about the damage to your yard than taking to your bed and crying all day.

"I've been a widower for fifteen years," he continued. "In that time, I haven't met another woman with a strong enough constitution to take on a cop. You seem like you might be able to handle it. Not to mention, your green eyes are the prettiest I've ever seen. I'd like to get to know you better. Tomorrow's my day off."

I didn't know what to say. Thomas had been gone a little over six months, and I'd given absolutely no thought to dating. But there was something about the sergeant that made me feel comfortable.

Cooper had been following our exchange with bright eyes. I looked down at him. The fact that *he* liked the sergeant was a major point. *Why the hell not?*

"I'd like that, Sergeant," I replied.

"Then, if we're going to be friends, you should call me Dave. Unless I'm on official business and there are other uniforms around. Should I pick you up, or would you feel more comfortable meeting me?"

"I'll meet you," I said, being prudent and all.

"Good. Meet me at the Whistle Stop at noon. Bring Cooper – they have an outdoor patio where dogs are welcome. Here's my personal cell in case there's a problem." He handed me a slip of paper with a local phone number on it. His eyes did indeed twinkle as he gave me a smile and short salute. "See you tomorrow!" He was whistling when he let himself out of the house.

"*What happened?*" Cooper asked. "*I could understand you but not him. And your face is red, and your heart is beating faster. Are you okay?*"

"I think so," I told him as I put the two men's mugs in the dishwasher and poured myself yet another cup. "We are going to meet the sergeant for lunch tomorrow."

"*We? I get to go with? Which one is the sergeant? Where are we going? Is it a long car ride? Will there be treats?*" Coop's tail was wagging so hard he was moving the chair he was standing next to an inch or so each time his tail hit it.

"Yes, you get to go with. The sergeant is the older man who just left. It's not a long ride, and yes, I'll make sure you get a treat."

I sat down with my phone and group-texted my kids and mother. **I have a date tomorrow for lunch,** I told them.

The replies were fast and furious. **With whom? Are you ready for a date? Be careful!**

Before I could reply to any of them, my phone rang, and caller ID said it was Samantha. "Deets, Mom, deets!"

I had learned through trial and error with her generation that "deets" meant "details."

"He's a sergeant, a watch commander with the Sheriff's Department," I told her. "I met him yesterday morning. He appears to be a few years older than me, just shy of six feet tall, I'd say, still in nice shape, graying black hair, and twinkling Sinatra-blue eyes. He told me today he's a widower. Not much else to tell at this point."

"But there must be more to make you want to go out with him!"

"Not really, sweetie. Just a comfortable feeling when I've been around him. It might just be his air of quiet authority. Or maybe because he called his nephew to fix the damage to my yard all the cars caused yesterday."

"I want to hear about that, too, but next week when Jay can be in on the call. You'd better call me tomorrow when you get home. I want to hear all the dirt!"

I promised, and she hung up to go back to work. Within seconds, she'd added what I'd told her to the group text and promised to fill her brother and grandmother in the next day if I didn't.

I sat at the table, coffee cup in hand, brain in a fog. I was going on a date!

Then I looked at the hand holding the cup. For over thirty years, I'd worn a wedding ring. The first one was a simple silver band – Thomas couldn't afford anything more. For our tenth anniversary, he got me a wedding set with a proper engagement ring. I hadn't taken it off – until now. If I'd accepted a date, that meant I accepted the fact I was single again.

I heaved a sigh and walked into my bedroom. I opened the jewelry box on my dresser and placed my wedding set in it. Since I was accustomed to wearing a ring on that finger, and it would feel naked if I didn't, I replaced it with my grandmother's topaz. We'd shared a birthday, and Mom wanted me to have it after she'd passed. It would take time to get used to seeing that, I knew. But I also felt good about my decision. I returned to the kitchen table and contemplated my life going forward.

Friday morning found me in a tizzy. I hadn't been on a date in thirty years and had no idea how to dress or act.

After my shower, I stared at the mirror in horror. I hadn't paid any attention to my appearance since my last charity board meeting a month after Thomas had passed. My hair had grown out, and my roots were no longer right at my scalp, but the gray and brown mix was almost to my ears. There was no time for a hair appointment this close to lunch.

"*What are you worried about?*" Cooper asked from his position guarding the bathroom door.

"I've let myself go," I moaned. "I look like crap."

In a moment of insight I didn't think was usually found in dogs, he said, "*You had just gotten out of bed when you met him a week ago. Why do you think you look any different than you did then?*"

I had learned in the intervening months dogs have an awful sense of time, but there was no use trying to correct the "week" to "two days." However, he was right. Sergeant Anderson – Dave – had seen me in my bathrobe with no makeup and severe bedhead. I just shrugged. He'd get over it – or not.

I pulled my hair back into a bun, which limited the amount of dyed versus natural visible. Then, what to wear? Even the fanciest restaurants in town catered to people on vacation, and about the only dress code was "shirts and shoes." So I pulled a clean pair of jeans from the closet, paired them with a casual buttoned shirt, blazer, and loafers. A quick swipe of blush, mascara, and lip gloss completed my "casual dating" look.

I was about to head to the car in the garage when I heard a loud bleating noise coming from outside. I knew the investigators were still over at the campsite, but this sound hadn't come from any human, and it was too close to the house. I went out to the deck to see if I could locate the noise.

When I stepped outside, it wasn't difficult. Standing at the foot of the stairs to the deck was a six-point buck, staring directly at me with no fear in his eyes.

"Were you trying to get my attention?" I asked, maintaining a safe distance from those sharp antlers.

"*I was,*" I heard. "*Your assistance is needed in the woods.*"

"I was about to leave the house," I told him. "Is it an emergency, or can it wait a while?"

The buck snorted. "*I would not have approached a human if time would solve the problem.*"

I motioned to the buck to lead on. He didn't run at full speed, but I was hard-pressed to keep up because I wasn't used to running, nor could I leap over obstacles in my path but had to go around.

Cooper and I followed him south, almost along the same path as we'd taken the day of the murder. This time, however, we didn't turn but continued straight.

About three minutes of trotting and stumbling brought us to a clog of dead trees and underbrush. I heard faint cries coming from somewhere close.

"*There is the problem,*" the buck said, tipping his head to indicate the pile of detritus in front of us.

I dropped my purse and clambered over a couple of dead trees. On the other side of a pile was a small, probably juvenile raccoon, its head stuck through one of those six-pack rings. If it had been hairless, I would have assumed its face to be blue at this point because it was choking. I was outraged that someone would have left such garbage behind them. Even with the supposed redesign so wildlife would be able to get themselves free, I couldn't pull one apart but had to cut them, either with a knife or scissors.

Thankfully, my purse was full of things women didn't normally carry, including a pocketknife.

"Cooper, I need my purse, and quick!" I said. My dog dutifully picked it up in his mouth and climbed the pile of wood, dropping it at my side. I got my pocketknife out and, squatting down, said, "Hold still. I'm going to cut this off you, and I don't want to hurt you."

Sliding the knife under the plastic meant it tightened on the coon's throat even more, but I kept the blade sharp, and it was only a moment of worse pain than it had been in. When I freed it, it lay there a few minutes, panting hard. While I waited for it to recover, I put the offending plastic in my purse to be properly disposed of at the house.

"Will you be okay?" I asked. "Is there anything else I can do?"

"*I think I will live*," it replied in a croaking voice. I still couldn't tell if it was male or female. "*I would not have if you had not come. Thank you.*"

"*And I thank you, as well*," the buck said. "*Humans do not normally help creatures such as us.*"

"How did you know to come get me?" I asked.

"*Birds and squirrels have spread the word that a decent human lives among us. I came upon this creature just as he was approaching the tree, but he did not heed my warning about the human trash. As soon as he got stuck, I went to where you live, hoping you would help. And you did.*

"*Do you need me to guide you back to your shelter?*"

"No, Cooper can get us back. Thank you for coming to get me." The buck dipped his head and bounded off deeper into the woods.

"If I can't help any further, I'll go home," I said to the raccoon.

"*I will be fine after I rest,*" he said. "*You have removed the danger, and I can now get at the food in the pile. Thank you again.*"

"In that case, Cooper, let's get back to the house. I'll need to clean up a bit before we leave."

I had to get some leaves and twigs out of my hair and change my socks, but otherwise there was no damage to my appearance. I texted Dave with an apology, that we were on our way, and would see him in fifteen minutes.

After I'd pulled onto the road, I looked at Cooper in the rearview mirror. "If you can only speak to your own species, how are the animals of different species in the forest communicating?"

"*I don't know. I only spoke to dogs at the big house. Cats and squirrels aren't worth the effort. Perhaps I can speak to others, after all. I should try.*"

It took a few minutes of driving around to find a parking spot. It was a glorious spring Friday, and the tourists were out in force. Between the raccoon and the parking problem, I was a half hour late and hurried toward my destination. I was breathless as I approached the stairs down to the Whistle Stop, which was below street level. Cooper was straining against his leash, eager to get to the cooked food even I could smell.

As a consequence of hurrying and Cooper's eagerness, I missed a step and almost tumbled head-over-heels down the rest of them. Thankfully, I was able to catch myself on the railing, but managed to wrench my shoulder and twist my ankle. I let go of Cooper's leash, but he stayed put at the foot of the stairs. Dave and another man were at my side in a heartbeat, both asking if I was okay and helping me to my feet.

My face was, I'm sure, beet red. It's bad enough to be a klutz at home but in public? It was mortifying.

"I'm fine," I told the men. "Embarrassed, is all."

"*Did I do that?*" Cooper asked, hanging his head. "*I didn't mean to hurt you.*"

I hopped down the rest of the stairs, hanging onto Dave's arm. When I reached the bottom, I gave Cooper a scratch on the head to let him know he was okay, too, and picked up the end of his leash.

Dave led us to a table behind a fenced-in area where there were several people with dogs already seated. Cooper dutifully lay on the floor at the side of the chair Dave had pulled out for me after lapping at the water bowl under the table.

I plopped into the chair and immediately regretted the action. The chair was wrought iron with no cushion, and my butt complained. However, that was the least of my pains. I could feel my ankle start to swell and wasn't certain I could reach the glass of water waiting for me on the table. I managed, however, because I got some ibuprofen out of my purse and swallowed a few pills.

"Are you sure you're okay?" Dave asked with a concerned look on his face.

"Not entirely," I replied truthfully. "I think my ankle is swelling, and my shoulder hurts like the dickens. It's probably just slight trauma. I'll wait a bit to see if it gets worse.

"I truly am more embarrassed than anything else. I'm a klutz on a normal basis at home. Just ask my kids. But in public? I'd like to be an ostrich right about now."

Dave laughed. "I've pulled some horrifying stunts myself. But if it gets worse, please let me know, and I'll take you to the doc-in-a-box out on the highway. Okay?"

The other man who had helped me on the stairs approached with a bag of ice and a bar towel in his hand.

"Thanks, Jack," Dave said as he took it. "I think her ankle could probably use it." He pulled another chair around, lifted my leg onto the seat, hitched up my pants leg, draped the bar towel over my ankle, and placed the bag of ice over that.

I looked at the man and proffered my thanks. "Jack here owns the place," Dave said. "Jack, this is El, and her dog is Cooper. They're new in town."

Jack shook my hand. "Welcome to Blue Ridge," he said with a smile. "I hope your near-tumble won't make you think less of us. I know those stairs are steep."

"It was entirely my fault. I was in a hurry because I was running late and wasn't watching where I was going closely enough. Not to mention, even I can smell something delicious. Cooper was eager to get to it, too."

Jack left us, and Dave finally settled back in his chair. "So are you hungry, or has your appetite fled after that?"

I chuckled. "I haven't eaten since breakfast, and it's been an eventful day so far. Yes, I'm hungry."

We looked at the menus and made our choices just as the waitress returned. After ordering (including a plain burger patty for Cooper), we turned to each other.

"So what can I tell you other than you know I'm a klutz?" I asked. "I've been out of the dating scene for thirty years and have no idea what should happen."

Dave smiled at me. "You've already mentioned you have kids. I've seen no evidence that anyone other than you and Cooper are living at your house, so you're single? From Atlanta? Why did you move here?"

"Two kids. Boy, thirty, lives in LA; girl, twenty-five, lives in New York. My husband passed last August from a heart attack.

"Our house in Atlanta was too big after the kids left and *way* too big after Thomas passed. I wanted a place small enough I could keep up with on my own rather than have an army of housekeepers. We'd rented a cabin up here ten years ago, and I liked the peace and quiet of the country. So, I sold the monstrosity and moved. You don't have a stereotypical southern accent. Are you from around here?"

Dave took a drink of his soda before answering. "I'm a native Atlantan. My wife was killed in a car accident fifteen years ago. I couldn't stand the house after she was gone and wanted a change of scenery. There was a job opening up here, so I took early retirement from Atlanta, got hired on here, and moved thirteen years ago. Haven't looked back since.

"Sadly, we had no children. Amy was a social worker and claimed the kids she took care of were enough for her.

"As to my lack of accent, I have my mother to thank for that. She ensured we spoke 'properly,' correcting us every time our speech slipped.

"I hate to ask in case it's personal, but what made you late?"

I grimaced, then reached down to my purse and pulled out the offending plastic that was still there.

"This was wrapped around a raccoon's neck," I huffed. "I had to get it free. Why in the world people don't take better care of their garbage is beyond me. Hell, they even talk about the dangers of these things on social media!"

"It didn't bite you, did he?" The dangers of raccoons and rabies were well-known in these parts.

"No. I think it was too worried about breathing to think about me," I said, declining to talk about my abilities with an almost-stranger. "I cut it off and backed away. It` lay there for a few minutes then wandered back into the woods."

"That was really nice of you, but please be careful where wildlife is concerned. Rabies is a real problem up here – even more so than down in the city."

I made a face. "Dave, you seem really nice, but we need to get one thing straight from the get-go. I can take care of myself and don't need someone telling me what to do and how to do it."

He at least looked contrite. "Sorry. Habit. Cops are trained to be protective. I should know better, though. Amy yelled at me multiple times. Most of her kids lived in not-so-nice neighborhoods, and I always worried about her. Nothing ever happened, though."

"Apology accepted," I said. "Now, on to more pleasant subjects."

Our food arrived and looked just as delicious as it smelled. "Do you say grace?" Dave asked as I put Cooper's basket on the floor for him.

"No, but I'll sit quietly if you do." He shook his head, and we dug in.

Before I could even finish chewing one bite, Cooper had inhaled his single burger patty.

"*More?*" he asked, looking up at me with a plaintive look on his face.

"No," I said, reaching down to pat him, my hamstring protesting at the unwelcome stretch. "That's enough treat for one day."

He plopped his head down on his paws and looked at me forlornly. Dave chuckled and after swallowing, said, "I imagine it take a lot of food to keep that one fed. What kind of dog is he?"

"Cooper is mostly Newfoundland with some Retriever, we think," reiterating what I'd told the investigator. "He has a Newfie's size, build, and coat, a Retriever's face, and lacks the webbing between the toes that a purebred Newfie has. In addition, and luckily for me, he doesn't drool much at all. He likes water as much as any Newfie, except baths. He'll jump in a mud puddle with no qualms, but it's a struggle to get him into the tub."

Dave threw back his head and guffawed. "I haven't yet met a dog who likes baths. Even our K-9 handlers have issues with that."

After our food baskets had been cleared, we sat a while longer with a cup of coffee each. We chatted quietly about our lives, his job, and my kids. I found myself relaxing more and more with each revelation.

We'd finished our coffees, and Dave cleared his throat. "I need to ask you something about what's been happening around your place. In a semi-professional capacity."

"Okay," I said, rather sorry the conversation had turned. "Shoot."

"You mentioned Caleb – Ranger Doyle – had visited you. We're a small law enforcement community up here and usually share virtually anything of interest, yet there's been no reports to us of problems along the hiking trail.

"I called his supervisor yesterday when I got back to the office, and he wasn't aware of Caleb's concerns, either. Can you reiterate what he said, leaving nothing out?"

I told him about the alleged attacks, both along the trail and at campsites. Then aloud, I wondered if that and the killings were related.

"That's what I'm wondering, too," Dave said. "I'm going to look further into it on my own. I'll let you know if I find anything that should concern you."

Finally, it was time to wrap up and head home. "I had a wonderful time," I said after Dave had paid the bill. "Thank you." Then I attempted to stand. *That* was a mistake. My ankle wouldn't hold my weight.

"Okay, that's it," Dave said. "I'm taking you to the clinic."

"I can drive myself," I said. "It's my left ankle."

"Maybe so, but I'd feel better if *I* did the driving. Sit back down and let me go get my truck. I'll be back in a minute."

I sighed and sat. "*Are you okay?*" Cooper looked up at me.

"No. I hurt my ankle bad when I tripped on the stairs. I need to have a doctor look at it."

"*I'm sorry,*" he whimpered.

"It wasn't all your fault," I reassured him. "I missed a step."

Then I realized the people at the table next to me were staring. I'd inadvertently had a conversation with my dog in public. So I was crazy. I just glared at them, and they finally turned away.

Dave returned a few minutes later and without ceremony, grabbed my purse and Cooper's leash, then picked me up from the chair.

"Hey," I said. "I can limp."

"No weight until we know it's not broken. I can carry you."

My face turned red again as eyes followed us up the stairs. His truck was idling in the street, the passenger door already open. Another bonus of small-town living. In the city, it would already be gone.

He let Cooper in first, then settled me in the passenger seat. He climbed in the driver's side and after buckling in, headed for the four-lane.

"This is so embarrassing," I moaned, thinking to myself this was *not* the way a first date should go.

"Don't worry about it." Dave smiled but never took his eyes off the road. "Like I said, I've done some stuff in my time, too. I'll tell you about some of the more humiliating instances while we're in the waiting room. Laughter will make you forget the pain."

When we got to the clinic's parking lot, Dave asked if Cooper would stay in the truck if the windows were rolled down.

"Yes, if I ask him to," I said.

"Good. Otherwise, I was going to have drop you and take him back to your house. I think he'd prefer to stay close."

I told Cooper to stay in the truck and we would be out as soon as we could. He whined a bit, then lay down on the seat as soon as Dave had scooped me up again.

Dave had me howling at some of his more notorious accidents over the years, including breaking a finger the first time he'd handled an automatic rifle. That took talent! It did help me forget my own humiliation – for a bit. It took an hour, but x-rays showed there was no break, just a sprain, and not even a bad one at that. I was discharged with an elastic wrap and a pair of crutches to be used for a couple of days.

Cooper sat up with a worried look on his face when we emerged from the clinic, me getting used to the crutches. Dave had slung my purse over his shoulder, unconcerned about the unmanly appearance of it.

"Should I take you home?" he asked.

"No, I need to get my car," I said. "I don't want to leave it parked downtown even overnight."

"I'll admit, I forgot we drove in separate vehicles. Where did you park?"

He dropped us at my car, then informed me he'd be following me home to ensure I was settled. I hoped he wasn't the hovering type.

My fears were unfounded. He followed me into the house, got me settled in my chair with my foot up on the ottoman and an ice pack on my ankle. After asking me where things were in the kitchen, he set a glass of water on the table next to me, then kissed me on the top of my head.

"I had a *great* time," he said. "Can we do it again when you're feeling up to it?"

"I'd like that," I replied. "But someplace without stairs the next time? I don't think I want to chance a repeat experience."

"I'll call you tomorrow to check in. We'll set a date and time when you're ready." Once again, he whistled as he let himself out of the house.

I spent a fairly sleepless night. "Minor sprain" or not, my ankle hurt, and I couldn't seem to get comfortable. Not to mention I usually slept on my left side, and my shoulder complained every time I rolled over on it. Finally, about five, I heaved a sigh and got up. Jostling the bed when I left it didn't wake Cooper, but the thump of the crutches did.

"*Why are you up?*" he asked sleepily.

"I hurt and can't sleep. Go back to sleep if you want."

He got out of bed and followed me to the kitchen. "*I will watch over you,*" he said.

I managed to get myself and a cup of coffee over to the chair using only one crutch. However, I couldn't sit down. There was a cat snoozing in my spot.

"You missed this?" I asked Cooper.

"*No. She asked if she could come in where it's safe. She was scared. I didn't think you'd mind.*"

"So you speak to cats now?'

"*I guess.*"

I looked down at it. A quick check told me it was a female. Based on her size, she was perhaps three or four months old. She was thin, filthy, and somewhat bedraggled. "So what's your story?"

The kitten opened one eye then, slowly, the other. "*You speak to me?*"

"I can, yes. Didn't you know?"

"*The others said you could, but I did not believe them.*

"It is frightening in the woods. There is something that chases those such as you. My mother was abandoned by her humans near here and was killed by a dog. I am the only one of my litter to survive.

"I met a raccoon who said you might be able to help me. I came here, and your dog said I could come in."

I eyed Cooper. "So how many other *guests* should I expect?"

"None. I told everyone else they could shelter under the porch but not come in the house. I know cats are okay — several of the people near the big house kept them."

Oh. Em. Gee. More animals wanted to come in my house? What was happening out in the woods?

And my dog was almost as soft-hearted as I was. "You'll have to share your food until I can get to the store and get proper cat food," I told him.

"Whatever. As long as she doesn't eat all of it."

"Okay then," I said to the cat. "Come in the kitchen and let's find you something to eat."

I set my cup down and thumped my way back to the kitchen, Cooper and the cat following. The cat kept a close eye on my crutch, ensuring she didn't stray too near it. A few minutes later, she had inhaled a half can of his wet food and a whole bowl of milk as both Cooper and I watched.

I made my way back to my chair and gratefully sank into it, laying the single crutch I was using on the floor next to me. I lifted my sore leg onto the ottoman and groaned with the movement. The cat, obviously unafraid, hopped into my lap and started giving herself a bath.

I turned the television on to get the morning news and was shocked when the lead story was "Murder in the Mountains." Turning the volume up, I listened as the news anchor described not only the two deaths by my house but one more about a mile away on the hiking trail.

"Authorities are at a loss as to motive," he said. "In addition, it appears all three deaths were due to blood loss."

"Holy shit," I exclaimed.

"*What?*" both Cooper and the cat asked.

"There's another body," I said.

"*Yes,*" the cat said.

"You knew?"

Both animals replied in the affirmative. "*All the animals are talking about it and are scared,*" Cooper told me. "*That's why they all wanted to come in the house. They think they will be killed, too.*"

"How…how many are out there?"

Cooper put his head on his paws. "*I don't know. Foxes, raccoons, mice, voles, coyotes…I think there might be a bear or two at the edge of the woods. They don't fit under the house or through my door.*"

"No squirrels or deer?"

"*I didn't see any squirrels. I think they are all in the trees with the birds. I haven't seen any deer.*"

So animals who lived on the ground and couldn't run faster than a human. Putting all the information I had together, I had to assume it was a vampire feeding on the humans. However, from what I knew, or at least read, they wouldn't slash their victims such as the one in my back yard. The one who had most of his blood when he left the campsite, if the trail that led to my property was any indication. That meant there was something or someone else out there besides the vampire.

As much as I knew, which admittedly wasn't a lot, all I could do was keep an eye out for myself and my charges. Speaking of, I looked down at the cat.

"Do you plan on staying here, or will you go back outside when the danger has passed?"

She paused in her cleaning to look up at me. "*It is warm here, and I do not have to hunt for food. I will stay if you will have me.*"

"You may stay, but there are conditions," I warned her.

"*Yes?*"

"You will have to go to the doctor to be checked out. There may be medication you will have to take so you stay healthy.

Eventually, you will need to be spayed so you do not bear any children. There will be drops on the back of your neck every month so you do not get fleas or ticks. Cooper tells me it is uncomfortable for a few minutes until the liquid works its way into your skin, but as I told him, it is better than the itch that comes with fleas or the sickness that comes with ticks.

"Also, you will relieve yourself outside until I can get a litter box for you. Once I have that, you may use it instead of going outside, but *no* peeing or pooping anywhere else."

"I do not know this 'doctor' you speak of, but I do not wish to bear children. I saw what happened to my mother and siblings. I will agree to your terms." She resumed grooming.

"One more thing," I added. "Humans call animals by names. Just like I call that dog there 'Cooper.' I will come up with a name for you, and when you hear it, you should respond."

"If it suits me, I will," she said.

I wasn't sure if she meant if the name suited her or if she would, like most cats, "take a message and get back" to me. I took a good, long look at her. I was pretty sure when she was clean she'd be a long-hair calico. "Patches," I said. "I will call you Patches."

The three of us sat in comfortable silence as I watched the rest of the morning news, checked social media on my phone, and occasionally thumped back and forth to refill my coffee cup. The first time I rose and displaced her, Patches glared at me then, with a flick of her tail, moved over to the sofa.

I was just figuring out how I might take a shower and not fall over as I tried to keep the weight off my foot when my phone rang. It was Dave.

"Mornin'!" he said. "How are you feeling?"

"Still sore, but that was to be expected. I was about to take a shower."

"Don't forget to wrap your bandage in plastic before you get in," he admonished.

"Actually, I was going to take it off for that short period of time. I *do* know how to wrap an elastic bandage."

"Of course. Sorry. That over-protective thing again. I actually called for another reason. They found another body yesterday afternoon."

"I know. I saw it on the Atlanta news this morning. How awful! Do they have any leads?"

"Not that I'm aware of, but then again, I'm not in the investigative division. We just got a bulletin handed down to keep our eyes and ears open in that part of the county.

"Since you live over there, I'm rather concerned about your safety."

I harrumphed. "I'm stuck inside the house for the next couple of days, all the doors lock, and I have a very protective *large* dog. I'm not worried."

"I know. Like I said, that over-protective thing. I get off at four-thirty. Can I bring you anything?"

"I did grocery shopping three days ago, so I'm set." Then I had a thought. "This is going to sound weird, but could you pick up some cat food, a litter box, and litter? Three or four cans of food ought to be enough until I can get some delivered. I could make it to the store, but hopping around the aisles on crutches might get difficult. Those floors can be slick."

"*What?* When did you get a cat?"

"Um. This morning? She was on my chair when I got up. I assume she came in through the doggy door. I fed her some of Cooper's food, and she seems content to stay."

Dave laughed. "And Cooper let her in? Your dog isn't as protective as you claim! Of course, I'll be happy to pick up supplies for her."

He didn't know just how protective Cooper really was. Then again, I hadn't looked outside to see what sort of menagerie was around the house, so I couldn't really confirm his story.

"I'll get cat supplies *and* dinner. I should be there by six. Will that suit?"

I said it would, and we hung up.

Once it was fully light, I hobbled to the deck to look around. I could see nothing out of the ordinary, but there was a lot of rustling in the leaves piled up underneath. I gingerly made my way down the stairs and crouched to get a look. Eyes. Lots of eyes looked back at me from small and medium-sized bodies.

A fox nosed its way from out of a pile of leaves. "*Will you protect us?*" it asked in a quivering voice. "*We are frightened.*"

"I'm not sure what I can do," I replied. "But you are welcome to shelter here as long as you feel necessary.

"I would ask that the various species do not fight, though. I don't want the noise *or* to have to clean up messes."

"*We have called a truce for now,*" it said.

Cooper and Patches had come out of the house and stood at my side. I looked at them. "Did you hear what I said? No fighting, no chasing. Not until these folks are back to their normal homes."

Patches sniffed. "*As long as they don't bother me, I will not bother them...for now.*"

Cooper whined. "*There are coyotes under the front. They are difficult to ignore.*"

"You'll manage. Go back in the house for now because I need to talk to the coyotes, too."

With only one crutch it was easier to go back through the house where I had furniture to hold onto. Once out the front door, I crouched to look under the porch and gave the coyotes the same spiel. *They* were not happy with my orders, but on the other hand, they didn't want to go back to the woods, either. Cooper had ignored my request and followed me outside. He growled something I didn't understand, but I think he was telling them he'd be the house police. All eight coyotes cowered so whatever he said, I think he got his point across.

With the ground rules laid down to my refugees, I felt I could finally take my shower. That was an adventure. As I'd told Dave I would, I unwrapped my ankle and felt it immediately start to swell again. I knew I should probably only take a bath, but I couldn't wash my hair that way, Since I was having company for dinner, I didn't want to look like a bum with greasy hair. So I teetered on one foot and washed just as fast as I could.

It took me a half hour to re-wrap my ankle and dress. By that time, I was ready for a painkiller or six. I hadn't had the prescription filled, thinking I would be able to get by on ibuprofen, and if both legs had been working, I'd probably have kicked myself. Not wanting to stand at the stove to cook, cereal sufficed for breakfast, and after downing a handful of pills, I re-settled myself in my chair with another ice pack. It was going to be a boring day.

I got cat food ordered for Patches, adding it to my monthly order for Cooper, and picked up the book I'd been reading. It hadn't truly held my interest when I started it, and it still didn't. I turned the TV back on to find nothing had changed there, either. Daytime television was just as bad as it had always been. Thankfully, with the advent of cable and satellite, I could at least watch movies. I fell asleep sometime in the middle of *Indiana Jones and the Kingdom of the Crystal Skull.*

Dave arrived a few minutes before six. One of the benefits of country living is being able to hear his truck pull up the drive. He hollered as soon as his foot hit the ground. "Don't get up. I'll let myself in." He'd forgotten, or didn't know, I kept my doors locked even, or especially in the woods.

I made it to the door just as I saw the knob turn. Laughing to myself, I unlocked the deadbolt and opened the door to see him balancing a bunch of shopping bags while reaching out for the door.

"You probably would've dropped something anyways," I said, holding the door open wide enough for him to get in.

He walked past me and dropped his armload on the island counter. "Go. Sit. I have more to bring in."

I obeyed and watched with curiosity as he made two more trips from his truck to the house. The cat box and litter were obvious, but what was the rest of it?

As he was unloading, Cooper banged through the doggy door and stood at attention, eyeing the bags on the counter with extreme interest. Patches came out from wherever she'd been napping and started winding her way around Dave's legs. The contents of the bags must have smelled divine.

"Hey!" he said as Patches nearly tripped him. "If you want what I have in the bags, you need to give me some space!"

He turned to me. "Where do you want the litter box?"

"I can do some of that," I complained.

"Nope. Stay off your ankle. You've probably been hopping around all day, and it hurts like hell, right?"

Sheepishly, I nodded.

"Right, then. Where do you want it?"

"In the second bathroom. There should be enough room between the vanity and the commode."

"Gotcha." He took Patches' accoutrements into the designated bath. Surprisingly, neither animal followed him.

Quietly, so Dave couldn't hear me, I asked, "What's up? You two would normally be trailing him to watch."

"*He has food,*" they said in unison. Patches even hopped up on the counter and started nosing in the bags.

"No nosing around," I admonished. "He'll give you whatever he thinks you can have when he's ready."

I got a glare in return, and she continued her exploration. Until, that is, Dave returned and lifted her off the counter, placing her back on the floor. She jumped back up and the process was repeated twice until she got the message.

"I brought ingredients for Hungarian goulash," he said as he emptied the bags. "I hope you like that. I also got cat food and both cat and dog treats. Where should I put those?"

"I don't think I've ever had Hungarian goulash," I replied. "But I'm always open to trying new stuff.

"You can put the animals' food in the long cupboard next to the fridge. Cooper's food is already in there. Can I help?"

"No. Like I said, stay off your ankle. Do you mind if I rummage in your cupboards for all the pots, pans, and utensils?"

I shook my head and turned back to the evening news. Thankfully, there was nothing more about the murders in our county and instead, was more focused on what was happening in the big city. The clanking of pots and pans was background noise, and soon, I heard the sizzling of meat in a pan and the chopping of vegetables on the cutting board.

An hour later, my stomach rumbled as Dave set a plate of a stew-looking mixture poured over egg noodles on my side table. It smelled delicious. Next to it he placed a glass of wine. Shortly, he brought his own plate and glass back and sat on the sofa across from me.

I moaned with pleasure at the first bite. "You'll have to give me the recipe," I said. "This is awesome!"

He wiped his mouth with a napkin and said, "I can't take credit. It's my grandmother's recipe. She was from the Old Country. I was told this was a staple dish – cheap and filling. But sure, I can write it down for you."

I cleaned my plate in no time and put it on the floor for Cooper to "wash." Patches sniffed at it and turned away. Dave went back for seconds, but when he was finished, Cooper got to clean his plate, too.

Dave still made me sit as he cleared the plates, loaded the dishwasher, and started it. He brought the bottle and refilled my wine glass.

"How did you get to be so domestic?" I asked.

"Mom. When we were growing up, she was of the opinion if you liked to eat, you could learn to cook your own food. If you didn't want to trip over anything or find lost socks or shoes, you could clean up your own messes. I can sew a button on and iron my own shirts, too."

"I think I'd like your mother," I said. "I'd like to know her secret. No matter how hard I tried, Jason just couldn't be bothered to learn to cook or clean. I honestly shudder to think what his condo must look like before I visit."

"She'd like you, too, I think," Dave smiled. "She likes independent women, those who are like her."

"There's something I failed to ask yesterday," I said. "Why did you become a cop?"

"Dad was an Atlanta City cop for thirty-five years. He spent a lot of his free time down at the homeless shelters and on the streets, trying to help those who, for whatever reason, couldn't help themselves. My older brother, John's dad, is a detective in Houston; my younger brother is a firefighter in Breckenridge,

Colorado. My sister, the baby of the family, is a public defender in Albany, New York. Dad led by example, I guess.

"He's the reason Mom instilled domesticity in all of us, I think. Between his actual job and his volunteer work, he wasn't around much. We all had to pitch in and help."

"Are both your parents still alive?"

Dave shook his head. "Dad was killed eighteen years ago when he was trying to help a meth addict to one of the treatment facilities downtown. It was a gang shooting, and he got caught in the crossfire. Mom is in a memory care home in Marietta. She has Alzheimer's."

"Oh, I'm so sorry." I really was. I'd read all sorts of stories about how that disease affected not only the patient but the family and was grateful my mother still had all her marbles.

Dave shrugged. "It's tough, but she's well taken care of. I go down once a week to see her. Some days she remembers me; some days I'm just a friendly face. What about you? Parents? Siblings?"

Thinking about my family was a downer, but he asked, so, "I had an older brother. He enlisted and was killed in Iraq in 1990.

"Dad retired about ten years ago, and he and Mom moved to Florida for their 'golden years.' Dad died of cancer four years ago. Mom's still alive and kicking down there."

"That's really a bummer," he commiserated. "Change of subject. What do you do?"

"What do I do?"

"Yeah. For a living, to fill up time…that."

"Oh." I squirmed. "I'm trying to figure that out.

"Thomas left me comfortable if I'm careful with my spending. I don't *have* to work, but once the garden is completely in, that'll only take a couple of hours a week. I *do* need to fill the days. I haven't decided what, yet."

Dave sat forward on the sofa, cradling his wine glass in his hands. "I'm just going to throw something out there. Take it with a grain of salt if you want.

"Have you thought about maybe you and Cooper joining the search-and-rescue teams up here? Most of them are volunteer – there's a club for them. Will – Inspector Woods – mentioned how good Cooper was at following the blood trail and you keeping him in check. Those are skills we can use on occasion.

"It would require training and certification, but after that, you'd only be needed once in a while, and only if you want to do whatever search the EMS folks ask about."

I shook my head. "While I think Cooper would be really good at it, I don't think my knees could handle hiking through rough country. Hell, I don't even think I could get all the mowing done before they complained loudly. I'm also not very outdoorsy. I've been camping exactly twice in my life and found I like my creature comforts."

Dave shrugged his shoulders and sat back. "It was an idea. If you change your mind, let me know. I can hook you up with the trainers."

I was just about to take another sip of wine when Cooper, Patches, and all the animals outside started yelling. I heard *"Go away!"* and *"Danger!"* I'm pretty sure all Dave heard was barking, yipping, yowling, and squeaking.

"What the hell?" Dave was out of his seat in a flash. "What's all that noise?"

I watched Patches scamper into my bedroom as Cooper flew through the house to the doggy door. "Cooper!" I called. "What's going on?"

"There is a noise outside. It sounds like it is near the garden. It's walking around. I am going to investigate."

"No! Cooper, come back!" I yelled. I didn't want my dog to become a victim of whatever or whoever was out there. He ignored me.

As the noise from the animals continued, Dave ran out the front door and returned moments later with his sidearm and a flashlight. "Stay inside," he admonished as he raced through the house and out the door to the deck.

I grabbed both crutches and followed – as far as the deck. Dave was out in the back, shining his flashlight this way and that, trying to see what had set the animals off. The light caught Cooper, pacing the back of the drain field in front of the trees. His growl was audible even from the house.

"What is it, boy?" Dave asked Cooper as he slowly made his way back to where the dog was stalking. The other animals were now quieting, but I could hear the coyotes' yips and growls still coming from the front of the house. Dave continued to shine his flashlight along the woods' edge but finally turned back to the house.

"Come, Cooper," I called as Dave mounted the steps to the deck. He still ignored me, and I could still hear him growling and the occasional *"Do not come into my yard."*

"I don't know what set the animals off," Dave said, "but whatever it was seems to be gone. At least, it's quieting down out here. Where did all the animals come from? Are you running a zoo? I've never heard so many in one place."

"They all appeared this morning," I said, trying to figure out how to tell him but not give my secret away. "When I looked under the deck and the porch, I saw dozens of animals, and they were all trembling. With fear, I think."

"As long as they don't fight, I'm not worried about them being there. What I *am* worried about is what caused them all to take shelter under my house at the same time…even species that would normally eat one another."

Cooper finally trotted back to my side. "Okay, bud?" I asked.

He head-butted my right leg, nearly causing me to lose my balance even with the crutches. *"It is gone now. It did not smell right. The foxes and coyotes tell me this is what is scaring them."*

Forgetting myself, I asked, "What do you mean, it didn't smell right?"

"*It smelled human, but not. Dead, but not.*"

"Explain."

"*I'm not sure how. Humans smell warm and sweet. This one had a human smell but…old? Sort of spoiled, like the meat you don't want to eat after you've had it a while. It didn't smell warm, either.*"

"Hang on a minute," Dave interjected. "What's going on?"

Oops. I did it again. I sighed. "I need to sit down. Come back inside, and I'll try to explain."

I hobbled back to my chair and sat with a sigh, lifting my leg onto the ottoman. Cooper settled himself on the floor next to me, on the other side of the chair from where I dropped my crutches. Dave, after locking the doors again, got a fresh ice pack out of the freezer and draped it over my ankle before re-seating himself on the chair opposite, eyes boring into mine.

"Okay. You were talking to your dog and not the way most people talk to theirs. Explain."

I took a big gulp of my wine. "You probably won't believe me, but here goes.

"You know how you talk to pets as if they were human, but not really expecting an answer?"

Dave nodded.

"About two weeks after Thomas died, I started hearing Cooper answer me. I thought I was going crazy, but he told me my mother and aunt converse with him, too. So I called my mother.

"She said women in our family can hear, um, higher orders of animals. It usually starts around menopause, but Mom thinks Thomas' death threw my hormones out of whack and I started early.

"I believed her, but on the other hand, it was just my dog, right? Then I rescued a wren stuck in one of the screens of this house the day I looked at it. I was already at the car in front when

I heard a child-like cry for help. The bird was stuck on one of the windows overlooking the deck. I don't think I would have heard its little "cheep" amongst the rest of the bird calls unless I heard the "help," too.

"And I can talk to the animals in the woods. That raccoon I rescued yesterday wasn't at the edge of the drain field like I told you. A six-point buck came to get me, and the poor guy was about a three-minute trot into the woods.

"One thing I can do my Mom or aunt can't is talk to trees. Well, one of them anyways. There's an old oak at the southern edge of the clearing that speaks to me."

I steeled myself to lose a new friend. "I wouldn't have said anything about it to you except for what happened tonight. If you don't want to deal with a crazy woman, I'll understand. Thank you for the shopping and dinner."

Dave drained his wine, went into the kitchen to open the second bottle he'd brought, refilled his glass, and drank half that down before sitting again.

"You're still here," I observed.

Dave nodded. "You forget, I worked in Atlanta for twenty years. I saw and heard all sorts of weird stuff. There are also folk up here in the mountains who have…unusual abilities. Some like yours. I've learned not to discount anything just because I don't understand it. And I can't *not* believe you after hearing your side of an exchange with your dog that would have made no sense if he wasn't replying.

"So this ability of yours. What are you hearing from the animals and what did Cooper say?"

I finished my wine. Dave refilled my glass. "The animals know what has happened to humans along the hiking trails, and they're scared they're next. They say something walks on two legs in the woods, but don't know what it is.

"Cooper told me whatever, or *whoever* was outside tonight didn't smell right.

"Mom told me along with the ability to talk with animals also comes the ability to see creatures for what they really are. Apparently, vampires, werewolves, gnomes, and all the other fairy tale creatures really do exist, and now I can see them. Haven't yet, as far as I know, but so I was told.

"If what I've garnered from the news reports and what Cooper tells me is correct, I think the murderer is a vampire."

Dave opened his mouth to speak, and I held up my hand to quiet him. "*However*, the vampire has help of some kind because as far as I know, they don't cut their victims, just bite them. What or who that help is, I don't know."

"Can I talk now?" Dave asked. I nodded.

"I believe you."

I almost choked on my sip of wine. "You do? Why? I mean, I'm relieved, but why?"

He smiled. A wry little smile. "First, like I said, I've seen some weird stuff in my time. But more importantly, some information about two of the murder victims wasn't released to the public, yet you already figured it out.

"The body in the tent and the third one they found yesterday? Neither of them was cut up badly like the guy in your back yard. But both died from severe blood loss. There were two holes that looked like the bite of human canine teeth on both. And both were bit on the neck.

"The hiker found yesterday had a few slices on his legs; one hamstrung him. But the coroner says none of the cuts were deep enough that the guy would have bled out.

"So along with this odd ability, did anyone tell you how to kill a vampire?"

I shook my head to clear it. Had I just heard him agree with me and ask my advice? I drank more wine.

"Sorry, no. And I don't know which, if any, of the methods you read in books work. I'd think, though, lopping off the head would work. I mean, if you can't bite and drink…?"

"Yeah, I thought about that, too. However, neither I nor any of my deputies have a sword handy."

I thought for a minute. "Do you have any sharpshooters? If you shot across the neck in a line, that would work. Maybe?"

Dave thought for a minute. "We're all really good shots, but no one is considered a sharpshooter. However, there's a type of load that, if packed into a high-velocity bullet, explodes on impact. I'll have to talk with the sheriff about that."

"You know, this is a really morbid conversation for two people who've just met," I said, conversationally.

"And it doesn't seem to bother you," he commented. "See what I mean about you being able to handle a cop?

"Sort of on the same subject, can you handle a gun? I don't like the idea of you being alone here with whatever it is stalking around your house."

I nodded. "I can, but they terrify me. They're so *loud*. My grandfather taught me to shoot a rifle when I turned fourteen, and he thought I was mature enough to handle a gun. The noise scared me, and I had a bruise on my shoulder from the recoil for a week afterward. I didn't and don't like them, and still don't want them in the house."

"Too bad. Then I'll have to rely on Cooper to keep you safe, but I'm not certain *he'd* be safe from a vampire."

I ruffled Coop's fur, and with that motion, Patches came out from under the chair and stuck her head between Coop's back and my hand. I scratched her head for a moment until she left to go do…whatever it is cats do.

Dave looked at his watch. "It's getting late. I should go. I'm driving into Marietta to see Mom in the morning, then taking the middle shift for a guy who's on vacation.

"Is there anything I can do or get you before I leave?"

I shook my head. "No. And thank you for a delicious dinner. You really didn't have to do that, you know. And the protection. And the worry. All that. It wasn't necessary. By the way, are you okay to drive?"

Dave stopped on his way to put his glass in the dishwasher, turned, and looked at me with concern in his eyes. "First, I'm fine to drive. A glass of wine an hour isn't enough to impair me, and I think the adrenaline burned off the first two glasses. But more importantly, didn't your husband help out when you were sick or injured? Didn't he worry about you?"

"Thomas wasn't the domestic sort. I rarely get sick and never bad enough I'm laid up in bed. After each kid was born, he threw frozen dinners in the oven for a couple of days until I could get up and around to cook.

"Worry? I'm not sure there was anything to worry about. We had an easy life."

"That's not what I'm talking about. I assume you were never in any dangerous neighborhoods or anything like that. I'm talking about everyday concern for your spouse's wellbeing. Just, *care*. I don't think I'm saying this right."

I shook my head. "I think I know what you're saying. Mom and Dad were like that. Refilling her coffee cup if he was getting his own, pecks on the cheek for no real reason, things like that."

I thought for a moment. "I think Thomas and I loved each other but weren't *in love*, if you know what I mean. We liked and were comfortable with each other, but there wasn't a lot of outward affection like what I saw with my folks."

His look of concern changed to one of pity, and he turned to put his glass in the dishwasher. I couldn't see his face when he said, "You're a beautiful, strong, smart, nearly fearless woman. Any man should have been proud to call you his wife and showed it at every turn – both publicly and privately.

"Now, I really do have to go. Like I said, I'll be in Marietta tomorrow morning but back up here by one. Call if you need anything. I mean *anything,* okay?"

I nodded. "I'll be fine. Thanks."

With a kiss on the top of my head, he whistled his way out the door, pausing long enough to say, "Lock up after me."

I grabbed the crutches and thumped my way over the door to lock it. Back in my chair, I pondered what he'd said while finishing my wine. He really was concerned for me, and I don't think I'd ever seen that from Thomas. Granted, we'd never lived somewhere a vampire was on the loose, but still. Even when I miscarried a girl between Jason and Samantha, Thomas was sad but buried himself in his work, seemingly not concerned about either my physical or emotional wellbeing.

I looked down at Cooper, who was observing me. "He's nice."

"*I like him,*" Cooper said. "*He likes you, too. Otherwise, he wouldn't have cooked for you. I heard the word 'treats.' What did he get me?*"

I laughed. "I don't know. Let's go look, shall we?"

I went into the kitchen, crutch in one hand and empty wineglass in the other. After putting it in the dishwasher, I opened the cupboard where I'd told Dave to put the animals' stuff. It was a crowded cupboard. I saw not only Cooper's dry and canned food, but a half shelf was full of cans and pouches of moist cat food, a whole bag of dry, and four pouches of treats for both dogs and cats. It was all organic and grain-free. He didn't get that at Walmart!

I grabbed a pouch each of cat and dog treats. At the shake of the pouch, Patches zoomed out of my bedroom and twined between my legs. *"Is that for me?"*

I opened both pouches and put a handful of each on the floor, about six feet apart. I didn't want Cooper inhaling his then going over to filch Patches' and told him so. He just grunted as he ate his, then stared at Patches as she daintily ate one piece at a time. But she ate all hers on her own with no help, so I was satisfied.

Before I put the coffee together for the morning, I texted Dave. **Where did you get the fancy cat food and why?**

A laughing face emoji answered with, **There's a small pet supply store downtown that carries all that. I heard you tell John you didn't want any chemicals on your yard and assumed you'd be all healthy-stuff with your animals, too. Did I do right?**

Yes, I replied. **But I forgot to reimburse you for it. How much do I owe you?**

Zilch. My gift to the new resident. Get some sleep.

I felt guilty. I ordered Coop's food online to save money and yes, it was all organic. It was also expensive. Buying the same sort of stuff locally would've had me choking, I assumed. I'd have to find a way to pay him back.

Thankfully, my sleep was uninterrupted. I had gone to bed in trepidation, thinking whatever was out there would come back after the house lights had been turned off and was awake for nearly an hour, anticipating a clamor from the animals outside and in. But when everything remained quiet, I drifted off and didn't even notice whether my ankle or shoulder hurt. Thank you, wine!

My ankle was finally feeling better the next day, and I chanced limping around without a crutch to do some housework. After turning on some 80s music (that my kids would grimace at), I got the dusting done. I even swung a dustmop around in time to the music before my ankle told me it was time to sit. Then I grabbed my list of plants and seeds for the garden. I didn't know if garlic hurt vampires, but I changed the planting arrangement around a little to include more of it, just in case. I could always use the extra in cooking.

After lunch, I decided to check on my refugees. Trying to be prudent, I used the crutches to get outside and down the stairs so I could peer under the deck. Sure enough, there were countless eyes staring back at me.

"Are you okay?" I asked in a general way. "Are you able to get food and water?"

"The oldest of us are taking turns to collect food while it is light outside," a fox, I think, replied. *"They are the most expendable. But we cannot all go out for fear we will be hurt or killed."*

"Hang on," I said, and thumped my way back into the house. Once inside, I dropped the crutches and grabbed my largest mixing bowl. I took that out back, placed it next to the deck stairs, and filled it from the hose.

I hopped back up to the deck and watched as, one by one, about fifty animals of various sizes crept out from underneath and lapped at the water. Almost immediately, I realized the smallest couldn't drink from that large bowl. I went back in and got a shallow baking pan for them. I had to refill both containers twice before I heard sighs of relief.

I returned back inside and took my next-largest mixing bowl out front and repeated the process. I heard a chorus of *"thank you,"* from underneath the porch. It was the least I could do.

Once back in my chair, I realized I hadn't seen Cooper all morning. He had risen with me, as usual, and gone outside. But on a normal day, he would be in and out, having a nosh on his dry food or getting a drink of water. Today, though, the in-and-out hadn't happened.

I went back out to the deck and called his name. Three times. There was no answer. I called down under the deck. "Hey. Have you seen my dog?"

A small, squeaky voice replied, "*He left some time after it got light. He went into the woods.*"

Oh. Shit. I went back in the house, re-wrapped my ankle as tight as I could get it without cutting off circulation, and pulled on my outside boots, lacing the left one tightly around my ankle, too. Slipping my phone into the back pocket of my jeans, I headed for the old oak.

After placing my hand on its bark to get its attention, I asked, "I am looking for my dog. I understand he went in the woods this morning but has not returned. Can you help me find him?"

The leaves rustled but there was no reply. "*Please,*" I said. "He is important to me."

"*We know. We are looking. Patience.*"

Patience had never been my strong suit, but I had learned it raising two kids. After what seemed like an hour but was probably only about ten minutes, I heard, "*He is lying some distance from here. Follow the leaves to him.*"

"*Follow the leaves?*" I thought. Then I noticed even though there was only a slight breeze, the leaves of several trees were waving as if the wind were gusting this way and that. Even the trees that were only budded out waved their branches. I made my way into the woods, looking up to watch the trees and down so I wouldn't trip on anything.

It took me the better part of a half hour to limp my way to where I saw Cooper lying on the ground. Ignoring my ankle, I ran to him. He was breathing but unconscious. I saw no blood, but he didn't stir when I put my hand on his side and spoke his name.

There was no way I could carry a dog that weighed as much as I did back to the house. I pulled out my cell. Thankfully, I had one bar of service. Crossing my fingers that my signal didn't disappear, I called Dave.

I didn't bother with pleasantries. "Cooper's in the woods, and he's hurt," I said, choking back the tears. "I can't carry him back to the house."

"Calm down, El," he said in a soothing tone. "Do you have GPS turned on?"

"I don't know. I don't know how to do that."

He walked me through getting GPS coordinates on the map function of my phone. "Okay. I have where you are. I'm only at the beginning of my shift, so I can't come. I'm going to send Deputy Sorenson to get a retired vet I know. He'll be faster than trying to get someone from the clinic. It'll take about fifteen minutes."

"Okay," I said, my voice breaking.

"I'm not going to hang up, but I'm going to put you on speaker so you hear me making the calls. I'll stay with you until they arrive."

I heard Dave on a phone, describing what the problem was and how big Cooper is. Then I heard the crackle of a radio as he gave his deputy instructions. I continued to stroke Cooper and speak to him. "It'll be all right, bud," I said. "They're bringing a doctor who will make you better."

By this time, tears were streaming down my face. Cooper had been my only companion since Thomas died. I couldn't lose him. I just couldn't.

"How's he doing, El?" Dave asked. "They're about ten minutes away now."

"Nothing's changed. He's still breathing but unconscious. I can't hear him, Dave. He's not speaking to me!"

"Doc Martin knows what he's doing," Dave continued to soothe. "He'll get Coop to the hospital and fix him up."

I heard some rustling in the dead leaves on the forest floor. Then a warm body bumped my back. Patches came around my back to lean against my side, and I saw two foxes, a rabbit, and one skunk making a circle around me.

"We came to keep you company," Patches said. *"We know your heart hurts."*

I sniffed. "Thank you," I said. "I appreciate it. But there are humans coming to help." I looked at the not-cats. "You may not want to be around when they arrive."

"We will stay with you until we hear the humans," the skunk said. *"Then we will leave."*

"What's going on?" I heard from my phone's speaker. "I heard meowing and squeaking, then you talking."

"Patches and a few animals have come to keep me company until your deputy and the vet arrive."

"Wow. Kinda cool."

I sniffed again. "Yeah."

I felt Cooper stir beneath my hand. My heart leapt. "Stay still, Coop," I said. "Help is on the way."

"Hurt. "

"I know. But don't move. You might hurt yourself worse."

"Okay." I continued to lightly stroke his fur.

A lifetime later, I heard the loud crashing of humans through the woods. The wild animals melted away, but Patches stayed, still leaning against my side.

"Ms. Mackay?" I heard a gruff voice call.

"I think they're here," I told Dave. "You should probably get back to work."

"I'm good. I'll stay on the line in case I can help further."

"Here!" I yelled. Then I looked down at Patches. "Can you guide them here?"

Her tail lifted. *"I will try. Most humans are stupid, though, and they may not follow."* But she took off in the direction of the voice at a run.

It took a minute or two, but when I heard footsteps close, I looked over my shoulder to see Patches, her tail still in the air, walking toward me with two men behind her. One was tall and lanky, with weathered features indicating he'd spent a lot of time outdoors. The other man, as big and brawny as Hulk Hogan, wore a uniform. The tall man carried a doctor's bag. The deputy carried a portable stretcher in one hand and his cell phone in the other.

"Your cat?" The vet said. "Smart. She came right up to us then turned in this direction. I'm Alex Martin, Dave's veterinarian friend."

"I guess she's mine," I said as she leaned against my side again. "She showed up in the house yesterday. Can you help my dog?"

"Let's see what we've got," he said as he crouched on the other side of Cooper from me.

"Hi fella." His voice was quiet and soothing. "I can see you're awake. I want to shine a light into your eyes, then I'm going to move my hands over you to see what's wrong. You let me know if I hurt you, will you?"

I looked at him in amazement. "You can talk to animals?"

"All my life," he replied as he shined a small flashlight back and forth at Cooper's eyes then slowly worked his hands over Cooper's body. Cooper twitched a couple of times when the vet touched his legs and side but didn't cry. "Makes being a vet a lot easier, I can tell you!"

He got to Cooper's head, and when he probed the side lying on the ground, Cooper whined. "*Hurts.*"

Doc Martin's hand came away bloody. I gasped. "Is he going to be okay?" I cried.

"He'll be fine. It's not deep. And just like humans, dogs' heads bleed a lot.

"Mark, help me turn him over onto the stretcher."

I stood and moved out of the way and fidgeted as the men worked. Deputy Sorenson laid the stretcher alongside Coop then gently, the men rolled him over onto it. Doc Martin looked up at me.

"Surprisingly, he isn't concussed. Hard head, that one. He really doesn't need a hospital if you're willing to stay up with him tonight. We can take him back to your house, and I can stitch him up there."

"Please." I knew I sounded like I was begging. "I know I can't stay with him at the clinic, and I'd like to. I'll stay up all night if that's what it takes."

"Hey Doc?" Dave's voice came from my phone.

"Yeah? What'cha want, Dave?"

"If necessary, I can relieve El when I get off shift."

"I'll be okay, but thanks, Dave," I said. He'd done enough already.

"Okay. Call if you need me, though. I'm happy to help." We hung up. Just in time. My phone had been warning me for ten minutes and ran out of battery as soon as I hit the 'end' button.

The men picked up Cooper on the stretcher. "Which way?" Deputy Sorenson asked.

Shit if I knew. I was somewhere in the woods. I hadn't been paying attention to exactly where I was going in my effort to get to Cooper. All of a sudden, though, the tree branches started swaying as they had, showing me the way.

Bless the trees. "This way," I said and started limping in the direction of home.

"You're hurt!" Doc said.

"I sprained my ankle a couple of days ago," I replied. "It *was* better, but I walked and ran to find Cooper. I'll get off it as soon as I know he'll be okay."

It took us twenty minutes to get back to the house by which time my ankle was screaming. I could feel the inflammation straining against the boot and wrap.

I hobbled into the house, the men and Cooper right behind me. When I gestured, they laid him on the island counter, and Doc Martin started pulling supplies from his bag.

"Would you like some coffee while you work?" I asked. "I'm going to be sucking it down and had planned on making another pot anyways."

Both men jumped at the chance for caffeine, so I limped around and got a new pot going. While I worked, the vet gave Cooper a shot in his hip, cleaned the blood away from a gash in his temple, then swabbed a sharp-smelling liquid on the spot that had Coop whining.

"I know," the vet soothed. "But this is to dull the hurt. I have to sew your wound closed."

"*Okay. Thirsty,*" Cooper said.

"In a minute. Let me get you stitched up first."

The vet worked quickly, and in only about ten minutes, the area around the injury had been shaved, the wound sutured closed, and a bandage applied.

"What's your dog's name?" I was asked.

When I told him, he crouched down so he could look Coop in the eyes. "Cooper, your head is going to hurt a lot then itch terribly in a few days. Do *not* paw the bandage or scratch at the itch.

"I am going to give your human some pills that will help with the pain and also the healing. Take them when she gives them to you. Don't spit them out.

"She will also have to change your bandage once a day. Don't fight her on it. If you do, she will have to call me, and I am not as nice as she is."

"*You are nice,*" Cooper said, still slurring his words a bit. "*You help me.*"

I watched Deputy Sorenson through the whole exchange. He didn't even bat an eye.

"Hey," I said as I handed him a mug of coffee. "Aren't you weirded out by the doc?"

He took a sip then drawled, "Nah. Doc Martin's ability is known throughout the county. At least, by those of us who grew up here. It's not all that uncommon. My granddad could talk to animals, too."

I think my eyes bugged out. "Really? It's not rare?"

Doc laughed. "I can tell just by your speech you ain't from around here, as the saying goes. There's a lot of folk with different abilities up here. Some like me, some can find water by dowsing, things like that. We just don't advertise it. Where do you want us to put Cooper, Ms. Mackay?"

"El, please. And on the floor in the living room by that chair. That's where I'm going to park myself in about five minutes."

The men gently lifted Coop off the counter and carried him over to where I'd indicated. The vet pulled a squeeze bottle out of his case, filled it with water, and gave Cooper a drink from it. He then put the bottle on the table next to the chair. Deputy Sorenson inhaled the rest of his cup of coffee, grabbed the stretcher, and waited expectantly by the door.

"Thank you for all your help," I told him. "I couldn't have carried him out of the woods by myself."

"All part of the service," he said with a smile.

"Now, El, let's get you looked at," Doc said.

"I'm fine. It's just a sprain I've aggravated. Some ibuprofen, some ice, and a lot of rest, and it'll heal."

"Nonetheless, I'm a doctor, and what's wrong with you is no different than a dog's ankle. Let me make sure it's not any worse than you think. Sit."

I sat, and he gently removed my boot, then the elastic wrap. He probed my ankle, and I winced.

"This time, you're right, young lady." He rewrapped my ankle then, without asking, went into the kitchen and brought back the hand towel I had hanging on the oven door and an ice pack from the freezer. After laying them across my ankle, he stood and looked at me critically.

"You should have a pair of crutches."

"I do. They're in my bedroom. I dropped them there when I went to change shoes to go looking for Cooper."

Deputy Sorenson turned toward my bedroom, and I winced again – this time out of embarrassment. I hadn't made my bed in three days, figuring I'd be the only one in there.

He returned with the crutches in his hand. Doc Martin took them and laid them on the floor on the other side of the chair from Cooper, saying, "Okay, I'm going to ask because I *really* want to know. How did you find your dog? Y'all were awfully far back into Forestry Service territory."

Knowing *he* could speak to animals and *unusual* abilities not unheard of in the mountains made my confession a little easier. "I can talk to animals, too. But not just them. At least one tree talks to me. *They* were the ones to find Coop and guide me to him.

"They helped me find home, too, if you want to know the truth. I was so concerned about Cooper I paid no attention to where I was going and would have been lost. But they showed me the path.

"I have a question for you."

He smiled. "Ask. I'm generally an open book."

"How did you have all the necessary supplies with you? Most vets need a clinic nowadays."

He laughed. "You *are* a city girl, aren't you? I'm an old-fashioned country vet. Sure, I worked with others in a practice before I retired, but I don't deal with humans all that well, so they kept me on house calls. I treated animals their humans couldn't get to the clinic. Horses, cows, pigs, and yes, dogs and cats. I still work on occasion for folks who don't like my replacement or in odd situations, like this one. So I keep my license current.

"Now," he continued, holding out two small packets. "These are for Cooper. The big ones, one every four hours for two days unless he tells you he doesn't need them. Those are for pain. The little ones are antibiotics. One a day for ten days. He'll probably be groggy for another hour or so from the shot I gave him, and the pills are going to hit him, too, but allow him to get up if he needs to. Just watch to make sure he doesn't stumble or pass out. If he does, call me immediately.

"You heard me tell him you need to change the bandage once a day. I left supplies on the counter. You should be able to leave it exposed in two or three days, but watch it. If it starts to swell, turn red, or seep, call the clinic and get him in ASAP.

"You'll need to make an appointment with the clinic in ten days to get the stitches removed. I'll alert them."

"These are for you." He held out a third packet. "They're just a higher dose ibuprofen than you can get over the counter, but it'll save you from having to swallow a *bunch* of pills. You know how to treat your ankle otherwise, so I won't lecture.

"This is for you, too." He held out a piece of paper. It was his bill, which was less than half of what I expected for a house (woods?) call and stitches. "Send me a check when you can get to your checkbook, but don't get up unnecessarily. I can wait."

He held out his hand, and I shook it. "It was a pleasure meeting you, El. You can always call me if something comes up the clinic can't handle. That ain't much, but it does happen. Stay off your ankle as much as you can."

With that, he grabbed his bag from the counter, and both men headed out the door to wherever they'd parked their car – it wasn't in my driveway. I picked my crutches off the floor, thumped over to lock the door, plopped back in my chair, and rearranged the towel and ice pack.

"Aren't we a pair?" I mused. "Both hurt, and no one to really help us. We'll manage, won't we, bud?"

"*I will help when I can*," came the mumbled reply.

"I know," I reached down to stroke his back. "Sleep, now, and get better."

I didn't exactly stay awake the whole night but dozed on and off, waking to hourly alarms on my phone to check on Cooper. He seemed content to lie on the floor next to my chair and doze, too, only rising twice – once to get a long drink of water and another to go outside to relieve himself. He dutifully waited for me to hobble after him so I could ensure he was okay outside. Patches woke me with a soft paw to my cheek to remind me she was hungry then, once she'd eaten, curled up in my lap.

The sun was rising when Cooper slowly stood and looked at me. "*You did not sleep well. You should go to bed.*"

"How are you feeling?" I asked, suddenly more awake than I'd felt all night.

"*Tired. Sore.*"

"Do you feel well enough to talk about what happened? You were a long ways outside our boundaries."

He padded over to his food dish and looked at me expectantly. I grabbed a crutch, filled his food bowl, and while I was in the kitchen, started a pot of coffee. I watched him eat as I waited for my elixir to perk. He was obviously quite hungry because he ate all his food in record time. I was thankful his appetite had returned – that meant he was on the road to recovery.

"*More?*" he asked.

"Normally, I'd say no," I chided him. "But because you didn't eat last night, I will give you more this time." And I did. He ate all that, too. After he'd finished, I gave him an antibiotic and asked about the pain pill. He declined that one but dutifully swallowed the little one.

"That tastes horrible," he said, lapping vigorously at his water.

"Necessary," was all I said.

Once my coffee cup was filled, I returned to my chair.

"Now, about yesterday. Why did you leave our property?"

He limped back to his spot by my chair and lay down once again, this time with his head on his paws, looking up at me with an embarrassed expression.

"There was an odd smell," he began. *"It wasn't normal. Human, but not. A dirt and rock odor, too.*

"The path took me from near where I found the dead body, past the tree you talk to, and into the woods. It was a fresh smell, so I know it wasn't from the other day. I did not pay attention to where I was going. I just followed the smell.

"I came across a small man who looked but did not smell entirely human, with the dirt and rock odor I had smelled. He was as tall as your knee but bigger around than your leg. He told me to go away, and when I didn't, he attacked me with a weapon of some sort. I fought back but he hit me with something sharp, and that's all I remember until I woke up and you were there."

"I am glad you are still alive," I told him. "But you shouldn't have gone by yourself, nor should you have gone beyond our property line.

"Whatever is out there has helped kill three humans and now, probably hurt you. Please, from now on, stay close to the house until the bad guys are caught."

Just then, my phone rang.

"El?" It was Dave. "I didn't call too early, did I? How are you and Cooper this morning?"

"I'm up. We're both tired and sore," I said, "but he is awake and talking so I think he'll be okay."

"I'm so glad." There was relief in his voice. "I'd like to come over and question Cooper about what happened yesterday – with your help, of course. Doc tells me the injury to his head came from a crude knife of some sort, and I want to know more."

"You're welcome to come, but I can tell you what he said," I started.

"I know, but I may ask different questions."

I sighed. "Okay. Give me an hour to get myself together. Don't you have to work today?"

"I'm off again. The shift I worked yesterday was a trade with the guy who was on vacation.

"And I have some concerns," he said. "Inspector Woods, who is the local CID guy, and the GBI people don't think this is anything but a normal serial killer. I tried to insinuate a vampire into the conversation yesterday and was blown off.

"I need to do my own looking-into for my own peace of mind. So I want to talk with Cooper. Okay?"

"Okay," I said. "See you in an hour. Since I'll be up anyways, the front door will be unlocked."

I hung up and, grabbing my crutches, hobbled into the kitchen for some plastic wrap. I didn't want to chance taking the compression off my ankle, even for the length of a shower. Sadly, I didn't have any. A quick rummage in the recycling bin under the counter produced a plastic grocery bag that would work.

Once again, I did a balancing act in the tub. Trying to keep my weight off that ankle while turning this way and that to rinse was an adventure.

"*Do you want me to stand under you?*" Cooper asked from his supervisory position at the door. "*You could rest your leg on my back.*"

"I appreciate that," I sputtered through some shampoo, "but I think I'd be more off balance. Besides, you can't get your bandage wet."

Forty-five minutes later, I was presentable *and* had managed to change Cooper's dressing while keeping him from fidgeting as I did.

"*It hurts and itches,*" he whined.

"That's a good sign," I told him as I taped the last little bit of gauze down. "It means you're healing fast. But, like the doctor said, no pawing or scratching. If you do, I'll put a cone on you."

Dogs' memories, like their sense of time, weren't the best, but the "cone of shame" he'd had to wear after being neutered had made a lasting impression. I laughed when he said, "No. *I will be good. Do not make me wear one of those again.*"

I was grateful I'd already showered because as soon as I'd finished with Coop, a bobcat came rumbling up the driveway. I opened the door, and the man driving it waved to me, then started in on grading the mess left by all the vehicles the previous week. I'd totally forgotten about that!

Resigning myself to the roar of heavy equipment for a few hours, I'd just poured another cup of coffee and gotten myself settled with yet another ice pack when there was a loud knock at the door before Dave let himself in.

"I bring gifts," he announced. I could smell his gifts from where I sat. He'd stopped at the bakery downtown before coming by. I'd only had one or two of their pastries since moving, but they were well worth the trip into town anytime.

"Coffee's hot," I said. "It should go well with whatever you brought."

He poured himself a cup, and I heard plates rattling in the kitchen. "I see John's man is hard at work," he said. Shortly, he returned to the living room with two plates holding bear claws, and his mug.

"Y'know," I mumbled around a delicious bite. "I've never asked where you live. It must be close to downtown."

He swallowed then said, "I used to have a cabin about four miles south of town. I discovered I didn't really have the time to keep up with it, working so much, so I sold that and bought one of the new condos they built next to the railroad tracks downtown. It's a good bachelor pad. I'm close to the office, within walking distance, actually, *and* close to all the restaurants."

"Pets?"

"Not right now. Pinky, our hairless cat, died about three years ago. She lived to the ripe age of twenty. She was really Amy's cat but…

"Anyways, I never got around to getting another one. And, like I said, I work so much, it really wouldn't be fair to whoever I got. I'm usually only home to sleep and shower."

"All work and no play makes Jack a dull boy," I said.

"I haven't had much else to do," he countered. "I don't hunt or fish, hike, play golf or tennis. I spend some time with kids at the high school to try to keep them out of trouble. There's an after-school club for careers and community leaders I help with. Then, I read a lot. The librarians know me well."

"But you obviously work out," I said, giving him an admiring glance.

"I do. Not to excess, mind you. I'm too damned old to think I could be a body builder. But I need to keep in shape for the job, so I run most mornings and lift a few weights."

He finished eating and took both our plates back to the kitchen where he put them in the dishwasher.

"Need anything while I'm here? More coffee? Another ice pack? By the way, did you overdo it yesterday? You shouldn't still have needed ice based on the way you were moving on Saturday."

"I did. Of course I did," I said. "I was more concerned with finding Coop than whatever would happen to me. So yes, I'm worse off than I was two days ago."

"So where's my victim?" He thankfully changed the subject.

"Outside, I think. I heard the doggy door flap a few minutes ago. I'm surprised he wasn't here, begging."

Dave walked to the back door and, opening it, let out a piercing whistle before yelling Cooper's name.

"Come on, boy," I heard him say and soon, I heard Coop pad his way through the house to my side. He was still moving gingerly, as if his hip hurt him.

"Are you okay?" I asked. "You're walking like you hurt."

"*Still sore but not bad. Head's worse.*"

"Want a pain pill?"

"*No. I do not like the feeling it gives me. I will be fine without.*"

"Okay, but if it gets worse, you let me know. Dave would like to ask you some questions about yesterday. Will you answer?"

"*If it will help catch the bad things, I will.*"

I looked at Dave. "He says okay. Ask away."

Dave leaned over in his chair so he could look directly at Cooper. "First, I know El has taught you about property boundaries. Why did you go beyond them?"

When I asked the question, Cooper lowered his eyes and wouldn't look at Dave. But he reiterated what he'd told me about the scent.

"You are lucky your human can talk with trees," Dave chided. "Otherwise, she may not have found you."

"*I know,*" Cooper said. "*But it was so unusual, I had to find out what it was.*"

"Okay," Dave continued. "So when you found whatever it was with the scent, what did you see?"

Cooper described the being. While he was doing so and I translated for Dave, I pulled my laptop from its perch on the side table and started searching for images of fairytale creatures. Of course, there were thousands of them, and thousands of interpretations of what such beings might look like.

One, however, struck me as I thought of what Cooper had described. I turned the screen and angled it down so he could see. "Does this look like what you saw?"

"*Mostly like that, yes,*" he replied, a smile in his voice for the first time all day.

I turned the screen so Dave could see. "Cooper was describing a gnome."

Dave stared at the picture. "Really? There are gnomes around here, too? But why would they attack humans, or Coop, for that matter?"

"I have no idea," I said. "But now we know who the perpetrators are. We just need to find them."

"I have more questions." Dave looked back at the dog. "Can you describe what you were hit with?"

"*He had two weapons, one in each hand,*" Cooper said. "*One looked like that thing she uses to pound with. The other cut. Both were sized like he was.*"

"So a hammer and a knife?" Dave mused. "El, where do you keep your tools?"

I pointed him in the direction of the garage. "Toolbox on the floor next to the house door."

Dave excused himself and returned with my claw hammer and a grin on his face. "Pink? Really?"

"Hey. I needed tools since I no longer had workmen to take care of hanging pictures and such. It was on sale, okay?" My face felt almost as rosy as the toolbox.

Laughing, he held it so Cooper could see it. "Did the pounding thing look like this?"

"*No. It was…more. Like the can she takes my yummy food out of on top, not that strange shape.*"

"So probably a mallet," Dave interpreted Cooper's description with ease. "What about the knife?" He went to the block on my counter and pulled out the three largest, bringing them back and laying them on the floor. "Did it look like any of these?"

Cooper rose with a groan and looked at the knives. He laid his paw on the butcher knife. "*Like this but not as shiny. It was crooked, too, without the smooth edge.*"

"Thank you, Cooper." Dave ruffled the fur on his back, careful not to touch the bandage on his head or the obviously sore leg. "You've been very helpful."

Coop gave Dave's hand a half-hearted lick, then curled up in his bed by the fireplace. That, apparently, was uncomfortable because within seconds, he was back on the floor, stretched out next to my chair.

"Do you need anything?" I asked my dog. "A pain pill, maybe?"

"Will it help me sleep? I would like to not hurt for a while."

"It will," I said. I started to rise from my chair when Dave pushed me back down. "I'll get it. Stay off that ankle. What and where?"

"Top shelf of the cupboard where the dog and cat food is kept. Big pill, not little."

Dave picked a pill out of the pouch. "Does he need peanut butter with it?"

Coop's tail thumped. *"Peanut butter? I know that word, too! That is good!"*

I laughed. "This time, yeah. Make a pouch with a chunk of bread and bury the pill in it."

"I've seen that on television," Dave said. "I never understood how they swallow the pill with their mouths glued shut by the peanut butter. But it seems to work, so okay."

He grabbed a slice of bread from the loaf, smeared some peanut butter on it, put the pill in the middle, and folded it in. He held it in front of Cooper's mouth, and Coop damned near swallowed Dave's fingers with it.

"Mmmmm. Good," Cooper mumbled around his mouthful. After that, he got up to get a drink of water, then lay back down next to me. It only took a few minutes before I saw him relax. A minute more, and he was snoring.

"So Coop's taken care of, and we know who or what our bad guys are," Dave started. "Now we have to figure out how to catch them. The regular cops won't even look for anything not human. You up for some police work, El?"

"I'll happily be an armchair detective," I said. "I'm a good armchair quarterback on Sundays. But I'm not sure how much help I can be with my ankle."

"Ah, a Falcons fan," Dave replied.

"Nope. I mean, I watch them because that's what's on TV. I grew up a Vikings fan and always will be. I keep closer track of their score on the crawl than I do the game being televised."

"Then we will have to be rivals during some games. I'm a Falcons fan through-and-through. Now to the detecting part.

"We need to know all we can about gnomes and vampires. How to spot them, how to disable them, all that. I have a feeling with your ability, you might be better at this than I, a plain-vanilla human, will be."

"Hey. I've only had this ability for a few months," I retorted. "And I've never been an investigator of any kind.

"Hang on. I just remembered something I need to do," I managed to completely rise from my chair before Dave pushed me back down again.

"What? Whatever it is, I'll do it. I'm here and completely ambulatory. *Stay off your ankle, woman!*"

I sighed. "Okay. Fine. There are bowls front and back, and a baking pan out back that need to be filled with water. The critters sheltering here are venturing out in daylight to get food but not all can get water. Use the hoses."

"I can do that," he said and went outside. As soon as he was gone, I grabbed my crutches and thumped my way to the bathroom. *That* he couldn't help with.

We arrived back in the living room at the same time, and Dave gave me the stink-eye. When I explained where I'd been, he relented.

"Where do we start with all this?" I asked. "What's out there is probably myth."

"My granddad believed myths rose out of people's collective experiences," Dave replied. "Someone wrote what today would be a news article; others corroborated it. Then, over time because the story wasn't continually verified, they became fairytales.

"So we start with the fairytales and myths. Find similar threads between them.

"What do you want for lunch? I'm going to go home to get my laptop and can pick something up," he finished.

"I was just going to make a lunchmeat sandwich, so whatever you get will be fine," I said.

"Okay. I'll be back in about forty-five minutes."

While he was gone, I mused on this strange relationship. In just five days, I had been…adopted? I wasn't sure. I knew I liked the guy, and he certainly exhibited a lot of signs of liking me, but we'd spent more time together than most people in that short span. Perhaps this was the new way of dating? He seemed to have no problem with my talking to animals *or* letting me in on police business. It was all so weird.

Patches hopped into my lap. "Where've you been?" I asked as I petted her. I'd found she didn't like to be scratched but stroked, and rarely on her head, but her back was always okay.

"*Out. Away from the noise,*" was all she said. "*Why was that man here again?*"

"He enforces human law," I told her, wondering if she would understand. "He is also my friend. We are trying to find who is hurting people *and* the creature who hurt Cooper yesterday. He will return soon."

"*Oh*," she said. Then, having been petted enough, hopped off my lap and went somewhere else. Probably the bedroom. I'd found her napping on my pillow more than once in the two days she'd lived with me.

Dave returned, laptop case slung over one shoulder, carrying a bag that wasn't from any fast-food restaurant. When he opened the door, I realized the background noise from the bobcat wasn't there, and I hadn't noticed when it stopped.

"I figured you wouldn't want meat twice in one day, so I got fish tacos. I hope that's okay," he said, putting his case by the chair he'd been occupying and taking the bag into the kitchen.

"Dave?" I started as he laid the tacos out on plates. "What are we doing?"

"Huh?"

"I mean, I've only known you five days, and in that time, you've brought me in on an investigation you're really not part of but feel compelled to work on. More importantly, you're *taking care* of me, a virtual stranger."

He put a plate by me, then sat and put his plate on the table next to him.

"I hadn't really thought about it, but now that you bring it up…" He was quiet for a moment, then said, "I don't know. From the time I met you, you felt comfortable. Like I'd known you for several years.

"Nothing about me being a cop has seemed to faze you. Nothing about this weird murder has seemed to bother you at all, despite its, what do you call it? Paranormal aspects. You're just taking it all in stride. That's cool in and of itself.

"Then there's your stubborn independence, which is completely at odds with my desire to protect. In that way, you remind me of Amy. But…" he held up his hand when I opened my mouth. "That's the only thing that reminds me of her. She would've freaked if animals started talking to her, not to mention the vampire and gnome. She wasn't even entirely okay with me going after drug dealers and such, but knew it was part of my job, so accepted it.

"I'd like to think we are friends," he continued. "Where it goes from there, I don't know. I'm not looking for anything more at this point."

I nodded. "Friends are good," I said. "Especially friends that bring me food *and* give me a project to occupy my mind. I haven't had much of a challenge in the last few months, and it'll feel good to sink my teeth into something. Like these tacos."

Cooper didn't even wake at the smell of tacos. Patches, however, strolled in from the bedroom. "*Food?*"

I laughed. "None for you, all for me. Go back to sleep."

She harrumphed then meandered back to her nap.

We ate then divvied up the searching. He took the vampire; I took the gnome. After only five minutes, I asked him to get me a pad of paper and pen from the desk in the study. I thought better if I could write things down.

As soon as he left the room, my phone rang. It was my mother.

"Hi, El," she said. "Calling to check in on you."

"It's been…an eventful couple of days," I replied and filled her in on happenings.

"Holy cow! What have you gotten yourself into, girl?"

"Not sure, Mom." I motioned to Dave to sit when he made signs asking whether he should leave to give me some privacy. "Dave's not a part of the official investigation, but we both think we know better than the real investigators, who are looking for a human.

"What do you know about vampires and gnomes?"

I heard her choke on the other end of the line. "You think that's what's killing people and hurt Cooper?"

"The signs point to a vampire feeding to excess, and Cooper identified the gnome when I showed him a picture off the internet. So yeah."

"Well, I probably don't know anything more than you. I've only dealt with humans and animals my whole life. I'd look at fairytales and myths for starters, though."

I smiled. "That's what we thought and where we're starting. I just thought maybe you'd come across something more than that."

"Sorry, no, sweetie. I avoid anything that doesn't look human, know what I mean?

"Now, since you have company and have work to do, I'm going to let you go. Stay off your ankle as much as you can, otherwise it's never going to get better. If that Dave of yours doesn't want to hang around, I'll come up."

Even though she couldn't see it, I shook my head. "I have crutches, Mom. I can get around the house fine. There's no need for you to come. Love you!"

I hung up before she could get another word in. Mom hanging around and babying me was the last thing I wanted.

"Mom is being a mother?" Dave asked with a smile.

"Yeah. She'd be here in a heartbeat if I let her, and I wouldn't even be allowed to shower without help. I love her to pieces, but she can be a bit…bossy."

"Two peas in a pod," he said. "I'll bet you two butt heads when you're together."

"I am not bossy!" I protested. "Opinionated? Yes. I'll own that one. But I try not to be an overlord."

He just grinned and, taking his own pad of paper, started looking at his laptop. I did the same.

After only a couple of minutes, he went into the kitchen and started another pot of coffee. "I hope you don't mind, but I think

I'm going to need some this afternoon." I didn't mind at all and agreed with his assessment.

Three cups of coffee later, I was only a little ways into understanding the gnome. Or gnomes. Was there more than one trying to get rid of humans in this part of the country?

What I found was that they lived in clans in forested areas of mountains. They lived in caves, if they were available, or carved out underground cities from the mountain rock. They were known as miners but of what depended on who you talked to.

More searching told me this part of the Appalachians was riddled with small caves, most inaccessible to humans. So there was probably a clan living somewhat close by. I scoured spelunking sites looking for mentions and found several saying they'd found a cave, but it was too small to squeeze into. Pulling up a map, I marked those spots and hit 'print' so I could share the information with…whom?

"Have you found anything useful?" I asked Dave.

"Not really," he replied, looking up from his screen. "Apart from repeats of the Stoker story, you know, sunlight, stakes, garlic, crosses, there's not much different. The only alternative I can think of is beheading, and we've talked about that already. What have you got?"

I filled him in. "Someone needs to go visit all those caves and see if there's a gnome clan living in one of them, *and* see if they'll talk to us, *and* see if they know who's being a problem child, *and* see if they know how or can help stop him. I'd go, but there's no way I could walk all that far right now."

"I can't see them, can I?"

"I don't know, but I sort of doubt it. Mom and Cooper have implied only people with 'magic in their blood'…" I used air-quotes around those last words. "…can see the paranormal species."

Without speaking, Dave pulled his cell phone out of his pocket and, scrolling through his contacts, dialed one. "Alex? Dave Anderson here. I have an odd question for you.

"Yes, Cooper's doing fine. He's asleep on the floor next to El at the moment.

"I know you can talk to animals. But do you see other species? You know, creatures out of fairytales like vampires and such."

He listened, then, "Listen, we have a problem that CID and GBI won't acknowledge. Trust me, I tried."

Dave went on to tell the story of the bodies drained of blood, the slashed guy in my back yard, and Cooper's description of what hurt him.

"El has marked out on a map possible sites where a gnome clan might live. Obviously, with that ankle, she can't go with. I need someone who can not only see these creatures but also act as a go-between since I don't think I can see them, much less have a conversation."

He listened some more. "Okay. Have one of them call me. We'll have to look not only during the day but my off-hours. I doubt Tyler would give me time to do it when the beings I've proposed are the culprits aren't supposed to exist."

They exchanged a few more pleasantries, then Dave hung up. Slipping his phone back into his pocket, he said, "That was Doc Martin. He agrees with our assessment of the perps. Yes, he can see other species, too, but claims he's too old to go traipsing through the woods looking for trouble.

"However, he has two nephews up in North Carolina who are were-bobcats."

"What?" I exclaimed.

"Hey, I'm just repeating what he said. Anyway, he thinks they might be able to help and will call them. I'll see if they're willing, and if they are, will coordinate with them."

"Won't it be dangerous?" I was starting to panic on his behalf.

"I don't really think so. Based on what Cooper said, and what you found, these gnomes are small – much smaller than even you, much less me. Even if they came at us with knives, I carry a gun, which is much more effective and…scarier.

"It needs to be done, El," he continued when I shook my head with displeasure. "I swore an oath to protect the citizens of this county, state, and country. If my fellow officers won't do anything about it, I have to.

"My thought is to take care of the gnome, first, one way or another. Without help, the vampire might be more reluctant to actually kill. But he or she needs to be tracked down and stopped, too, somehow."

I fidgeted in my chair. I wasn't sure *what* I thought would happen once we figured everything out, but putting Dave who, in his words, was a plain-vanilla human, in the way of a creature he couldn't see bothered me a lot. Not that I was sure what *I* could do, but being stuck in the house with this damned ankle left me feeling frustrated.

Dave looked at his watch then went through the motions of shutting down his computer. "We've been at this for hours. I'm going to go home and leave you to *relax*. Read a book. Watch television. Do *something* that isn't related to the problem and stay off your ankle. That's an order."

I narrowed my eyes at his last statement. He saw and sighed.

"Okay. Not an order. A strong request? *Please*, El. I have this awful vision of you out in the woods on your crutches, trying to find the gnome or vampire on your own. Not that my training included dealing with fairytale creatures, but I *have* been trained to deal with violent humans. Let me do what I was trained for."

Once again, he leaned down and kissed the top of my head before whistling his way out of the house.

Coop woke me with a loud bark in the middle of the night.

"*Something is in the garden,*" he told me when I grabbed his ruff and asked him why I was awake when it was still dark outside.

I threw on a robe, put on a pair of slippers, grabbed the crutches, and on my way to the deck door, dropped one of those and grabbed a flashlight. I heard whimpering coming from beneath the deck but no words. What I saw when I shined the light in the direction of the garden pissed me off beyond words. There was a small man-looking critter taking a sledgehammer to my beds!

"What the hell do you think you're doing?" I yelled. "Leave my stuff alone!"

He stopped and turned to me. "You can see me? *Scheisse!*" But it didn't deter him. In heavily accented English, he continued, "Get out of here, human!" Then he turned back to hammering at the bed walls.

Coop had followed me out and made a beeline for the man, barking and growling all the while. Fearful the sledgehammer would be turned on my dog again, I called him off.

"Cooper, stop!" I called as I once again ran on my sore ankle. "If you harm my dog, I *will* kill you!" I yelled at whoever or whatever it was, brandishing the crutch like a weapon.

Closing in on the being, who only came to my knees, I dropped the crutch and grabbed him by his long hair, pulling him away from what he was doing. I let the flashlight fall to the ground and tore the wee sledgehammer from his grasp. That wasn't as easy as it sounded because he had a death grip on it. But I finally managed and flung it away.

"Coop," I said, "please pick up the flashlight and shine it over here so I can see what I'm holding."

While I said that, the man was wriggling in my grasp, trying to kick me in the leg. I was thankful for my weeks of hauling heavy stuff because my arm hadn't yet tired, although his movement almost threw me off balance. Coop dutifully picked up the flashlight in his mouth and turned so it was shining right in the face of what I held.

"Let me go, you *verdammt* human!" he cried. At least, I was assuming it was a male. Accompanying the long hair was an even longer beard.

"I'm not letting you go. As a matter of fact, I'm going to call the sheriff."

At that, he laughed. "*You* may be able to see me, but other humans can't. What're you going to tell him?"

I didn't bother telling him at least one member of the sheriff's department believed me. "So tell me, little man, what are you and why are you attempting to destroy my garden?"

"Stupid females know nothing! I'm a gnome!"

I assumed as much but, "Okay, you're a gnome. You answered the first question; now answer the second."

He wriggled even harder. "Let me go!"

"I can stand here all night if that's what it takes." I couldn't, but he didn't need to know that. "And even if I let you go my dog can smell you, and I promise his teeth are quite sharp." I didn't know if this was the same gnome who had attacked Cooper but was willing to believe he wouldn't be hurt a second time.

"You are on my property. I want you gone!" he cried.

"I'm not on your property, I'm on mine," I retorted. "You're the one trespassing."

"You stupid female," he repeated. "This has been gnome territory for hundreds of your years."

"Perhaps," I replied. "But you've shared it with humans for that entire time. First the Native Americans, then whites. This house has been here for eighteen years, and no one I've spoken with has mentioned random, invisible acts of violence."

My arm was finally tiring, and my grip on his hair was slipping. I had to do *something* to calm this guy and get him to stop destroying my garden.

"Listen," I said. "Why can't we coexist peacefully? There's plenty of room for everyone, and we can stay out of each other's way."

"*Nein!*" he spat. "You *all* need to go. Every last one of you."

I finally lost my grip, and he fell to the ground, quickly standing and running away toward the woods. I put a hand on Coop's back to keep him from chasing. "Let him go for now," I said. "He won't be back tonight, at least."

I took the flashlight from Coop, wiped the slobber off on my bathrobe, and shined it around until I saw the sledgehammer. It was no larger than my claw hammer but about twice as heavy. I slipped it into the pocket of my bathrobe, which immediately sagged. Picking up the crutch, I hobbled back to the house, the hammer banging against my leg with every step. I would probably have a bruise.

The clock on the stove glared the time of 3:55 a.m. I was too hyped up on adrenaline to go back to sleep, but it was too damned early to do much else. Sighing, I turned on the light in the breakfast area and flipped the coffeepot switch to 'on.' As soon as I had a full cup, I took that and yet another ice pack into the living room. At the rate I was going, my ankle would never fully heal. Middle-of-the-night television was no better than daytime, but I found another movie to watch.

Coop lay on his bed with a groan. "*You should sleep. I am.*"

"No longer tired. Is that the gnome who attacked you?"

"*I don't know. Smelled the same. Looked similar.*" He squirmed around until he found a more comfortable position.

I smiled and said, "By the way, thank you for waking me."

"*My job*," he said, then rolled over and presented his back to me. Shortly, I heard his snoring.

Once the sun was up, I dressed and went out to inspect the damage. He hadn't managed to actually destroy any beds, but there were deep gouges and cracks in the rock wall he'd been working on. I was certain, with a deft hand, I could repair them with dyed concrete, but it would take time.

Assuming Dave would be up and getting ready for work, I called him when the clock struck seven.

"El? What are you doing up so early?" he asked.

"I've been up for hours. I had a visitor just before four."

"What? Who?"

I told him about the gnome and my wondering if it was the same one who'd attacked the hikers and Cooper. "I didn't see any knife, though," I said.

"You could have been hurt!" he exclaimed.

"Nah. He didn't weigh even as much as a bag of the rocks I used for the paths. I got the hammer out of his hand, and once I dropped him, he ran off. I have the hammer if you want to look at it."

"Geez, El," he said. "I can't leave you alone for twelve hours! I'll come by after my shift to get it. I assume you ran on your ankle again. How's it doing?"

"Hurts like hell. But I had no choice. I wasn't going to let Cooper deal with him on his own. I promise to stay in my chair as much as humanly possible today. Okay?"

"Okay. See you shortly before five. But if something happens between now and then, call me immediately."

I wasn't lying when I said my ankle hurt like hell. Eyeing Cooper, who was still asleep, I hobbled into the kitchen and swallowed one of his pain pills. We were about the same weight, and it was Tramadol, so it should work on me. Then I crawled back into bed.

I woke several hours later to two warm bodies pressed next to me. Cooper was on one side, Patches on the other. My stomach growled, reminding me I hadn't eaten. The clock said it was shortly after three. No wonder I was hungry!

When I stirred, both animals woke. Cooper dutifully got up with me, but Patches just glared, and once I was completely out of bed, moved to my warm spot.

I finally made that sandwich with the lunchmeat, sharing bits with Cooper…and Patches, who'd deigned to come into the kitchen to see what I was doing. After only one bite, she went back into the bedroom. Apparently, human food wasn't as interesting to her as a nap.

"We're late with this. We should have done it this morning, but you need to take a pill, and I need to change your bandage," I told him when we were done eating.

"*I don't want to feel sleepy*," he said.

"Not that pill, the little one that will help prevent infection. You don't have to have a pain pill if you don't want, but you *do* need the other one."

He sighed. "*Okay*."

I allowed him a long drink of water after the pill before I had him sit on my ottoman so I could check his injury. He shook his head vigorously when I got the bandage off.

"*I don't like having that on my head*," he said.

The injury looked like it was healing well so I didn't bother to re-bandage it. "I'll leave it off but still, no pawing or scratching at it, okay?"

"*I'll try*," he said, but I'd have to keep an eye on him. I knew how difficult it was to not scratch an itch.

I remembered I was expecting company so made myself somewhat presentable. I'd just finished in the bathroom when there was a knock at the door. I opened it to find Dave, still in uniform.

"Hi," he said, leaning over to kiss my cheek before walking in past me. "How are you feeling?"

I shut the door and hobbled to my chair. "A little better. I took one of Coop's pain pills and slept most of the day."

"Good. You probably needed it." He stood in front of me, looking down. "Where's that hammer?"

I pointed to the breakfast table. He picked it up and examined it while walking back to the chair he'd occupied the day before.

"Looks handmade. See here?" He pointed to the joint between the handle and the head. "This handle was carved to fit the head exactly. And the head isn't machine-smooth. I'll keep this, if you don't mind. It might help identify the guy if we can get any others to talk to us."

"I don't have any use for it so sure," I replied. "Have you heard from Doc Martin's nephews?"

"One called me a couple of hours ago, and they're both on board. He and his brother, naturally, work, so we can't go out until Saturday, when we're all off. But we plan on starting out at daybreak to search out those caves you marked. Maybe we'll have some luck.

"In the meantime," he started.

"What?"

"I've been trying to think of a way to keep you safe until we can catch the perps. Have you thought about a motion-detector light and camera? It can be aimed at the garden."

I shook my head. "Jason suggested that when I moved in. We had a similar system at the house in Atlanta, but with as many wild animals around as there are, it'd probably be going off every whipstitch.

"And the gnome wasn't bothered by my flashlight. He didn't quit what he was doing until I picked him up and physically stopped him."

"Then my final suggestion," he said, "is for me to stay here at night." He raised his hand when I was about to protest. "You *need* to stay off that ankle, or it's never going to heal. You know this. And I don't think this morning will be the only visit that guy will pay you. Based on what you said, he's going to keep going until either he gets his way or is caught.

"Either way, you haven't mentioned anyone else that might help you out. I know your kids or mother would be here in a heartbeat if you asked, but I don't know what they could do that I can't, and I'm *here*. Other than your mother being able to see him, that is."

I sighed. I didn't really have any friends I could call on in the area. Oh, sure, I'd sort of bonded with Mary and Tim at the garden center over bed design, but they were acquaintances only and had no idea about my *gift* or all the BS that was happening around here.

Then there was Anne, a woman I'd met at the Whistle Stop bar about a month previous when I just *had* to get out of the house one evening. At first, we spoke because we were sitting next to each other, appeared about the same age, and were there alone. Then we found out we were both single and from the Upper Midwest. Over the course of several drinks (piña colada for me, margarita for her) we let slip that both of us had *unusual* abilities – me being able to talk with animals, and she being able to see and talk with ghosts.

She'd actually seen and spoken with two in town. Like me, she'd been fearful of revealing her secret, but once I told her about myself, we both relaxed and compared notes. That was the start of what I had a feeling would be a close friendship – my first in years.

She probably would have come over, but I knew she wasn't in town and didn't know when she'd return.

Mom wasn't a choice, and I didn't want to take my kids away from their lives. Or explain *why* they had to drop everything to come take care of me.

"But you can't see him either," I argued. "So what can you do?"

"I have a hunch Cooper has learned his lesson on how to fight a gnome, especially if there are no knives being used against him. If he can pin the guy down, I can probably feel to get hands on him. At the very least, I can brandish my weapon in the direction you point and maybe scare him off without you running around.

"Then there's the issue of the vampire out there. Cooper is probably known to be *your* dog, and he or she might try something to hurt one or both of you. I *know* I can see one of those. And I've made my own loads with armor-piercing ammunition which should give even a vampire pause."

I sighed. This was all getting to be too much. I said so.

"I'm sorry to put you through all this, El. I really am. Civilians shouldn't have to deal with criminals, human or not. I'm trying to do my job the best way I know how when my boss doesn't believe in the paranormal."

"I need to think. Can you fill the critters' water dishes while I do?" I wanted him out of the house for a few minutes. "I didn't get around to it today."

While Dave went to do as I asked, I chewed on his request. On the one hand, I knew I really couldn't protect myself from nasties. The gnome? Sure. But a vampire? Since I didn't know what *really* hurt or killed them, probably not.

On the other hand, it seemed too soon after Thomas' death to have a man stay overnight – even in the guest bedroom. In the last six months, I'd gotten used to my solitude (if you discounted a dog and cat who talked to me, or the refugees under the house) and I wasn't ready to give that up.

On the *other* hand, I liked Dave, and he seemed to like me. He was also right that I had to stay off my ankle if I wanted it to heal, and there was no one around to do things for me.

On the *other* hand (how many did I have?), I was quite capable of getting around the house with crutches. If the gnome came back, the garden beds could be rebuilt – if he actually managed to destroy one or more with another tiny hammer. If the vampire came to my house, well, I wouldn't let anyone in I didn't know, and I'd keep the doors and windows locked.

Cooper came out from the bedroom and put his head on my knee. "*Are you upset?*"

"I'm thinking."

"*About what?*"

"Dave wants to stay here to protect us at night until the bad guys are caught. I know neither of us is really up to par, but I don't want an almost-stranger staying here, either. What do you think?"

Cooper snorted. "*I am sore, yes, but it won't stop me protecting you. We will be fine alone. We have been for years.*"

I chuckled at his inability to keep track of time, but he was right.

Dave returned and standing in front of me, said, "Did I give you enough time to think?"

I sighed. "You did, thank you. I appreciate your concern, I really do, but my answer must be no."

Dave started to reply, but I cut him off. "You're a nice man and yes, I consider us friends. In theory, you being an officer of the law should make you trustworthy. However, I don't feel I've known you long enough to let you stay overnight in my house – even in the guest bedroom.

"If it makes you feel any better, I won't go farther than the front and back stairs until my ankle is better. I *do* need to give the critters water, but other than that, I'll stay in the house with the windows and doors locked. That includes the doggy door for now. Cooper needs to stay quiet for a few more days, anyway, and can let me know when he has to go out."

Dave sat in the chair opposite with a huff. "You know it'll take me about fifteen minutes to get here if anything goes wrong, don't you? Fifteen minutes is a long time when bad shit's going down."

"I know," I replied. "But I'm just not ready to have someone else here. Cooper and I will be fine. If the gnome comes back, he can do whatever damage he wants to the garden beds. Those can be fixed. And I won't let someone I don't know into the house."

"Okay," he sighed. "Your house, your decision. At least let me order pizza for dinner."

"*Pizza?*" Cooper perked up. "*I know that word, too! That means good snacks!*"

"*What is this 'pizza?'*" Patches strolled out of the bedroom.

"*Oooh, it's good stuff!*" Cooper apparently had decided speaking to cats was all right. "*It has gooey food, and spicy food, and…*"

"*Then I will try some,*" she said as she hopped into my lap to have her back stroked.

"It's not here yet," I told her as I gave her the required petting. "I will give you some when it arrives. You may or may not like it."

Dave watched me with interest. "What?"

"Cooper has explained to Patches that pizza, which is a word he apparently recognizes even from other humans, is good stuff. She has decided she will try it. So, I think pizza *is* on the menu tonight, but let me get it. You've been spending a lot of money on me. It's my turn."

"Fine," he said. "Where do you normally get yours from?"

"Dominos. They deliver here; Pizza Hut doesn't. Why?"

"Call Mountain Pizza. I'll go get it. It's worth the trip back into town."

"Another time? If you go get it, you'll pay for it. The idea was for *me* to pay for dinner. I have the Dominos app on my phone."

He acquiesced, then we had to figure out what to get. I usually ordered veggie; he usually had the all-meat special. We compromised at half-and-half. An extra-large would leave enough for the furry pigs and probably lunch for me the next day.

After dinner (Patches licked all the cheese off her piece and left the rest, which Cooper immediately inhaled), Dave walked around the house, ensuring all the doors and windows were locked. Although I understood the need for security, I was unhappy. It was a glorious spring evening, and I would have preferred to have the house open.

"I'll say it one more time, then I'll go," he said. "I don't like you staying here alone."

"I know. But you know what? I'm probably not the only solo female in the county. Unlike most of them, though, I have a fierce dog and can actually converse with him. We'll be fine. Go home, stop worrying, and get some sleep."

I followed him to the door on my crutches, Cooper at my side. Dave leaned down and gave me a peck on the cheek. "You're not the only solo female in the county. You *are*, however, the only solo female in the county I care about at the moment. Lock up after me."

I did as instructed and thumped back to my chair. Plopping into it with a sigh, I let my hand dangle over the arm and gave Coop a good scratch on his back. He immediately rolled over to expose his belly, which I dutifully rubbed while musing on the evening.

"Overprotective men," I muttered to myself. It had almost been better when Thomas had trusted me to look after myself and the house without a lot of input from him. But it was nice to have someone care that much.

I sat there musing for almost an hour, then decided to hell with it, I was going to bed early. I was just contemplating putting my PJs on when an alarm on my phone sounded. Looking over, I swore. I'd totally forgotten it was Tuesday and I was due for a Skype chat with my kids. I pulled my laptop off the floor and logged on.

Sam's first comment was to chide me for not calling her after my Friday afternoon date with Dave. I'd forgotten to do that, too, but once I explained about my ankle, I was forgiven. Then I had to assure both of them I was able to take care of myself and there was no need for one or both to drop what they were doing and tend to their infirm mother.

It was difficult not to tell them about the gnome, or our assumption about the vampire, or the authorities' lack of belief in paranormal beings, but that would have been more cause for worry on their part, which I didn't need.

I was pleased to hear Sam had a date the next night for drinks with a man she'd met at her gym, and Jason had been given a bonus for completing a project early and under budget. When I asked him about *his* love life, I was told there was no one on the horizon and he was fine with that for now. He'd be sure to let me know if he met anyone interesting, though. I just smiled. Knowing my son, I'd hear about that only when the relationship became serious.

A half hour later, I'd told my kids I loved them and finally started the preparations for bed. Cooper dutifully went out to do his business with me watching from the door, grumbling about being back to having to ask me to go outside as he did in Atlanta.

We, all three of us, settled down for the night. I stayed awake for a couple of hours, tensing for Cooper's announcement that something strange was outside, but that never happened, and I finally drifted off.

I was awakened by a soft paw batting my nose. *"That place you want me to use to do my business is disgusting,"* Patches said when I opened my eyes. *"I would like to go outside where I can find a clean spot."*

Having a cat was going to take some getting used to. I grumbled, but the sun was up, so it was time I was, too. Both cat and dog paced at the door while I poured a cup of coffee. As soon as I opened it, they raced outside in opposite directions. Neither went farther than the edge of the woods, for which I was grateful.

I stood on the deck with my coffee, eyeing the surrounding area. It didn't look like anything else had been disturbed during the night, but I sighed in frustration nonetheless. I could see weeds – unwanted plants – coming up in the garden beds. It would be a couple of days before I'd be able to get out there to work, and I still hadn't bought seeds or plants for what I wanted to grow.

Cooper raced back to the deck and danced in front of me. *"Can we play? We haven't played in months!"*

I chuckled. Technically, he was right. Ever since moving, his need to *play* had been greatly reduced because he ran in the woods.

"Okay," I said. "Go find me a stick to throw." He raced back to the edge of the woods and returned with a fallen tree branch – that was about four feet long. I broke it in half, dropped one at my feet and threw the other as far as I could. I laughed at myself when it landed only about ten feet away. I know it's politically incorrect, but my thought was *I throw like a girl.*

Patches also returned from the woods and watched Cooper retrieve the stick with interest. *"Does he always do this?"* she asked.

"Occasionally. Most dogs do like to fetch thrown things."

"They are strange creatures."

This from a feline who seemingly only napped if she wasn't eating or peeing. However, I felt it wasn't my place to point that out, so kept my counsel. Cooper tired out after only a couple more throws, and after I refilled the water dishes both front and back (choruses of *"thank you"* came from under both areas), we all trooped back inside.

I'd risen too late to get the morning news from Atlanta on the television, so checked the internet. There were a couple of sites that focused on mountain happenings, and I was shocked and dismayed to read they'd found yet another person suffering from blood loss but still alive, this time a lone hunter about a mile northwest of me. He, also, had been sliced and diced, and hamstrung. His shotgun had been discharged, but there was no body, either humanoid or turkey, anywhere nearby. Doctors were hopeful he'd survive and had put out a call for donations from people with AB-negative blood.

The one good thing, if it could be called that, was the guy had a hunting knife clutched in his hand, and it was covered in blood. They were hoping to get a DNA sample to link to the attacker if they could. They were also hoping once the victim recovered consciousness, he'd be able to identify the perpetrator. A police sketch artist was already standing by.

The rest of my morning was spent *slowly* getting myself ready for the day, then scooping Patches' litter box. At least Dave (or the salesclerk at the pet supply store) had gotten the scoopable kind, rather than regular litter, which would have required emptying the whole box out and putting in fresh. (Yes, I'd done my reading on the internet on how to take care of a cat.) She carefully supervised what I was doing, apparently to ensure I got every last piece of smelly crap. As soon as I'd finished, she anointed the clean box. I sighed, waited for her to finish, then scooped that into the bag, too, before carrying it directly to the garbage bin in the garage.

My ankle let me know I'd been up too much, so I gratefully sank into my chair and picked up the book I'd been slogging through. It *still* wasn't the most interesting reading, but as I had nothing else on the agenda, figured I might as well finish it so I could go onto a better one. I hated leaving a book unread.

Dave texted me about noon to check in. When I told him I was being a good girl and staying not just indoors but in my chair, I got a thumbs-up in reply.

Of course, I wasn't in my chair for hours on end as my ankle would have wished. Cooper had to go out several times during the course of the afternoon, and I felt I had to keep an eye on him when he did. I had to admonish him, twice, not to roll around in the leaf litter on the forest floor. It wouldn't do his head injury any good at all to get dirty.

"*But it itches!*" he whined. "*You said not to scratch it, but this would help, I know!*"

Therefore, some part of my afternoon was spent holding an ice pack wrapped in a towel to his head, which he also complained about…until the itching stopped for a while. This was one more benefit to my *gift* – being able to explain the situation and keep him quiet when necessary.

When I fell into bed that night, I was grateful for an uneventful day. Even though it had only been a week, it felt like months since I'd had a day to myself to do absolutely nothing.

The following morning, I was in my chair, sipping coffee and contemplating what I was going to do for the day. The ankle was feeling better, but I knew if I was up and around on it, it would just swell up and hurt all over again.

I was scrolling through the guide on the television, wondering if there was anything decent on, when I heard a car pull up in the driveway. Cooper and Patches both went to the living room window, and in a span of moments, Coop went from cautious attention to racing to the door and dancing around, his tail wagging a mile a minute.

I rose and looked out the window to see my son emerging from what, presumably, was a rental car. Grabbing the crutches, I hobbled over and got the door unlocked just as he was walking up the steps.

"What are you doing here?" I cried.

"Hi, Mom," Jason said as he dropped his bags to give me a big hug. "It's a long story, and I'm low on caffeine. Got any going?"

"Of course," I said, hugging him back. "You can have the guest bedroom, and you know where the coffee cups are."

While he brought his bags inside, I fell back into my chair, wondering why in the hell my son had traveled all the way from Los Angeles in the middle of a workweek.

A few minutes later, he'd gotten himself a cup, filled it, and topped mine off before sitting in the chair opposite. Patches had disappeared, but Cooper, after checking on me, went over to Jason for some attention.

My son heaved a sigh as he scratched Coop's back. "Something's going on here that you didn't tell me or Sam about on Tuesday. Now that I see Cooper limping and with an injury on his head, I *know* something's happening. I thought about it all day yesterday and decided I needed to come check it out for my own peace of mind.

"I can read you like a book, Mom. I always have been able to. Your facial expressions and body language during our chat said you were really worried, and it wasn't just about your ankle.

"More importantly, now that I'm here, I can *tell* something's going on," he sighed again. "You're projecting not just the pain from your ankle and worry about Cooper, but extreme concern about something else. You see, Mom, I'm an empath."

"You're a what?" That term wasn't familiar to me.

"I can feel other people's emotions as if they were my own. It's one of the reasons I'm so good at my job. Oh, sure, I can read blueprints and cost estimates with the best of them, but when I'm with a contractor, I can tell if they're lying, or hiding something, or happy."

I was flabbergasted. "How…?"

"It's inherited," he said. "Dad was. So was Granny Mackay. Didn't you ever wonder why he seemed so closed off most of the time?" I nodded. Thomas hadn't been a cold fish, exactly, but it was rare he exhibited emotion or reacted to others.

"He was shielding himself from others' emotions so he wouldn't get overwhelmed. I can tell you it *is* overwhelming to feel what everyone around you is feeling. Imagine, at Dad's funeral, how it would be to feel everyone else's sorrow on top of your own if you couldn't block them out."

"Why didn't I know anything about this?" I asked, trying to keep my jaw from dropping farther.

"I'm not sure, but I think Dad was embarrassed," he replied. "You know how he wanted to rise above his mountain roots? It's possible he saw his ability as, oh, I don't know, unsophisticated.

"When I hit puberty and started exhibiting signs of being empathic, he taught me how to shield myself from others' emotions, then told me not to mention it to anyone because it was 'too weird' and I'd be ostracized. So I didn't."

"And you've been living with this for more than half your life?" I was feeling so sorry for my kid. I couldn't imagine what he went through. Or was going through.

"It's not too bad once you learn to turn the volume down or in some cases, off." He gave me a wry smile. "But it can be very inconvenient. Like if I'm dating someone. I *want* to know how they're feeling about me, but on the other hand, not so much. Know what I mean?"

I nodded. I thought I remembered when all that started. Jay was thirteen, had started his growth spurt, and all the other things that come with puberty for boys. He became very withdrawn for about three months. I had suggested we might take him to a therapist, which Thomas vehemently disagreed with. The weekend after that conversation, Thomas took him camping – the only time I'd ever known Thomas to give up his modern conveniences. Jay came back a different kid. After that weekend, he started socializing again, smiling, and laughing with his friends. When I'd asked Thomas what had happened to change Jay in such a short period of time, he just smiled and told me it was the father-son bonding.

"He taught you, what do you call it? shielding? that weekend he took you camping, didn't he?"

Jay grinned. "You remember! I thought it was so weird when Dad announced he and I were going camping and proceeded to buy the sporting goods store out. We'd never done it before, and I thought he was off his rocker.

"But when we got to the campsite, he sat me down and explained what was happening to me. He told me about his experience and what Granny Mackay had told him. Then I spent the rest of the weekend learning to turn the noise down. We didn't really camp, you know. The place had comfortable cabins, and we drove out to a diner for our meals. All the stuff he bought was for show.

"Taking me out for meals wasn't just because he couldn't cook, although there was that. It was his way of making sure I'd learned the lesson. There were always people in the diner, and if I got jittery, he'd remind me to put my shields up. By dinner Sunday night, I was okay, and we headed home."

"And your sister?" I asked, concerned. This seemed like something Samantha would have great difficulty with. She was, after all, a "people person."

"Far as I know, she didn't get it. At least, she hasn't acted like it."

I breathed a sigh of relief. I knew once she hit my age, she'd have to deal with hearing animals. I couldn't imagine that and feeling emotions at the same time.

I made a move to get up, and he motioned me back down. "What do you want, Mom? Let me get it for you."

I just pointed to my coffee cup. At the moment, I was wishing I could add a shot to it, but it was only ten in the morning, so…

After refilling both cups, Jason sat and looked at me expectantly. "So what's *really* been happening around here?"

I took a deep breath and plunged in, telling him about the previous week in gory detail. He only raised an eyebrow when I told him about the vampire and gnome. When I got to what had happened to Cooper, he looked down at the dog with sympathy in his eyes. When I told him about Dave wanting to stay at my house, he glared at me.

"You should have taken him up on his offer," he chided. "You're not really in any position to defend yourself, and Coop's hurt, too."

"I know," I said. "But I'm just not ready to have an almost-stranger in the house. I've done – mostly – as he asked, staying inside. And no one, other than you, has shown up at the door."

"Yet," he scowled. "Sergeant Anderson is right. Coop is probably known as *your* dog. And that gnome or whatever it was knows that now.

"I don't *want* to take over, Mom, but I'm going to," he continued. "I had a hunch it was something bad, and I was right. For the time being, you're going to have a man around. Me. I've rearranged my schedule so I can work remotely for at least two weeks.

"Please ask your friend where I can get a rifle. Preferably a thirty-ought-six. If it's good enough to bring down a large buck, it should be good enough for this vampire or whatever it is. And I want him to make me some of those loads he told you about."

I was glad I was sitting down. "You know about guns?"

"Geez, Mom, do you think all Sam and I did for that week we visited Grandpa and Grandma Bixler every summer was swim in the pond at Uncle Joe's and bother their chickens? Grandpa taught both of us to shoot at fourteen, just like Great-Grandpa taught you.

"And I've been hunting in the Sierras with a former boss several times. Although I much prefer target practice to actually killing a living being. Yes, I'm quite comfortable with them."

I was seeing a side of my son I'd never seen. I said as much.

"There's a lot of things I don't tell you," he said. "Not that you wouldn't be interested, I'm sure, it's just that I don't think it's important. This is one of them.

"If you were completely healthy *and* comfortable with guns, I wouldn't worry as much. But you're neither. And since you won't let a *trained law enforcement professional* protect you, I will."

I harrumphed. But he was right. I finally admitted it. He came over to my chair and hugged me. "I know it's frustrating, Mom, but I am able and willing to do this. Now, I have to work for about five hours. Can I use your study?"

I waved him in that direction. As soon as he'd left the living room, I sighed audibly. *"What's wrong?"* Cooper came over from his spot next to where Jason had been sitting and put his head on my knee.

I told him what Jason had said and the fact that I not only felt helpless but managed. Coop cocked his head as he thought. *"He is right. I can protect you from that little man, but I don't know about a vampire. I have never met one, I don't think, so I don't know what I would do."*

I also mused aloud on the fact that even with his empath ability, Jason still couldn't hear Coop. *"I don't know what this ability is,"* Cooper said, *"but he has no magic in his blood that I can feel."*

So no magic. Maybe it was an odd wiring in his brain? I'd heard of people who saw and thought differently, like those who saw music as colors. I'd have to research to understand my son better.

I gave him a scratch on his back, then decided it was time to shower and start my day – whatever that was going to entail. Before that, however, I sent a long text to Dave, inviting him for dinner so he and Jason could talk. I received a quick response with a thinking emoji and **I'll be there about five-thirty**.

I was just about to undress and shower when I heard Jason at my bedroom door. "When did you get a cat?"

I pulled my robe back on and opened the door to see him with Patches in his arms. She seemed quite content. *That* was odd! She wasn't that affectionate with me. "Oh. I forgot to tell you about her, and the refugees, too."

"Refugees?"

"Yeah. Cooper let her in the house through the doggie door on Saturday. What he didn't let into the house is a *bunch* of wild animals, scared of what's happening in the woods. They're all under the front porch and back deck, hiding. I've been giving them water since they won't all go out to forage."

"That explains the bowl out front. Geez, Mom. What next?"

"I have no idea," I said. "Right now, the next thing is a shower. Her name is Patches, by the way. Oh, and you're going to need to go to the store for me later. I wasn't expecting to feed anyone but myself and don't have enough food for two, much less three. I've invited Dave – Sergeant Anderson – for dinner so you two can meet and talk about…whatever it is you need to talk about."

He smiled. "No problem. Just be sure to give me a detailed list. You know I have no idea about cooking." He turned, still with Patches in his arms, and went back into the study.

After my shower, I made a grocery list for Jason. I *knew* my kid had no idea of cooking beyond microwave dinners, so it was detailed down to size and brand. Looking at the clock, I assumed he'd be done working by mid-afternoon. I'd have time to make a pot roast for dinner. That would leave enough for sandwiches the next day.

A couple hours later, I was in the kitchen, making a late lunch: grilled cheese sandwiches – the only food I had available for two. As soon as I opened the package of cheese slices, I had an audience. Both Cooper and Patches were on the floor at my feet, looking up with pleading eyes. Laughing, I gave them each a slice, tearing one into little pieces for Patches, placing them in the middle of the island counter where Cooper couldn't snarf them up before she could. I heard murmurs of "*so good*" and something that sounded like "*yummy*" while they ate and I cooked.

Jason's table manners *still* hadn't improved, and he talked through his sandwiches. "I have about an hour of work left, then I'll go to the store, which is where? Also, what else do you need done around here? You're going to stay off that ankle for the next three days, at least. I know you have projects, and I'll help since I'm here."

"Do me a favor?" I said when he finished. "Pay attention when Dave is here. Don't talk with your mouth full. I don't want him thinking my children have no manners whatsoever."

Jason chuckled. "Your daughter learned her etiquette lessons well. I know them, too. I just don't worry about them when I'm not in company. Don't worry, I'll behave."

"Lazy," I said, slapping him on the arm. "Don't you think I'd prefer it if you behaved in front of me, too?"

"Probably," he grinned. "But you're my Mom, and you love me anyways."

I could've slapped him again but didn't. I honestly was grateful there was someone here, not only to watch out for the bad guys but to keep me off my foot as much as possible.

Dave texted me about four, telling me he'd be late. **Problem. All hands on deck. Should be there by six-thirty. Will fill you in then.**

That suggested something having to do with either the gnome or vampire. I was curious but decided asking questions at this point would not only be distracting to him but moot because he said he'd tell me what was going on.

He finally arrived at six-forty-five, looking disheveled and exhausted. "I need to clean up, then I need a stiff drink" was all he said before heading to the kitchen sink. As soon as he'd washed up and dried his hands, I handed him a glass of bourbon.

"I know we've only had wine when together thus far, but I think this will be better," I told him.

He downed it in one shot, then grimaced. "Not usually a bourbon drinker, but at this point, it'll do."

Dave finally noticed Jason sitting in one of the living room chairs, watching him with curiosity. He walked over and held his hand out. "Hi, I'm Dave Anderson. I presume you're Jason?"

Jason set down the glass of wine he'd been nursing, rose, and shook the proffered hand. "Yep. You're Mom's new friend. Nice to meet you."

I cleared my throat. "We should eat, unless you boys want burned food for dinner." I had been babysitting the food on the stove for the last half hour, trying to keep it warm without overcooking anything. This time, Jason didn't yell at me for standing. He knew he couldn't do what I could where food was concerned.

We all sat at the table after we'd filled our plates, Cooper and Patches migrating from wherever they'd been to the men's feet. Patches tried to jump into Jay's lap, but he pushed her off. She grumbled about being smaller than everyone else and not being able to see what was on the table that smelled so good.

"She's only been here a few days but has already decided she's queen of the house," I laughed.

"*This is* my *house*," Cooper glared at her. "*You're only here because I let you in.*"

I almost choked on my food. "This is *my* house," I told him. "Both of you are here because I want you here."

The men looked at me, then at Cooper. Both smiled. "Arguments between species? How *unusual!*" Dave said.

"So what delayed you?" Jason asked, this time between bites.

"After we eat" was Dave's reply.

Surprisingly, both men shooed me into the living room, cleared the table, and cleaned up the kitchen – after putting a plate of leftovers on the floor for Cooper and a smaller one on the counter for Patches. I had come to expect the domesticity from Dave, but Jason's help was unexpected. He really *was* on his best behavior.

Jason refilled my wine glass and his, offered the bottle to Dave, who shook his head. "I can't mix wine and hard liquor. Is there anything besides bourbon?"

Jay rooted around in the cupboard that served as my liquor cabinet. "She's got brandy, rum, and vodka, too." Opening the refrigerator, he added, "Coke, Sprite, tonic, plain water."

"Rum and Coke is fine. Thanks."

Jason played bartender, and if I wasn't mistaken, poured Dave a double shot before adding ice and the mixer. We finally all sat in the living room.

"So what's happened?" I asked.

Dave took a long swig of his drink. "A farmer about three miles northeast of here found a cache of bodies in a copse at the back of his property. He doesn't normally go there but was tracking a wayward steer with his dog.

"Yes, wild animals had gotten to them, but some were still recognizable. It's going to take the coroner's office and the GBI a long time to sort them all out, but it looks like there were about ten.

"At least three of them were missing kids from Atlanta," he continued, taking another gulp from his glass. "I don't know about the rest, but I saw bite marks on at least two necks."

"Damn," Jason said, drinking his wine down by half. "It's worse than you thought, then."

Dave nodded. "We've either got more than one vampire *or* he or she has been working in this area for longer than a week.

"My only consolation in all this is the sheriff is finally coming around to my – our way of thinking, as is CID."

I felt numb. From everything I'd read, vampires tried to live below the radar and didn't normally kill. And to have all this happen in a rural community *right* after I'd moved was…unsettling.

"So I was right to come help Mom," Jason said, rather smugly, I thought. "Along those lines…" He proceeded to tell Dave what he wanted.

"Not until I've taken you to the range to see how good you really are," Dave replied.

Jason opened his mouth to argue, but Dave forestalled him. "I have a duty to ensure everyone in this community is safe. That means making sure some hotheaded kid doesn't go around brandishing a firearm without being able to use it properly. I don't know you. I'm going to assume you're level-headed if you're El's kid, but nonetheless, I want to see for myself.

"I'll take you to the range tomorrow morning, say, around ten? If I like what I see, I'll then take you to a good place to buy a rifle. You have an out-of-state driver's license, which means they wouldn't sell to you unless you were with me."

"I know the laws. I've lived here," Jason retorted. "Any legal adult can buy a gun in Georgia after passing a background check, which I can."

"Yes, but the store I like is leery of out-of-staters. *Especially* California, which is *way* out of state and comprised solely of potheads, if you believe the owner. I can get you around that."

Jason sighed. "Okay, *Dad,* I'll prove myself to you tomorrow. Ten, you said?"

Dave chuckled. "You know, that's the first time in my life anyone has called me that. I know you meant it sarcastically, but to me, it means I'm behaving as I should with someone your age I don't really know."

"What about the loads you mentioned to Mom?"

"Depends on what caliber rifle you get. Some armor-piercing are available commercially, and we might be able to pick it up when we get the gun. If not, yes, I'll buy the appropriate supplies and make the loads myself."

I was swimming in a sea of gun talk. I know they meant well, but it made me uncomfortable. Worse, there would be a loaded gun in my house all the time, not just when Dave was in uniform. I might have squirmed a little in my chair. Cooper sensed my discomfort and padded over to me, laying his head on my thigh.

"*Are you okay?*" he asked.

"Not really," I replied. "I'm not comfortable with guns."

Both men turned to me on hearing my comment, Jason speaking first. "I know, Mom, but it's the only thing I can think of that might have a chance against a vampire. After all this is over, I'll sell the rifle back before I leave for home, okay?"

I nodded, still uneasy.

Dave finished his drink and rose. "I need to get home," he said. "It's been a long day, and I have a sneaking hunch I'm going to get called in tomorrow. Unless that happens, I'll be by to get you at ten, Jason."

After putting his glass in the dishwasher, he gave me a peck on the cheek and left.

"He's…interesting," Jason said after we'd heard Dave's truck leave. "Not quite what I would have picked for you, but I like him."

I stared at my son. "What do you mean, *picked for me?* Nothing's happening here."

He laughed. "Oh, come on, Mom. I can see the way he looks at you. The way he treats you. And you respond to it. Not to mention I get "like" vibes all over the place between you."

My kid and his empathic abilities. Quite frankly, I would have expected that comment from my mother or daughter, not my son. "Okay, fine. Yes, he's a nice man. But we just met and honestly, have sort of been thrown together by circumstance. I think I'd like to get to know him better when there aren't dead bodies all over, including my yard."

I yawned. It was only nine-thirty, and even though all I'd done that day was sit, I was tired. "Go to bed, Mom," Jason told me. "I'll be up for a couple of hours yet and can take care of Cooper and Patches."

I nodded. "Thanks. Would you put the coffee together, too? The timer's already set for seven. All you have to do is flip the switch. The doggie door is locked until the problem is sorted, so you'll have to let Coop know when it's time to go out."

"Did that in Atlanta. Can probably do that here, too, even though I can't understand him like you can. Go to bed. I'll see you in the morning."

I grabbed my crutches and made my way into the bedroom, trailed by both Cooper and Patches.

"*Food?*" they both asked when they saw I was getting ready for bed.

"Jason will feed you at the normal time," I told them. "And don't beg early. It won't help."

It wasn't long before I fell asleep. Unfortunately, it wasn't a good sleep. My dreams were filled with piles of chewed and dismembered bodies; grinning but otherwise blurry faces with elongated canines, smeared with blood; and a perpetual feeling of fear. Twice Cooper nuzzled my face to wake me with a mumbled comment of "*bad dream, wake up.*"

When I finally crawled out of bed shortly after seven, I felt as if I hadn't slept at all. Today would be a day for copious amounts of caffeine, and I hurried as best I could to my source. The thumping of my crutches must have woken Jason because he was right behind me at the counter.

"Did you set an alarm again?" I asked as I grabbed two mugs from the cupboard. "Or did I wake you?"

"Neither. I'm not used to sleeping with an animal, and she kept getting in the way when I rolled to one side or the other. I heard you get up so decided I would, too."

So Patches had *really* taken a shine to Jason. I chuckled. "She must really like you. She shadowed you almost all of yesterday. You might be better off sleeping with your door closed."

"I'll get used to it. I don't want a door between me and whatever might happen. Go. Sit. I'll bring your coffee in."

We sat in companionable silence, slurping coffee and watching the morning news. The news of the pile of bodies hadn't yet made it to the Atlanta market, but I was sure it soon would. That was too sensational not to.

After an hour and three cups of coffee, Jason brought his laptop from the study to the living room. While I checked social media on my phone, he was busy doing something that looked work-related.

"Isn't it a little early to work?" I asked.

"Client's in Delaware," he replied, distracted by whatever was on the screen in front of him. "I usually start working about six at home to keep up with the time difference better when I'm working with someone on the East Coast. *Being* on the East Coast means I can be that more on top of things.

"Plus," he said, finally looking up, "I'm going to be offline for several hours today so wanted to get a jumpstart."

I could understand that. When I'd been working with charities, I adjusted my hours when Thomas and I went on vacation so I could respond in a timely fashion to emails and phone calls.

With that thought, my heart skipped a beat. Thomas had adjusted his hours, too. Vacations were almost just a change of scenery for us, rather than an actual break. Watching Jason brought back painful memories…he looked so much like his father with his dark head bent to better view the laptop screen, a look of intense concentration on his face as he moved his finger around the touchpad.

Dave was right on time. The two men left without saying much at all to each other, but both had challenging looks in their eyes. I hoped by the time they left the range things would be smoothed out. I believed my son when he said he could shoot, but I also believed Dave would be strict in his assessment of Jason's skills.

That left me to my own devices. It was a bright, sunny day, and I was aching to get out in the garden, but my ankle said, "Not a chance." I tried to remember what my life had been like when I'd been a socialite wife and not allowed to play in the dirt. When I hadn't felt the call of duty, as it were, to the charity work, I'd done a lot of reading. Rather than pick up the next novel, I decided it was time to learn more about my husband and son.

A couple of hours later, I was feeling rather overwhelmed by the psychological definitions and observations of empathy (or lack thereof), contrasted with websites talking about *really* empathic people – those who not only identified with what others were feeling but actually absorbed those emotions into themselves. No wonder Thomas had seemed so cold. His lifestyle didn't allow him to get away from people much. On the other hand, I knew Jason enjoyed hiking and just the outdoors in general. Based on my reading, that helped him a lot.

I was in the process of making a sandwich when the animals raised a ruckus again. Cooper was yelling, "*Stranger!*" while I heard the refugees screaming in their higher voices, "*Danger!*" I hobbled to the deck door to see a gnome, either the first or another one, attempting again to destroy my garden – this time with a knife.

My first thought was to laugh at the thought of a knife doing much damage to the stones I'd built the walls with, then outrage at the attempt. Ignoring the pain in my ankle, I ran out to the garden as fast as I could, carrying but not using the crutches. Cooper followed on my heels.

"Stop that, you nasty little man," I screamed.

"You again! You should have left when I told you to," he replied, continuing his assault on the stone wall.

With another scream, I swung one crutch at his head, and surprised myself – I actually connected. Not that an aluminum crutch has much weight, but it was enough to knock him off his feet. As soon as he fell, Cooper pounced and pinned, growling menacingly. Before the gnome could raise his knife hand to hurt my dog, I grabbed the weapon and threw it toward the deck.

Watching the little man squirm under Cooper's greater weight, I almost laughed. Now that I could see him in daylight, I was amazed at just how closely ceramic garden gnomes resembled this guy. Except for the longer hair and lack of a hat, he could've stood stock-still and no one would be the wiser. However, he wasn't ceramic and continued to try to get out from underneath the much-larger dog.

"Let me go!" Cooper's prisoner cried. "Get your *verdammt* animal off me."

"Not a chance," I said with a nasty smile. "Cooper, don't let him go. I'll be right back."

I hobbled back to the house on one crutch – the other had bent when I hit the gnome with it, and I left it lying where I'd dropped it. I knew I had no rope, but I *did* have leather belts. Those should be good enough to secure the little bastard until Dave or someone else could do something about him.

I returned with three. Working around Coop standing on the guy's back (which was tricky), I wrapped one around his legs, another around his wrists at his back, and the third around his arms, pinning them to his side. Only then did I allow my dog to get off him. Cooper stood at attention, his eyes never leaving our prisoner, and every time the gnome moved, he growled.

I hadn't heard a car pull up, but just as I was trying to figure out what I could do next, I heard both Jason and Dave calling my name.

"Garden!" I yelled, and both men came running out the door.

"What the hell?" said Jason at the same time as Dave said, "Are you all right?"

"I'm fine," I replied to Dave. "Neither of you can see him, right?"

They shook their heads. "No, but I can see belts looped around in odd positions," Jason said.

"It's the gnome," I told them. "He was attacking the garden beds again. His knife is somewhere around here." I waved my hand in the general direction of where I'd thrown it.

"You took my hammer," the gnome growled. "I'd like it back."

I growled right back. "No way. And you're not getting your knife back, either."

I looked at Dave. "Now what? If you can't see him, how do we handle this?"

Dave thought for a minute, then pulled out his phone. "Tyler? You know we talked about a vampire, right? I have another fairytale creature for you."

Tyler was the sheriff. I held my breath as Dave told him about the gnome, wondering if we'd be believed.

"Yeah, I know. Call Alex Martin for clarification. In the meantime, we need someone who can see this guy to guard him, not to mention question him. I'm going to suggest one or both of Alex's nephews. I'll explain why once I get their acceptance."

He listened some more. "*Fine.* I'll do it on my own, then. This guy's been trying to destroy Ms. Mackay's garden for a week, and I suspect he's involved, somehow, with our dead hikers. Once you've spoken with Alex, call me back."

He hit the 'end call' button on his phone so hard the device flew out of his hand. "Damned stubborn, pig-headed…" He picked his phone back up. The epithets went on for almost a minute. He was creative!

"He doesn't think there's anything we can do with a suspect we can't see. I disagree." He thought some more. "Can you keep Cooper watching him while I go out for about a half hour?"

"Of course," I said. "What are your plans?"

"I'm going to get a large dog crate to put him in. Then I'm calling the nephews. They should scare the shit out of this guy, especially if they're in their were forms."

"You don't need to go out. Cooper has a crate in the garage. It's folded up against the far wall."

Dave disappeared into the garage. Jason moved toward me, picking up the damaged crutch in his hand. "Geez, Mom. I'm in awe. You must've hit him really hard with this to bend it that far."

"Yeah, well. I'm pissed. You can see the damage he did earlier in the week. It'll take me hours to repair it."

"I'm not being facetious," he said gently. "You used whatever weapon was at hand, which is what you're supposed to do."

Dave emerged from the garage with the crate in his hand. Cooper saw it and whimpered.

"It's not for you," I told him. "It's for your prisoner."

"Oh. In that case, it is all right."

Dave opened the crate, locking the sides in place. He placed it on the deck with the door open, then came back to the garden.

"Where should I put my hands?" he asked.

I pointed. "Between that belt and that one. That will keep your hands away from his mouth."

We all watched as Dave reached around Cooper, looking like a mime, placing his hands around what to him was thin air. It was obvious, though, that he had hold of *something*, and that was wriggling around. As soon as Dave had hold of the gnome, Coop stepped aside at my request.

"Let me go, you *verdammt* human!" the gnome yelled. Dave obviously didn't hear him, but he grunted with the effort of keeping hold of the squirming mass as he walked toward the deck. He dropped the gnome once, and I was pleased to see he landed face-down on the graveled path. That had to hurt!

Feeling around, Dave got hands on the back of the gnome's shirt and with a couple more grunts, threw his charge into the dog crate, slammed the door shut, and threw the latch.

"That ought to hold him for a bit," he said. "But." He looked at the belts in the crate. "I'm not untying you. You can sit like that until I get reinforcements."

I tried walking to the house with one crutch, but two hops in, collapsed, my ankle deciding to completely give way.

"Shit, Mom." Jason was at my side in an instant. "You were supposed to stay off it."

"I couldn't," I said as he picked me up. "There wasn't anyone else around."

"I'm taking you to the hospital," he said. "You've probably completely messed it up."

"Not the hospital," Dave told him. "There's a clinic on the four-lane that's faster and cheaper than the emergency room. Where's your purse, El?"

I told him where I kept it underneath the kitchen counter, and he went inside while Jason carried me to the rental car. Dave emerged with my purse and as he dropped it in my lap, said, "If you don't mind, I'm going to stay here and keep an eye on the gnome. I don't trust him to not get out of the cage. Will Cooper help me?"

"Coop," I said to the dog who'd followed Jason around the house to the car. "Please stay here and help Dave keep an eye on the gnome. You can see him; Dave can't."

"*But I want to go with you!*" he exclaimed.

"You can't this time, bud," I replied. "We're going somewhere you're not allowed, and you'd just have to sit in the car. You'll be more help to Dave than me. Don't let the gnome out of the crate. Use your teeth if you need to, okay? I'd rather the gnome be hurt than either you or Dave."

"*Okay,*" he said, obviously chagrined. "*I will help your friend.*"

"Thank you," I said, scratching his back. "We'll be back as soon as we can."

"As soon as we can" turned out to be three hours. I saw the same doctor at the clinic I'd seen a week earlier and got an earful as, after another x-ray, he removed the elastic bandage and put a cast on my ankle.

"You're lucky you only worsened the sprain," he said, hands busy rolling yards of sticky stuff over my foot and ankle and nearly to my knee. "You could have easily torn a tendon running after your dog."

Sorry, Coop, I thought. There was no way I could explain to the doctor what had really been happening, so I blamed the dog.

I had to wait until the cast dried before being allowed to leave. This time Jason took me to the pharmacy to get the pain prescription filled. "You're going to take these and sleep," he admonished. "Otherwise, you'll just be up and about on it."

At the same time, he purchased a new pair of crutches – these were wood. It took some fancy stepping on his part to convince the pharmacist he really wanted wood for me, not aluminum. "If these are your weapon of choice, you need more weight," he grinned.

When we got home, there was a second truck parked next to Dave's in front of the garage. Jason parked behind Dave and yelled when I tried to get out of the car by myself.

"The crutches aren't going to work well on gravel," he said as he picked me up.

Thinking, probably rightly, that Dave was still on the deck, he walked around to the back of the house to get help getting me in the door.

Dave rose from a chair when we appeared, as did a man about Jason's age. This man was shorter than either Dave or Jason but built like a brick…you know what. His hair was a tawny brown and his eyes so light brown, they looked amber. There was a slightly feral look to his expression, as if he were always on guard, watching his surroundings, as most wild animals did.

He held out his hand to me. "Hi, I'm Jonathan, one of Alex Martin's nephews. You know about us, I'm told."

I shook his hand. "I do. Thanks for coming. I'd hoped to be a better hostess, but…" I waved my hand at my leg then pointed my thumb backward. "This is my son, Jason."

I took a quick peek at the crate. The belts were off the gnome, but he was still in it, glaring at everyone and everything. Cooper wasn't in evidence.

Dave opened the deck door for us. "A cast, El? You really did yourself up good this time."

"Major sprain," Jason told him as he carried me to my chair. "Not as bad as it could have been, but she's out of commission for at least a week, maybe two if she doesn't behave this time."

Dave sat on the chair opposite while Jason went back to the car for my new crutches and purse. "Jonathan says the gnome isn't talking, despite scaring the bejeesus out of him when he shifted. Which, by the way, even with warning, scared me more than a little, too. It happens in the blink of an eye. One minute there's a man in front of you, the next a bobcat, snarling.

"He thinks the only way to resolve this is to find the guy's clan and let *them* deal with him. According to Jonathan, making yourself known to humans is breaking clan law.

"So we'll go out tomorrow as planned. I know you don't want strangers staying at your house, but I'd like to stay here tonight and with Cooper's help, spell Jonathan and Don, when he gets here, guarding the gnome. That way all three of us can get a little shuteye.”

“It seems I have no choice but to allow men to take care of things,” I said. I might have sneered a bit.

Jason had come back into the house during Dave’s spiel. “I can help guard, too,” he said, putting the crutches next to my chair and my purse on the counter. “As long as I have Cooper’s eyes, that is.”

“Hey,” I interjected. “Coop needs sleep, too.”

“Okay, shift rotation. This I know well,” Dave said. “Me first. Then you. That way Cooper can still get his beauty rest. The brothers can take the last two shifts and decide between them who gets which.”

“Nuh, uh,” Jason said. “Me first, then you. Someone has to cook tonight, and it won’t be Mom. I understand you can. I can’t unless it’s microwave.”

I had *not* planned on feeding four men, three of whom probably ate enough for two. There was no way I had that much food in my pantry. I said as much.

Dave laughed. “I already thought of that. I called Jack. I’ll go pick up a mess of rib tips and sides in about an hour.”

At least I was spared having to cook a full meal. I thunked my head on the back of my chair. “I guess I’m stuck with you,” I moaned.

“Sorry,” Dave said. “If I still had my cabin, I’d take him there, and we’d be out of your hair. But I don’t, and the boys live up in North Carolina. I want to keep the gnome in my jurisdiction.”

“Don’t worry, Mom,” Jason said with his head poked in the refrigerator. “You’re going to sleep through it all, even if I have to shove that pill down your throat like I did Thumper.”

Before he’d left for college, Thumper had been Jason’s responsibility. The monthly heartworm pill had been challenging until someone came up with the idea of tasty pill pockets. I laughed as I remembered Jason's struggles, trying to get the pill down Thumper's throat without getting bit in the process.

"You won't have to shove it down my throat," I promised. "I *want* to sleep, maybe not through whatever will happen out on the deck, but to forget my ankle for a while." I held up my hand. "But not right now. After dinner."

Jason came out from the kitchen carrying a glass of Coke. He returned to the kitchen and got two ice packs out of the freezer and grabbed the hand towel off the oven door handle. While he did that, Dave grabbed a sofa cushion and placed it on the ottoman to elevate my leg. Jason put one ice pack below my ankle and the other on top.

"That ought to hold you for a bit," Dave said on his way out the deck door. Shortly, I heard murmured voices as he and Jonathan talked.

Jason walked out the front door, and I heard a car door open and shut. He returned with a rifle in his hand. After parking himself on the chair opposite me, he rested the gun next to the chair, opened his laptop, and booted it up.

I eyed the gun. It wasn't a typical shotgun, as I had been expecting. This one was sleek and modern and all black. There was a small box between the stock and the trigger housing which, I assumed, was the clip. I wasn't happy having it in my house but understood the need.

"You can go work in the study," I told him. "I'll be fine."

"Nope. Gonna stay right here so I can keep an eye on you. Unless you have to pee, you're not moving until it's time for bed."

Cooper wandered in from the bedroom, Patches on his heels. She tried to jump into Jason's lap but encountered an obstacle in the form of his laptop. Another try, and she was lying across his arms. Jason just looked down at her, dumbfounded.

"Do they always do this?" he asked.

"No idea. My first cat," I replied. "But if you move her often enough, she ought to get the message."

"*What?*" Patches asked. "*This is comfortable.*"

"Not for him," I told her. "He needs to move his arms and hands on that machine."

With a "harrumph" she moved around until she was lying on the chair, squeezed between Jason and the chair arm. He grinned down at her, gave her a scratch, then proceeded to go to work.

Meanwhile, Cooper was busy sniffing the cast. "*What is this?*" he asked.

"It's to keep my ankle from moving at all," I told him. "I made my injury worse running out to the garden today."

"*You hurt yourself again,*" he grumbled. "*We won't be able to play for months.*"

"Not months. But Jason will be here to play with you for a little while. By the time he leaves, I should be able to play again."

Cooper lay on the floor next to the ottoman, looking up at me with sadness in his eyes. "*I will watch over you.*"

"You're going to have to do more than that," I told him. "Both Dave and Jason will need your help guarding the gnome tonight. They'll need your eyes. After they're done, you can come watch me sleep, okay?"

"*Okay,*" he sighed. "*No bad dreams tonight, though. You must sleep to get well.*"

I wouldn't have any dreams this night. Narcotics ensured that. But he wouldn't understand, so I just agreed.

About a half hour later, as I slumped in my chair, watching a mindless show on the television, another truck pulled into the drive. Jonathan emerged from the back of the house and greeted a man who, had he been two inches taller, could have been his identical twin. I assumed this was Don, the other nephew. They both waved at me through the window and went around back. Shortly, I heard more muted conversation.

Dave came into the house. "I'm going to get dinner. The boys will watch the gnome while I'm gone. Maybe having *two* shifters out there will pry some information from him."

"Hey," I said, sitting straighter. "It's still spring. It's going to get chilly tonight. You guys are going to just sit, so you'll need something to keep you warm. *And*, I know he's a prisoner and all, but the gnome shouldn't get cold, either."

"I thought of that. We all have heavy jackets with us, and Don brought a horse blanket if the gnome wants it. I suspect he won't, though. If they live underground, it's always a lot colder in caves than the air temperature will be tonight."

"And food?" I asked.

"I ordered enough for eight people," Dave smiled. "I don't know what he eats on a regular basis, but if he gets hungry enough, he'll eat human food."

Appeased, I sank back into my chair and turned my attention back to the television. Jason hadn't even looked up from his laptop during our conversation but now interjected, "Gnomes probably eat berries and stuff. Roots, too. If they live underground, they probably don't come out to hunt much."

"Then he'll eat the French fries and maybe the coleslaw, too," Dave said. "I'm not going out of my way for him. He is, after all, a criminal."

"Just making an observation," Jason retorted, eyes still glued to the screen.

Dave whistled as he walked out the front door. Based on the set of his shoulders, he was actually enjoying himself. Then again, I thought, he'd had mostly desk duty for the last however many years he'd been a watch commander. It probably felt good to get "out in the field" again, no matter how weird the circumstances.

One of the nephews came in from the deck. "Is there anything to drink? Jonathan says he's parched."

So this one was Don. I waved my hand at the kitchen. "Help yourself to whatever you can find. There's booze in the cupboard underneath the toaster, sodas and water in the fridge, and you're welcome to make coffee, if you want that. Glasses are in the cupboard above the dishwasher, as are coffee mugs."

"There's beer in the fridge, too," Jason said.

I looked at him in astonishment. "Beer?"

"Yeah. I bought some yesterday when you sent me to the store. I do drink beer on occasion."

"Okay, then," I said. "Beer, too."

"A soda will be fine," Don said. "We don't want alcohol if we're going to be on watch. If it's okay with you, we'll have coffee after dinner."

"Whatever you want," I replied. "I'm glad you've agreed to help us."

Don shrugged as he opened the fridge door and pulled out a couple of cans of soda. "It's different. We usually just shift and go hunting in the woods. This way, we get to scare something that isn't food. Well, not *quite* food."

I gulped at that last statement. "Are you making any progress with getting him to talk?"

"Nope. He's being as tight-lipped as a spinster."

My eyebrows raised. "As a spinster? I don't think I've heard that one before."

Don laughed. "Grandpappy used to say that when we got into trouble and no one would tattle. When I asked him what he meant, he said it came from *his* pappy who knew a spinster. Everyone wanted to know why she wasn't married, and she wouldn't say, just pressed her lips together. Most of us say it now, although I'm not sure about anyone outside our family."

All of a sudden, we heard a banging and clattering coming from the deck. Don dropped the cans on the counter and raced back out the door, Jason on his heels. I looked over to the chair Jason had been sitting in, and his laptop was on the floor. Patches was eyeing it with a curious look, then hopped down and stretched across the keyboard.

The noise stopped, and both men returned to the house just a moment later. "What was all that about?" I asked.

Jason picked up his laptop, complete with cat, and sat back down with a snicker. "Seems Jonathan told the gnome he looked tasty… much better than the small game they normally hunt. For *some* reason, the gnome got upset and started rattling the cage. When Don told him unless he started talking, the two of them would certainly have a feast tonight, the cage stopped moving. Jonathan says the gnome is huddled in the back corner of the cage, as far away from him as possible."

As he moved Patches back to the spot next to him, I turned in my chair so I could actually see Don. "You wouldn't really eat him, would you?"

"Nah. We promised Dave we wouldn't. 'Sides, I'm told they're really not that good eating. Lots of fat and gristle, not enough meat."

I shuddered. That means someone they knew had actually eaten one at some point. I didn't want to know the particulars.

Just then, Dave returned with an armload of Styrofoam boxes and a couple of paper bags. "Dinner!" he yelled when he walked through the door. Jason rose to help him as I looked on helplessly.

Dave dumped his armload on the island counter. Jason grabbed plates and forks, and they set it all out buffet style. Jason kindly loaded up a plate for me, but he must have been thinking about his own stomach because it contained about twice the amount I normally ate. However, Cooper solved that problem by coming over to my side and making puppy eyes at me.

"*That smells good!*" he said.

"You can have my leftovers," I told him. "But not until I'm through. Me first, then you." I gave lie to my statement by giving him a rib tip before I'd even taken a bite. He inhaled it then sat watching me like a hawk as I ate.

Dave, Jason, and Don sat at the breakfast table to eat, and I could hear them strategizing not only for the night, but the next day. Don said gnomes usually didn't travel far from home, so chances were, the clan they were looking for was within about three miles of my place. Dave pulled the map I'd made out of his pocket, and they decided which caves would be the most likely.

As soon as I was done eating, I put my plate on the floor, and Cooper proceeded to demolish my leftovers. Patches had come sniffing but decided it didn't smell interesting and had resumed her seat on the keyboard. When I asked her why, she told me it was nice and warm. I left it for Jason to convince her his keyboard was *not* a good resting spot.

"Come on, Mom," Jason said when he picked up my now-sparkling plate. "Let's get you settled in bed. Because I'm not going out tomorrow with the other three, I'm taking the late shift. Will you tell Cooper I'll come to get him when it's time?"

I nodded, then protested as he picked me up. "I can make it with crutches!"

"I know. But better if you don't as much as possible," he chided me.

He carried me into my bedroom and sat me on the edge of the bed before going to the hook on the back of my bathroom door to get my nightclothes. While I changed, he went back for my crutches, both Cooper and Patches following when he returned.

"Dave's taking the first shift. The other two will go home to sleep for a few hours before returning. Will you ask Cooper to go outside now?"

I relayed instructions to Coop, who seemed reluctant to leave me. "I'll be okay," I told him. "As I told you before, you can be of more help being the eyes of the men who can't see the gnome. And I know you can hear anything in here from the deck. We'll unlock your door just for tonight so you can come in if you need to."

Patches leapt onto the bed. "*I will watch her,*" she said to Cooper. "*I will call if you are needed.*"

Jason brought me a pill and a glass of water, setting those on my bedside table before bringing cushions in from the sofa to elevate my leg. I was looking forward to not feeling my ankle for several hours. Despite the bravado, it really did hurt…and I was already itching under the cast.

He kissed me on the forehead. "That's from me." He kissed me on the cheek. "That's from Dave. He's really a good guy, you know. Get some sleep." Then he left me to my own devices.

I dutifully took the pill and settled down as best I could. I didn't normally sleep on my back and wasn't quite as comfortable as if I'd been able to lie on my side, but I couldn't do that and keep my leg elevated at the same time.

Once I'd stopped fidgeting, Patches curled up next to me. "*The dog is right. You need to sleep to heal. I will keep watch.*"

Soon, the pill took effect, and I knew nothing more.

I woke as it was just getting light, still groggy from the pill but determined to be up and about as much as I could. Cooper stirred when I rose but immediately went back to sleep. I didn't blame him. He'd probably had a longer night than he was accustomed to, being the eyes-on-the-gnome for both Jason and Dave.

Someone, probably Dave, had put the coffee together the night before, and the pot was ready for me. I was grateful I didn't have to wait for my first cup – I needed the caffeine to dispel the remaining narcotics in my system.

I managed to get both myself and a full cup over to my chair using only one crutch. I settled with a sigh. The fiberglass cast was lighter than a plaster one would have been but still more awkward than a simple elastic bandage. It took me a bit to get my body into proper position, keeping my ankle elevated on the extra cushions someone had left on my ottoman.

As soon as I was sitting still, Patches hopped into my lap. *"You slept last night. That is good. You must continue to heal."* She turned a few times, lay down, then rose slightly again because it was, apparently, time for a bath.

We sat in companionable silence, she grooming herself and me sipping my coffee, looking out the front window. Although it was overcast, the weatherman had said it wouldn't rain until late. At least it looked like the men would have a dry day for exploring caves.

About a half hour later, Jason came out of his bedroom, hair still tousled and eyes still sleepy. Without a word, he poured himself a cup of coffee and sat on the chair opposite.

"Mornin'," he mumbled into his cup.

"Mornin', sweetie," I replied with a smile. "Did you sleep okay?"

"I should have taken one of your pain pills," he grumbled. "We rearranged schedules because Don and Jonathan didn't want to split up. I'd just got off my shift and was drifting off when the gnome raised a ruckus. It took forever to get back to sleep."

I'd totally forgotten there were two men out on my deck watching the little creep. I was also amazed the pill worked that well because I didn't hear a thing. But as soon as Jason was done complaining, Don walked into the house with two cups in his hand. He proceeded to fill both.

"I hope you don't mind, but we already drank one pot of coffee this morning, so I made another. We also helped ourselves to the milk in the fridge."

I laughed. "I don't mind at all. Whatever it takes to keep you awake and happy until all this is resolved."

"We're waiting for Dave to return, then we're going to go find his clan. So one of us is watching the little bugger at all times, Jonathan and I will go out with Dave separately, unless we get lucky and they live in one of the first couple of caves we check."

He turned to go back to the deck, but before he took a step, the door opened and Dave walked in. He was in full uniform, the only difference being he wore brown hiking boots rather than the usual black work shoes. He had a travel mug in one hand and two boxes in the other.

"You're up!" he said. "How are you feeling this morning?"

"It's sore but not as bad as yesterday," I told him. "You look mighty chipper for not having gotten a full night's sleep."

"I've managed on less before. And the fact that I was able to sleep in my own bed helped.

"I brought you a roll of plastic wrap," he continued. "It'll be easier to use that than taping a grocery bag around that cast when you shower."

"And the other box?" I asked.

"For Jason," he said, handing it to my kid. "Ten rounds. Hotter load so the kick will be a little harder but nothing you can't handle."

Jason just nodded and took the box of ammo with him to the chair. He sipped his coffee then changed the rounds in the gun from what had been in there to what Dave brought. He casually leaned the rifle back against the chair and opened his laptop.

Dave placed the box of plastic wrap on the counter then turned to Don. "Y'all ready to go?"

Don drained his cup in one go. "I'm going first. Jonathan will stay to watch the gnome. If we don't find anything in two hours, we'll come back here and switch off."

"Why just two hours?" I asked.

"It's risky for us to stay in our were form for long periods of time."

"Explain?" My curiosity was piqued.

Don sighed. "The lure of being in that form is strong. It's tough to really explain to a full human, but it feels *right* to be on four paws instead of two and to have the enhanced senses. If we stay that way for a long time, chances are we'll lose ourselves in that form and not change back.

"Pappy told us the longer we stay in our were form, the more we lose our humanity. There are stories of weres who've gone completely feral, not returned to their human form, and were lost to their family and friends.

"Four hours is the longest I've ever stayed in my were form, and I could feel the pull to not change back. When I did, I felt like I'd lost something precious. So we try to limit our time."

Dave topped off his travel mug then waved it in my direction. "We're off. I'll call if there's any news…or trouble."

They left, and I could hear a murmured conversation out on the deck before it was quiet again.

I turned the television on, wanting some noise. Jason's fingers were busy on the laptop keys. It being Saturday, the Atlanta news was still on and I listened for any further updates on the killings in the mountains. Thankfully, none was forthcoming in the last hour. Either the locals were keeping it quiet, or there had been no new developments. I suspected the latter.

Jason had just returned from refreshing Jonathan's coffee and refilling my cup for the third time when Cooper padded out of my bedroom. He immediately went outside and after, I presumed, doing his business, returned to stretch out on the floor next to my chair. Patches opened one eye suspiciously then returned to her nap, still curled up in my lap.

"*You are better this morning,*" he said, looking up at me.

"I am," I told him.

"I still can't get used to one-sided conversations," Jason said, pausing the clacking of the computer keys for a moment.

"I don't know about the one-sided conversations," I replied with a grimace, "but after six months, I *still* can't get used to hearing other animals."

"You seem to take it in stride, though."

"It's weird, but it's an *is* so yeah, I'm just trying to go with the flow. I think it's easier because I'm alone so much of the time. I don't have to worry about what others might think."

"You shouldn't ever worry about what others might think," my son chided me.

"It's different now that Dad's gone," I told him. "When he was alive, I was concerned about appearances – for *his* sake. Now I'm not *that* worried, but still, I do try to watch myself, at least in public."

"Nonetheless, be yourself, Mom. You've earned that."

"What do you mean?" This was another side of my son I hadn't seen – maybe it had to do with his empathic abilities? His next statement proved me right.

"Once my abilities manifested, I could see how hard you worked to be the perfect wife for Dad. A lot of it went against your nature, and I could feel the conflict. Like wanting to play in the garden but not doing so because of Dad's opinion on that subject."

My jaw dropped. I thought I'd hidden all that. Then again, Samantha had noticed. Why not Jason?

Jason smiled. "I know Sam thinks I worshipped the ground Dad walked on. I admired him in a lot of ways, yes, but the truth is, I could also see how he stifled you. It wasn't my place to speak out, and he would have probably thrashed me for doing so, being his kid and all.

"It was even more obvious once both Sam and I were out of the house and you didn't have to play Mom all the time. You *still* did everything necessary for Dad and nothing for *you*. The conflict in your emotions was more evident every time I visited.

"Since Dad died, you've been a lot more relaxed. At least, since his estate was settled and you decided to move where *you* wanted to live. So I want my Mom to be herself – whatever that might be.

"And frankly, it's easier on me, too. I don't have to shield as much when I'm around you now.

"So now that I've lectured you for the first time in my life, what can I do to help you around here? You still need to stay off that ankle as much as possible."

I thought first about what he'd said. I was glad both my children wanted me to do whatever I wanted to. I knew a lot of women who kept up a façade "for the children's sake." It was a relief to know I wouldn't have to be one of them.

Then, I tried to think of a project for him. And came up empty.

"Sorry, but the only project on my list right now is the garden, and I know that's not your thing. It'll just have to wait until I can get out there again."

Jason looked at me thoughtfully. "What about foundation planting? It's a blank page, now. I'll bet you have ideas."

"That was one of next year's projects," I said. "But sure, if you're up for a lot of digging, I can tell you what I want and where to get it."

He stood and stretched. "There's no gym nearby, so I'll do whatever you want that involves exercise. Let me change clothes, then we can talk about it."

"Let me shower first," I picked Patches up and put her on the floor next to Coop. She yowled in protest then ran out the doggie door. "I think better after coffee and shower."

"Okay. Let me help you wrap that cast, at least."

I laughed. "I can do that. I know how, if you remember when you had a cast on your arm when you were ten?"

Jason had decided the tree in front of the house in Smyrna would be perfect for climbing. In his defense, it probably was – the lower limbs were sturdy and just at the height a ten-year-old could grab to swing himself up. However, that same boy lost his grip and fell, landing on his arm and breaking it in two places. He wore a cast for two months, which had to be wrapped each time he took a bath.

"I remember," he said with a wry smile. "But I can at least carry the roll for you so you can use both crutches."

"You don't even have to do that," I grinned, then looked down at my dog. "Coop, there's a skinny box on the kitchen counter. Would you carry it into my bathroom, please?"

Cooper went into the kitchen, looked to find the box, stood on his hind legs, and gently took the box of plastic wrap in his mouth before dropping to all fours again. He trotted down the hall, and shortly, we heard a 'plop' as he put it on the vanity. I knew it would have dog slobber on it but kept that to myself. I wanted my kid to know I *could* get along without him.

"Helpful," Jason said as he watched.

He walked behind me as I thudded down the hall on my crutches. "He is," I said. "And being able to ask him for help is a boon at times."

After I'd showered (and hung the plastic on the shower rod to dry before being used again), we went out onto the front porch. I showed him where he'd have to dig up wayward grasses, told him how deep to dig, then gave him instructions on augmenting the clayey soil. "There's a spade on the wall in the garage," I told him. "Sorry, I don't have a pickax, which would help you break up the soil faster. I can't handle one of those."

"No worries," he said. "The spade will do just fine. Go. Sit. Can I get you anything before I get started?"

I shook my head and hobbled back into the house. After re-situating myself in my chair, I picked up my novel and tried to read. It was nearly impossible, though, because I was jealous of my son being able to work in the dirt when I couldn't. Visions of *me* doing the work kept creeping into my thoughts.

Suddenly, I heard Jason laughing uproariously and "What a good dog!" coming from the front. Grabbing my crutches, I went back out onto the porch to see what was so funny.

Jason stood to one side, leaning on the spade. He was wiping tears from his eyes as he watched Cooper digging enthusiastically in the area I'd shown Jason I wanted dug up. Jason looked up as I came out the door.

"I started breaking up the soil, and all of a sudden, Coop came running around from the back of the house, pushed me aside, and started digging." He was still chuckling.

Jonathan also came around from the back of the house to see what the commotion was about. When he saw what Cooper was doing, he laughed, too.

Coop stopped digging and looked up at me. *"What? You won't let me dig but you will him? I can do it faster than he can."*

I started laughing, too. "You wanted to dig in the garden beds, which isn't what I want. You can help Jason here all you want, provided you stop when and where he tells you to."

"Want some help, Coop?" Jonathan asked. "I have good claws, too."

"Aren't you supposed to be on guard duty?" I asked.

"I can guard from here, too," Jonathan said with a smile. "If I'm in were form, I'll hear anything out back before you do, and he's not fast enough to outrun me if he should actually escape, which I don't think he can. I twisted the latch on the cage."

"Hey," Jason interjected. "The whole point of this was so I could get some exercise. If you two do it with your claws, I won't even break a sweat."

"Oh," Jonathan said. "In that case, I'll leave you to it." He turned and disappeared around the corner of the house.

I sighed. If Jonathan twisted the latch, that meant the crate would be unusable to me because it would probably break off when put back into its proper position. Not that I had any plans to need it in the near future but nonetheless…

Jason resumed his digging at Cooper's side, more or less outlining the area I wanted cleared, leaving the heavy work to the dog. I watched for a few minutes, noting that Coop really did a good job. However, Jay was going to have to pick up after him: Coop paid no attention to what was happening behind him, and clumps of dirt and grass were flying out into the yard. I chuckled to myself and went back into the house.

I'd no sooner settled myself back into my chair when I heard the clomping of boots on the deck. Before I could rise to see what was happening, Dave came into the house.

"Any luck?" I asked.

"I think so," he replied as he sat at the breakfast table to take off his boots. Refilling his travel mug once again, he padded into the living room in stocking feet and sat in the chair opposite.

"We found a clan about a mile and a half from here. It was the second cave we checked. They were reluctant to talk, at first, because of me, but Don convinced them…he had shifted into human form when he picked up their scent at the cave mouth but shifted back when told they didn't want to talk to us. The shifting, by the way, is still really creepy.

"The opening was large enough for him to get all the way in when he was in cat form. He got halfway in, retreated, and came back to his human shape.

"Don said the gnome he spoke with believes our prisoner is one of theirs. A guy named Gloomy or something like that. He disappeared a couple of weeks ago, but before that, he'd been spouting off about humans ruining the woods."

"That might be our guy, then," I said. "If it's the same gnome, he said he wanted all humans gone when he was attacking the garden beds."

"Probably. They're going to call a council meeting to discuss the issue. Apparently, it's not unusual for one of them to leave one clan and move to another, so they paid no attention to this Gloomy's disappearance. However, once informed about the damage to your garden beds and the possibility of a gnome helping a vampire, he got all agitated, according to Don."

"So what now?"

Dave sighed. "Don gave them some convoluted instructions on how to get here – landmarks and scents. We wait for them to come to us. Someone is supposed to come inform us of the council's decision *and* make sure our prisoner is their man. If his actions were deemed appropriate, they will demand the prisoner's release. If they decide he needs punishment, *they'll* be the ones to administer it."

I heard a truck's engine start and the crunch of tires on gravel. When I looked out the window, Dave said, "That'll be Jonathan leaving to go get some rest. Don is going to stay for a couple more hours on the off chance his shapeshifting will be needed in that timeframe. But he's going to tire out, too, and I told him you and I could handle things if he had to leave."

I looked at him in amazement. "You think *I* can handle all this?"

Dave nodded. "With backup, of course. I can't see the gnomes, nor can Jason, but you have a large dog who can. Based on what I was hearing, Cooper scares this little guy just as much as Don and Jonathan do when they're shifted. I can speak to the legal end – the human end, anyway. You can translate."

I sat back in my chair, stunned. I was actually going to get to help in resolving the mess. Thomas would have had me locked in the bedroom, rather than get involved in…police matters. Was that what this was? I wasn't sure, but with Dave sitting there in full regalia, I guessed it was.

"I have a question," I started. "One I wanted to ask this morning, but you left before I could."

"What?"

"Why are you in full uniform? Didn't the sheriff say it wasn't a departmental problem?"

Dave shrugged. "He did. But I thought maybe seeing a human law enforcement officer might carry some weight. I'm not sure if it did, but I don't think it hurt matters.

"I also know there's at least one more criminal hanging out in this area. If he or she happened to see me, they'll know we're serious about catching them. It was a thought, anyway.

"Now, while we wait, are you hungry? I ate before I left home, but having been hiking for the last two hours, I could eat again. Don's probably starved, too. And I know Jason didn't cook breakfast."

I nodded. "I could eat. Jason probably could, too. He and Cooper have been hard at work this last hour." I pointed out the front.

Dave looked out the window, then back at me. "Put him to work, I see. Good for you! Bacon and eggs?"

I waved him in the direction of the kitchen. "Works for me. Whatever you can find will be fine."

He set to work, whistling all the while. It wasn't aimless whistling, either. I was pretty sure what I was hearing (albeit in a much higher tone) was a Bach concerto – one of the Brandenburgs, I thought. Classical music, huh? The man continued to surprise me.

Fifteen minutes later, he called Jason in, then took two plates out to the deck. One was piled high with bacon, scrambled eggs, and toast. The other, smaller plate had just eggs and toast. Presumably for the gnome.

Cooper followed Jason into the house and sat at his feet while he washed at the kitchen sink, looking longingly at the stove. As soon as Jay dried his hands, he laughed, put a small amount of bacon and eggs on a plate, and set it on the floor. While Coop inhaled that, Jay put together another plate and brought it to me before returning for one for himself.

Dave got his own plate and joined us in the living room. Cooper finished his plate and stared alternately between the three of us, hoping one of us would drop something, I'm sure.

It was mid-afternoon before I heard a male voice calling from the deck with Cooper's *"What do you want?"* answering. Dave had just returned from taking Don home, so it was only the humans and dog to deal with whatever was happening. Jason and Cooper were out on the deck, presumably guarding the gnome, but the voice I heard was different than the guy in the dog crate.

I grabbed my crutches and made my way to the deck, Dave on my heels, still in stocking feet. "I'm guessing there's someone else out there? I heard Cooper bark," he said before we'd even made it to the door.

"Yeah. Another voice."

When I finally got to the deck, Jason was looking at Coop, who was in full guard mode at the head of the stairs, staring at three gnomes standing on the path between the deck and garden.

"Down, Cooper," I said to get my dog to back off. "How can I help you?" I asked the three on the ground. I decided to be polite – until and unless they became aggressive. Coop relaxed his stance somewhat but was still wary.

"You can see us?" the elderly-looking gnome asked, looking first at my dog, then me. His English, while still accented, wasn't as difficult to understand as the perp's. "Where is the shifter who came to us this morning?"

"He's gone," I replied. "You'll have to deal with me."

"Highly unusual. Well, it seems we have no choice. We, the three chosen by the elders, have come for our clan member," he said. Despite them *all* looking like garden gnomes minus the hat, it was easy to tell them apart. Two had white hair and beards; the third new one had black. The one in the crate was a brunet. Their faces were different, too, although they were all wrinkled, so determining age was problematic. The one speaking looked to be the eldest of the four.

"The council determined he has committed transgressions, and we have identified him as a missing clan mate," he continued. "It is our duty to take him back to the clan for punishment."

"Wait a minute, please, while I tell the other two what you have said," I told them.

The speaker harrumphed, said something to his compatriots in a guttural language I thought might be a German dialect, then all three closed their eyes and appeared to be concentrating. Moments later, I heard both Dave and Jason gasp.

"I can see them!" Dave said with amazement, while all that came from Jason was, "Wow."

The speaker reiterated what he'd told me, and both men's jaws dropped. "I can hear him, too," Dave was awed.

"Unveiling is a skill some of us possess, but since it is now forbidden to interact with humans, we do not use it," the gnome told us. "I am making an exception in this case because you are obviously human law enforcement and need to know what will happen without the possibility of error in the woman's translation."

Dave moved from my side to sit on the top stair so he was closer to eye level with the gnomes. "You are correct. I *am* human law enforcement, and if I am right, your clan member has committed more than just destruction of property."

"We have seen the destruction. It will be repaired. What else do you believe he has done?"

Dave told him about our theory of a vampire attacking humans and a gnome helping him.

"This was not relayed to the council earlier today. If he has indeed assisted a *nachzehrer* in its wicked ways, his punishment will be much more severe."

While unfamiliar with the term they used, I knew "nacht" was German for "night," and vampires were generally considered to be creatures of the night, so assumed it was their word for a vampire.

Dave was quiet for a moment then said, "I could use your help."

"In what way?"

"Most of my colleagues do not believe in the supernatural as I do, making it difficult for them to investigate. We need to catch the vampire but do not know where it may be hiding or who it may be. I am probably the only one who is willing to believe in that which I cannot normally see and want to do what I can to stop the killing.

"This gnome…" He pointed to the dog crate where the captive was sitting in a corner, arms crossed over his chest, still glaring at everyone and everything. "…may be able to help with the vampire's capture. He could tell us what it looks like, and even perhaps where it could be found. But he will not talk to anyone, not even after being threatened by the shifters."

"A moment, please," the older gnome said, then turned his back on us to confer with his…friends? Colleagues? I heard murmuring but could not understand what they were saying to each other.

Finally, they turned back so all three were facing us. "This is a larger decision than we are empowered to make. We will take Gloomy back to the clan, tell the council what you have said, and allow them to determine the next steps.

"Should they decide to assist you, I will return with whatever information is gleaned. Will that be acceptable?"

Dave shrugged his shoulders. "It will have to be. I hope you have more luck than we did."

The older gnome's eyes gleamed. "It is rare for one of us to commit such heinous transgressions, and the council does not look kindly on those who do. We *will* know what he has done and with whom."

He turned to me. "You are obviously kind to the animals," he said, indicating the refugees still under the deck and the pans of water. "That is rare for a human, and we appreciate it. Your walls will be repaired within the rising of four suns."

I smiled. "And I thank you for it. As you can see…" I gestured down at my cast. "…it will be more than four days before I could do it myself. May I ask a question?"

The gnome thought for a moment then nodded his head. "If it does not violate our laws, I will answer."

"You said it is *now* forbidden to interact with humans. Was it not forbidden in the past? If so, what changed?"

"You listen well for a female." I gritted my teeth at that statement. "Yes, we once had friends among humans. They did not look as you, with darker skin and hair. They revered the land as we do, and we traded with them.

"Then, about ten or so of your generations ago, new humans arrived. They had fairer skin and hair as you all do. They drove away the original humans, took from the land, giving nothing back in exchange. In addition, they invaded our homes, taking our livelihoods for themselves."

I interpreted this to mean white humans started mining in their caves. It didn't surprise me in the least.

"Our master council met and decided we would no longer be friends with humans. A spell was devised to hide us from human sight. We also split into smaller clans and moved into caves the humans could not access. Since then, we have looked on humans with wariness. It is rare for one to have the power to see us, much less treat us with respect."

"I hope you will not think that of me," I said. "I would have left your clansman alone if he had not tried to destroy my property. Thank you for explaining."

The gnome simply nodded without answering further.

We all moved back to give the gnomes space as they walked up the stairs and over to the crate. Dave took a multitool from his pocket and used it to untwist the crate's latch before opening the door. The gnome inside, Gloomy, I supposed, tried to make a run for it. Before he could get to the stairs, the black-haired gnome muttered something, and Gloomy froze in place.

"Cool magic," I said.

The black-haired gnome smiled. "It is useful on occasion."

He and the other white-haired gnome shouldered Gloomy as if he were a log, walked down the stairs, and headed toward the woods. The one who'd been speaking with us looked at Dave.

"I do not know how long it will take to get the information you require," he said. "I will return when I have news to impart."

"I do not live here," Dave told him. "But you can tell El, and she will relay the information to me if I am not here."

The gnome's eyebrows raised a bit. "We do not normally bring women into such serious matters. Perhaps the other man?" He looked at Jason.

"I may not be here, either," Jason said, speaking for the first time. "I do not live with my mother. I am simply visiting."

I could've kissed my kid. I knew he had no plans to leave in the next week, but between him and Dave, they were giving the gnome a lesson in women's independence.

The gnome harrumped. "Fine. I will relay the information to whoever is here when I arrive, then. But do not blame me if she tells you incorrectly."

He followed his clan mates into the woods, leaving us alone on the deck. I turned to go back inside. Jason opened the door for me, and we all trooped back into the house, Cooper following me closely.

"That was…awesome," Jay said after we'd all sat in the living room. "I never thought I'd see one of them move and talk!"

I laughed. "I don't think they're really statues come to life."

"No, but you have to admit they look like them. Minus the hat, of course. Whoever designed the first garden gnome must have had some interaction with real ones. I wonder if these guys know they've been made into caricatures?" Dave was chuckling.

"They're obviously a patriarchal society, looking down on their women," I grumbled. "'Do not blame me if she tells you incorrectly.' Geez."

"Don't worry, Mom. *We* know you'll relay correct information, even if they don't."

Dave yawned. "I don't think they're going to be back immediately, so I'm going home for a nap. Call me if anything more happens." He changed his seat from the sofa to the breakfast table, put his boots back on, and left out the back door.

Jason rose, too. "I'm going back out to work on the foundation. I presume Cooper will join me?"

I laughed. "Probably. It's the only chance he gets to legitimately dig in dirt."

Cooper did indeed barrel outside as soon as Jason exited out the front, and I was left to my own devices. My ankle was throbbing, and my shin and calf were itching. I grabbed my crutches, hobbled over to the coat closet, and pulled out a wire hanger before returning to my chair. It took some doing without a pair of pliers, but I was able to unbend it. Sighing in relief, I stuck the straight end down the cast and scratched the itchy parts.

"*I could scratch your itch*," Patches said as she hopped into my lap, turned a couple of times, then settled in.

"I'm not sure you could get your paw down there," I told her. "It's a pretty tight fit. *And* your claws are sharper than this. I don't need to bleed to stop itching."

"*Don't say I didn't offer.*"

I didn't feel like reading so turned the television on and found an afternoon baseball game. It wasn't the Atlanta Braves or Minnesota Twins, and really held no interest, but it was noise.

Patches' purring was soothing, and I soon followed Dave's idea of a nap.

Cooper woke me an hour later with a lick to my face, his dirty paws on the arm of my chair. Jason was sitting in the chair opposite.

"*We finished digging. It was wonderful!*" Coop said, tongue lolling in a doggy smile.

I rubbed my eyes. "You're all done? Already?"

Jason chuckled. "Yes. Well, he is. I have to clean up after him, but that won't take long. Are you hungry? I can't cook, but I can make sandwiches."

"I could eat, but before that, will you clean Coop's paws?" I eyed the pawprints on the chair arm. "I don't need him tracking any more dirt around the house."

"Sorry. Come here, Coop." Jason grabbed the hand towel off the oven handle and wiped paws down before proceeding to wash his own hands. I groaned both at the pawprints going from the front door to my chair, then into the kitchen; and at him using the wrong towel, but it was too late to avert a mess.

"I'll clean everything up," he told me. "After lunch."

"Lunch" consisted of peanut butter and jelly sandwiches. Thirty years old and that was the best he could manage with fridge and cupboards full. I wondered where I'd gone wrong in the parenting department. He did, however, pull out the vacuum and clean up the tracked dirt, as well as change out the kitchen towel, so I gave myself points for that.

"I'm going to finish up outside for today. Are garden stores open on Sundays around here? I could go get your plants tomorrow if they are. What else needs doing?"

"You could put Coop's crate back in the garage. If it's still useable, that is. I don't know if the latch will still work after being bent and unbent."

He went out to the deck, and I heard the crate being folded. Rather than walk around to the side garage door, he carried it back through the kitchen.

"Latch is fine, at least for several more uses," he called on his way into the garage. "It'll eventually break, but not right now."

I heaved a sigh of relief at that. Again, I had no plans to use it in the immediate future, but one never knew. Especially, it seemed, around this house.

I dozed again and didn't wake until the sun was sinking below the trees. Jason had obviously showered and was sitting in the chair, doing something on his laptop. Patches had moved from my lap to his side and was intently watching his screen.

"What are you doing that has her so intrigued?"

He chuckled. "Watching a deep-sea fishing video one of my friends posted on Facebook. I saw her looking at it, and this is the third time I've run it. She hasn't taken her eyes off the screen for the last ten minutes."

"Must be wishful thinking," I mused. "I don't think she's ever seen anything like that in real life."

"*I have not, which is why I am looking,*" she said. "*I would like to see food like that in real life.*"

I laughed, then looked at my phone for the time. It was nearly six, and I needed to figure out what to have for dinner. I wasn't about to eat peanut butter and jelly sandwiches twice in one day. Thinking on what I'd had Jay pick up at the store, I decided I could manage hamburgers and French fries.

As I stood, Jason looked at me in alarm. "What are you doing?"

"Going to make dinner. I'm not eating sandwiches twice in one day."

"Sit. I already ordered a pizza on your phone. *And* a salad because I know you like them."

I sat, grumbling. I'd already had pizza once this week. I liked a little more variety in my menu, but he was trying to take care of me. With that realization, I stopped grumbling.

My phone pinged with a text. It was from Dave. **Called into work. Another body, less than a mile from your place. Stay inside. Will come by when I can with what info I can share.**

I showed it to Jason. "That's not good," he said, heading into the bedroom he was using. He returned with the rifle, leaning it against his chair. Then he went around the house, locking windows and doors that had been opened in the last day with so many able-bodied men around, including the doggy door. Cooper watched him warily.

"Sorry, buddy," Jay said to the dog. "But we need to keep you and Patches safe. That means you have to stay inside, only going out with human supervision."

I had to translate what he'd said for the dog and cat, both of whom were upset at being confined to the house again.

"It's for your own good," I admonished. "We don't know if the bad guy is around here, but I don't want either of you hurt. We *all* have to be careful."

A car pulled into the driveway, and Jason looked out the window to confirm it had a Domino's sign on top before opening the door to accept delivery of dinner.

We ate in silence, Jason wolfing down his food and me picking at mine. With the text from Dave, my anxiety had ratcheted up a couple of notches, and I had difficulty swallowing. But knowing I needed sustenance, I choked some of it down.

Jason put a *lot* of leftovers into the fridge, then stood by my chair with a pain pill in one hand and a glass of water in the other. "You should take this."

I shook my head. "No, I want to be awake if and when Dave gets here. Just get me some ibuprofen and a couple of ice packs. That'll be enough to calm my ankle down to manageable levels." Then I reached for the coat hanger again.

That, at least, got a laugh out of my son as he returned to the kitchen to exchange pills and get ice packs out of the freezer. "It's been a long time, but I do remember how bad casts make you itch."

After getting me situated with ice, he sat back down, and we turned our attention to the television and another baseball game. After moving to the West Coast, my son had developed a fondness for the Los Angeles Dodgers (much to my chagrin), and he was animated as he watched the game, groaning when the Atlanta Braves did something good and whooping when the Dodgers played well. My emotions were just the opposite, and we were in a competitive mood.

The game ended (the Braves lost – Jason was ecstatic), and I was about to give up on Dave and go to bed when I received a text from him. **On my way. I'll knock twice only so you know it's me.**

"Make a pot of coffee," I told my son. "I have a feeling we're all going to need it."

He rose to do my bidding and hadn't even finished pouring the water into the machine when headlights shined through the living room window. We heard a car door shut and shortly, two brisk knocks at the door.

Cooper beat Jason to the door, but after a sniff, moved aside so he could open it. "*It's your friend,*" he told me, and I relayed to Jay that it was Dave on the other side and not a stranger.

Dave was not whistling when he came in. Instead, he had a murderous look on his face.

"Sit," I told him. "We have coffee brewing, and whatever you have to say can wait until it's done."

"I could use some. Thanks. I hate to impose, but is there anything to eat? I didn't get dinner."

While waiting for the coffee to finish, Jay put the rest of the pizza in the microwave. "*This* I can do," he crowed.

That, at least, brought a slight smile to Dave's face. "It's better than a sandwich," he said, but as soon as he spoke, his face returned to its thundering look.

Jay gave Dave the pizza and returned to pour us all coffee. When he'd distributed the mugs, he sat and gave Dave a concerned look.

"You look like you could kill something."

"I could," Dave said between mouthfuls. "This time it was your neighbor, El, Harvey Jackson. He'd gone out for an afternoon walk and didn't return. His wife went looking for him and, unfortunately, found him."

"Oh my god," I cried. "How is Myrtle holding up?"

The Jacksons were my nearest neighbors, owning the land that sort of abutted mine on the southwest side. Their house was almost a half mile away through a finger of woods owned by the Forestry Service, although only a couple of tenths of a mile separated our two driveways out on the road. We'd only met once – the day I moved in. Harvey had seen the moving truck when he'd checked the mail, and they'd come by briefly to introduce themselves. They were in their late sixties or early seventies, I guessed, and they inherited the place, which had once been a vacation cabin, from Harvey's parents. Harvey and Myrtle had made some major improvements to the house, making it fit for year-round habitation.

"She's not," Dave said. "The EMTs had to sedate her. We've called their daughter, who lives in Savannah. Until she can get up here, an off-duty female officer from Cherokee County is staying at the house."

Dave finished eating and put his plate in the dishwasher before sitting again on the sofa. He leaned forward, cradling his coffee mug in his hands, and stared at the floor as he spoke. "Harvey was found on a trail he liked because it was level, about a hundred yards from their house and right next to the boundary between their property and the Forestry Service's. Like the first body in the tent, he wasn't marked much at all…just the two holes on his neck.

"And *all* of the media is apparently now listening to our scanners. Not only the local guys, but CNN showed up. It's becoming a nightmare, both on the investigative side *and* the bad publicity for law enforcement up here.

"Everyone is at a loss on how to catch this criminal. All the higher-ups have finally bought that it's a vampire. But whoever it is doesn't fit the stereotype completely, because this killing happened in broad daylight.

"We got some DNA off the first three bodies – it's one person there. Harvey had skin and blood under the nails of one hand, so he managed to scratch his killer at least once. We're pretty sure it'll match the other DNA."

"So what now?" Jason asked. "From what I've heard, the perp is preying within about two miles of this house. Do I take Mom elsewhere? Twenty-four-seven police protection? What?"

"I'm not leaving," I said firmly. "Except for the one guy dying in my back yard, everything else has happened in the woods. I can't go into them, anyway, in my condition, so I should be okay sticking by the house.

"And since the gnome is no longer a problem, at least I don't think so, it should be easier for the police – or sheriff – to catch someone out where they're not supposed to be. You should be able to see a vampire, even if you can't a gnome."

Dave nodded. "The problem as I see it is none of us really knows what a vampire looks like. I doubt they look just like Bela Lugosi with their hair slicked back in widow's peaks and wearing capes. So they basically look like anyone else, unless we find someone with elongated canines and blood dripping from their mouth. It's a tough go if we can't catch someone in the act.

"In conjunction with the Forestry Service, we're trying to shut down the hiking trails. They're open to the public which means that'll be difficult, but there will be officers stationed at the usual entry points to warn any hikers away. If there *are* any hikers after the news breaks nationwide.

"I hate to do this, El, but because you're centrally located to this mess, we'd like to use your property as a staging area."

"And mess up my yard again with all the vehicles?" I was indignant.

"No," he shook his head. "Two patrol cars in your driveway will be all, and you'll see them walking from the cars to the woods alongside your house. They'll have no need to come inside. Four officers will fan out from here on a rotating basis, patrolling the woods and trail behind your place. Four others will come from north and south along the same trail. They won't actually come in the house. We just need somewhere to park the cars that isn't right out on the road."

"I guess that would be okay," I said.

"It's all hands on deck until the killer is caught. We have more than forty officers from three different departments working in concert with each other. It also means extended shifts and no off days."

He stood and looked at his watch. "I have six hours until I have to report in again. I'm going to get what shut-eye I can."

He eyed the gun leaning against Jason's chair. "Keep that handy," he said. "Let no one into the house. *No one.* I don't care if they're wearing a uniform or not. Except me if I'm able to come by. I'll text you beforehand, El, and knock only twice, as I did tonight.

"And you," he eyed me. "Stay off that ankle. Let your more able son handle whatever comes up. Unless, that is, you want to be in the hospital, which will happen if you don't take care of it."

He leaned down, kissed the top of my head, and let himself out. Jason locked the door behind him.

"Okay. You've seen Dave. Go to bed. I'll be up for another hour or so, but then I'm headed to bed, too. I'll feed the kids and let them out before I go, but would you tell Coop not go out of my sight, and the house is locked up tight? He should be able to sleep tonight, too."

I nodded, and after giving Cooper all the information he needed, including the fact that there would be strangers walking through the yard, grabbed my crutches to head into bed. Jason followed shortly with the pain pill, which I took as soon as I was under the covers. He kissed me goodnight, and once again, the pill did its trick and I drifted off, not even feeling when the dog came into bed sometime later.

I woke the next morning with a pain pill hangover again, which was one of the reasons I didn't like taking them in the first place. I blearily made my way into the kitchen, only to discover no one had bothered fixing the coffee the night before. I had to wait fifteen minutes before I could get some caffeine into my system to counteract the narcotic effects.

While I waited for my elixir to brew, I hobbled over to look out the front window. There were indeed two patrol cars parked in my driveway…one was a Fannin County Sheriff's Department vehicle, the other a sheriff's car from the neighboring county. I didn't see any people, though, so assumed they were out on patrol. At least they had been quiet about their business because I'd heard no one, and Cooper hadn't barked.

I heard a noise and turned to see Jason pouring coffee into two mugs. He set one on the table next to my chair before joining me at the window.

"Go and sit down, woman!" he commanded. "Based on recent developments, I think it's best I stay home today rather than go to the garden store to get plants. I don't want to leave you alone."

I obeyed his instructions and sat in my chair, lifting my leg onto the cushion still resident on the ottoman. I noticed the rifle had reappeared at the side of the chair he normally occupied. He must have brought it with him from the bedroom.

"The cops arrived about midnight," he said without turning. "They were quiet as they walked around the house, but I heard them, nonetheless. I assume there will be a shift change sometime soon."

Cooper came out of the bedroom, looking first at Jason, then me. "*Out?*"

"Coop has to go out. Would you supervise him, please?"

Jason headed for the deck door without a word, Coop on his heels. A couple of minutes later, I heard the dog barking furiously, and Jason's voice trying to calm him. The barking consisted mostly of *"Go away!"* Grabbing my crutches, I headed for the deck as quickly as I could.

Jason was out in the yard, holding my dog by his collar - barely. Cooper was straining at the collar, nearly choking himself to get at the strangers. Jason was hanging on with all his might to keep Coop in check. Four uniformed officers in full riot gear were standing together at the edge of the woods, looking at my dog with alarm.

"Cooper!" I yelled. "Down! Allow those men to pass."

He stopped barking and looked at me. *"They are strangers on my property. I will protect."*

"Remember I told you last night there would be strangers in our yard? These men are okay. As are the four who will change places with them. Let them pass!"

Coop stopped straining and allowed Jason to walk him back to the deck. Jason, however, did not let go of the collar.

"My apologies, gentlemen," I said to the cops. "He is a bit overprotective. You can get to your cars now."

The officers started walking toward the front of the house, all four keeping a wary eye on the dog standing alert on the deck. One, who looked to be the youngest of the four, stopped at the corner of the house. "You have an admirable dog. We change shifts at eight, four, and twelve. You might want to keep him indoors during those times.

"And did you just *talk* to your dog as if he were human?"

"Dogs understand more than you think, officer," I said by way of explanation. "He responded to my voice, which is all we really want, isn't it?"

"Yes, ma'am," he replied, still looking a tad confused. He joined his comrades out front and shortly, we heard the two cars leave the driveway. Just a moment later, two more pulled in. They must have been waiting out on the road to swap places. I was going to give Dave a kiss for whatever instructions he'd passed on to keep my yard in decent condition.

The three of us went back into the house, staying at the deck windows to monitor the new officers as they walked from the drive back into the woods. They split off in pairs as they got to the woods, two veering to our left, two to the right. Coop didn't relax until they were out of sight.

"I'm glad I'm not the one on patrol wearing all that gear," Jason said as we sat back in the living room. "That shit gets heavy after a while."

"And you know this how?"

"I read an article some time ago on how much weight a police officer carries on a normal basis. All the stuff on their belt weighs about twenty pounds. Add in the Kevlar vest and helmet, and that's another six or ten pounds, depending on what they're wearing. Let's say a round figure of thirty pounds. Carry all that while walking through woods on uneven ground for eight hours and tell me how you'd feel."

"Exhausted," I replied. "I hauled that and more between the driveway and the garden when I was building the beds. Even using a hand truck, it didn't take long for me to wish I'd designed a smaller garden. And that was in spurts – I rested a bit between trips. I can't imagine doing it nonstop."

"Exactly. I don't mind lifting weights but not for eight hours straight. Still, I suppose you get used to it after a time.

"So since I'm not going anywhere today, what's on the agenda?"

I stared at him. "I'm supposed to keep you occupied? I thought you were self-sufficient."

"Normally, yeah. But I'm not really a couch potato on weekends. Since I sit at a desk so much during the week, I'm normally at the gym, swimming in the ocean, or hiking with friends. I don't do enforced inactivity well."

I gestured at the cast. "And I do?"

"Point." He grinned. "But I need to do *something*. Do you still have board games?"

Growing up in the snowy Midwest, my family played a lot of board games in the wintertime. My southern-born husband, on the other hand, only knew of Monopoly, and that was from ads in magazines. As a child, he was outside nearly year-round. But it rained a lot in the winter in Atlanta, and there were even snow days once every few years for the kids. I had taught my children how to play a variety of games to keep them occupied when the weather kept them indoors. Thomas had just snorted at the idea, opting instead to read industry magazines.

"There's a deck of cards and a cribbage board in the lower left drawer of the desk. I didn't keep any of the others when I moved, thinking I wouldn't need them."

"That'll work. You might have to remind me of the rules, though. It's been a few years. After breakfast and showers?"

I nodded. "What do you want for breakfast?"

"You're not standing at the stove," he told me. "Talk me through making waffles. I can do that, I think."

I laughed. "I don't make homemade waffles anymore. It's too much work for just one person. You'll find a package of frozen ones in the back of the freezer. You pop them in the toaster."

"Oooh. I know frozen pastries. How many do you want?"

After we'd eaten and showered, Jason got the cards and board out of the desk, moved one of the other side tables to the left of my chair, and pulled his chair closer. I had to turn in my seat to see the game, which wasn't comfortable. I decided I really needed to sit square so my back wasn't twisted and told him to grab his laptop. Closed, we could use that as a table on my lap. It wasn't ideal, but my back was happier for it.

Jason needed no reminding of the rules of cribbage. It only took two hands before he was way ahead of me on the board. The animals, however, needed reminding this was a *human*'s game, not one for a cat or dog. Cooper pawed at the deck of cards, making them fall in a mess on the floor. Because we'd already had a starter, we had to begin again. Patches was fascinated with the pegs. She managed to pick one of the loose game pegs up with her teeth and before Jason could grab her, had taken it to bat around the kitchen floor. It did, I'll admit, make what was probably a satisfying rattle as it rolled around. Jason rescued the peg and pocketed it, much to Patches' chagrin.

She squeezed herself next to him and watched as he lay down a card to start the game. Cooper rested his chin on the arm of my chair and did the same.

"I think they've taken sides," I opined as I discarded. "And it seems Patches has taken a shine to you."

"I noticed," he replied wryly. "She keeps trying to sleep with me, too. I put her on the floor twice last night yet woke up with her sleeping on the pillow next to me."

"Probably because once you're asleep, you don't move much. I know I do, especially now because I'm not used to sleeping on my back. She's small enough to get rolled over on."

"And fast enough to not. She *did* sleep with you the other day."

"I think she's just a man's cat. I'm a poor substitute, but she'll take it when I'm the only one."

We played several games, splitting the wins between us. When Jason's stomach growled, I knew I had to feed him. I put the laptop aside and rose.

Before he could protest, I held up my hand. "I've been sitting on my duff for nearly three days and, despite your company, I'm *bored*. I can stand long enough to make us some lunch. I promise to balance on my right leg as much as possible."

He muttered something under his breath that sounded a lot like "stubborn woman" but continued to sit. I let the comment pass and took it as a good sign he was going to let me do *something* on my own…other than going to the bathroom, that is.

I wasn't thinking about anything fancy, so grilled cheese sandwiches and tomato soup were on the menu. Naturally, as soon as I went into the kitchen, both animals followed.

"Sit over there," I said, pointing to the edge of the island where I wouldn't run into them. "I'm not well balanced and don't need you to trip me."

"*But, but, you're doing something with food!*" Cooper whined.

"Yes, and you'll get a treat when I'm done, provided you behave."

It took no time at all to heat up the soup and make the sandwiches. I made an extra sandwich and gave it to Coop, while Patches got part of a slice of cheese on the counter. That kept them busy so Jason and I could eat in peace.

We spent the afternoon playing cribbage and keeping one eye on the baseball game on television. Once the game was over, I decided to take a nap. All that inactivity had tired me out.

I must have been tired. I slept nearly fourteen hours. I was undisturbed, thanks to my son's presence, feeding the dog and cat and letting them outside as necessary. Then I wondered what he'd had for dinner…there were no prefab meals in my freezer.

I hobbled out to the kitchen, thinking I'd have to fix the coffee then wait for my first cup. But the pot was already full. The light indicated Jason had set it up the night before and used the timer function. I was honestly impressed. He wasn't usually that domestic.

I did a lot of hopping around, setting one crutch next to my chair before returning to the kitchen to carry my coffee mug. Before I could sit, Cooper padded out of Jason's room.

"*Out?*" he asked. I slowly made my way to the door to the deck, unlocked it, then let him out with a "stay close." He, thankfully, went no farther than the edge of the woods, quickly did his business, and returned. As I turned to go back to my chair, I noticed there were no police cars in my driveway.

"What happened while I was asleep?" I asked, not sure Cooper would be able to give me a coherent answer.

"*Nothing,*" was his reply at the same time as I heard, "I'm not sure" from Jason as he padded to the coffeepot, sporting one of the worst cases of bedhead I'd seen in a while. "Second shift left at midnight, as scheduled, but no one came in after them."

"Hmm," I said, finally sitting down. "I wonder if they caught the vampire."

"No telling what's going on," Jason mumbled into his cup, sipping coffee as he leaned the rifle against the chair he normally occupied. "We're only ordinary citizens, and unless Dave gives you an update, we get to sit and wonder."

"What did you have for dinner?" I asked. "I don't have frozen meals."

"PB and J sandwiches. A staple in any bachelor's kitchen."

I grimaced then reached for the television remote at the same time as Jason reached for his laptop. It seems we got our news from different sources these days. I mused on that, and thought it was probably a generational thing.

I watched, he scrolled, all in perfect companionship. After I'd had enough caffeine to feel slightly more human, I asked, "So what's on your schedule for today?"

Jason shrugged his shoulders. "It's Monday so I do have some work…about four hours, maybe a little more. Then I thought I'd go get those plants you want and put them in the ground. It's the only way I'm going to get some exercise around here. You should be okay by yourself for a couple of hours with Cooper here."

I wanted to argue I'd be okay by myself *anytime* but didn't. With a cast weighing me down, I knew I wouldn't be able to run, or fight if it came to that. I *would* have to rely on my dog, which wasn't a comforting thought because I wasn't sure Cooper could handle a vampire on his own.

An hour later, Jason had showered and taken over the office for his own. As I made my way to my shower, I heard him speaking on the phone, talking in the language of real estate development: "square footage, market saturation, build-out." They were terms I was familiar with, having overhead similar conversations from Thomas. I teared up again at the similarities between my husband and son.

"*Why are you sad?*" Cooper asked as he padded just behind me in the hall.

"He's so like his father in so many ways. It reminded me of my husband, that's all. I'll be okay," I told him.

I showered – awkwardly, given the plastic-wrapped cast and only putting my weight on one leg – and sat back in my chair. Although I had a feeling the vampire crisis wasn't over, it appeared I wasn't supposed to worry about it. Otherwise, someone would have told me *something*, wouldn't they? It was time to contemplate my future again.

I wondered about selling fresh herbs – perhaps in the local farmers' market? Looking at the room I had for a garden, I would have to specialize in just one, if I wanted enough plants to be able to make money off them. Then I thought about what was being sold at the garden centers by the big growers, how much they retailed for, and decided it really wasn't worth the effort.

I was turning from that back to wondering if I should actually design gardens (and whether I could make money doing that) when I heard "Hello!" coming from the back of the house.

Before I could get completely erect with my crutches in one hand, Jason was in the living room with gun in hand. "Let me find out what's going on," he said, pushing me back down. I resisted his efforts and was almost on his heels as he went out to the deck.

The three gnomes from Saturday were back, standing on the garden path in their same triangular formation with the oldest-looking one at the front. Ignoring me completely, he looked first at the rifle in Jason's hand, then at his face.

"Your weapon is not necessary," he chided. "We are here in good faith."

"You'll forgive my caution," Jason replied. "I didn't know it was you."

"We understand. We have come to tell you we failed in our attempts to extract information from our clanmate."

I was aghast. They'd promised they had ways of getting their kind to talk. I said so.

The designated speaker only flicked his eyes at me before addressing my son. "He chose death over betraying a confidence, no matter how misplaced that confidence may have been. We regret his choices, and our clan mourns his loss.

"I was told to tell you no unnatural being has been near our cave or those of our neighbors. We will, however, keep our ears open, and if new information is available, we will pass it on. We do not like the *nachzehrer* any more than humans. They prey on us, too, if they catch us out in the open."

Jason nodded and thanked them for their help, such as it was.

"We have delivered our message and will leave now." All three scrunched up their faces as they had before, then turned in unison and quick-marched toward the trees on the northern end of my property.

"I'm assuming they left," Jason said. "They did their disappearing act on me."

I watched as the gnomes made their way into the woods. Once they were beyond my sight, I nodded. "They're gone."

"*That* was singularly unhelpful," he grumbled as he walked back into the house. "You should probably tell Dave." Then he chuckled. "They still look like garden gnomes to me."

Jay disappeared back into the office, and when I'd gotten comfortable in my chair again, I pulled my phone to me and opened up the text thread with Dave.

Gnomes just left. Gloomy died rather than give up his secrets. There's no 'unnatural creature' in their neighborhood, they said. BTW, where are the cop cars that are supposed to be parked in my driveway?

I put my phone down and went back to my musings. Then I grabbed my laptop and started looking up local garden designers on the internet. There were too many and all well-established. I doubted I could compete with them. One more idea down the tubes.

My phone pinged with a reply from Dave. **Thanks for the info. LEO redeployed elsewhere. Fill you in at dinner?**

Dinner's fine. I can bake some chicken & potatoes. Is it okay for Jason to leave for a few hours?

Stay off your foot! I'll bring food with me. Should be OK for J to leave.

I was getting mighty tired of being coddled but if I protested to either man, they'd just chastise me – again. I slumped in my chair. Then realized it was almost lunchtime. Jason was still working so couldn't yell if I fixed the midday meal. I went into the kitchen and grabbed a couple rashers of bacon out of the freezer. A few minutes later when the sizzle and smell reached the rest of the house, I had an audience.

Cooper and Patches were both sitting at my feet, looking up at the stove. Jason was leaning against the island. "You're supposed to stay off your foot," he admonished.

"I am," I replied while slicing tomatoes. "See? I'm balancing on my right foot."

While we ate the BLTs I'd fixed, I told him what Dave had said about it being okay for him to leave.

"Good. I'm glad he thinks it's safe. Nonetheless, I'm leaving the rifle where you can get to it."

I opened my mouth to protest.

He held up his hand to forestall me. "I know, I know. You hate guns. But I know you can handle one. A lot of noise is preferable to something worse."

"Okay," I said, dubiously.

"I have another couple hours' work left. In the meantime, draw up an exact list of what shrubs you want out front and where to find them. I'll leave as soon as I turn my computer off."

I dutifully created the requested list and included directions to the two garden centers he would need to visit. One was an hour away, and depending on traffic, he may not make it back in time for dinner. With an afterthought, I added two loaves of bread to the list. We ate a lot of sandwiches. When he emerged from the office, I told him about returning in north Atlanta traffic.

"I'll go there first then hit the local stores. If I'm not back in time, just keep some food warm for me. Can I use your car? I don't think the rental is good for hauling three- to five-gallon pots."

"Keys are on the hook next to the garage door."

Cooper heard the jangle of keys and ran to Jason's side. "*Car ride?*" he asked eagerly.

Jason laughed. "I don't have to understand him to know what he wants." He ruffled Coop's fur. "Sorry, buddy. Not this time."

The dog swung his head around to me. "*What did he say? Can I go with?*"

"Sorry. He's going to stores for me. You can't stay in the car that long…it's too hot outside. Now, come over here so I can look at your head. I want to make sure your injury is healing properly."

Cooper hung his head as he padded toward me. "*I want to go for a car ride. And my head itches, but I haven't scratched, just like you said.*"

Jason exited the house as soon as the dog's back was to him. I heard the garage door open, the car start and back out, and the door close again as tires crunched on the gravel outside. I looked at Coop's stitches and declared he was healing nicely. Another couple of days and they'd be removed. Which reminded me. I grabbed Doc Martin's invoice from the stack of paper piling up on the table next to me and called the veterinary clinic to make the appointment. While I was at it, I needed to get Patches checked out, too.

"Doc told us you'd be calling," the receptionist said after I'd identified myself and the reason for the call. "He didn't say anything about a cat, though. So two appointments. How does Thursday at three sound?"

I agreed to the time, hung up, and put the appointment in my phone. Then settled back with the book I was still slogging through, determined to finish it and move onto one more enjoyable. Cooper curled up on the floor next to me, on the other side of where Jason had leaned the rifle. Patches came out from the bedroom Jason was using and after a few attempts to get between me and my reading, finally settled in my lap.

The book *really* wasn't holding my interest, and I nodded off despite having slept so long the night before.

Sometime later, I was awakened by a knock at the door. Both Cooper and Patches were alert. I grabbed my phone. I hadn't received a text from Dave, and it was more than his standard two sharp raps.

A face looked in the front window. It was Ranger Doyle, and he smiled and waved at me. Cooper stood, hackles raised, and growled. Patches launched herself from my lap and made a beeline for the bedroom.

I put my hand on his back. "It's that Forestry Service officer that was here a couple of months ago. Calm down."

"*He smells bad. I have smelled this before, but I don't remember when.*"

I yelled loud enough to be heard through the window, gesturing at the cast on my foot. "Sorry. What can I help you with?"

"I have news about the vampire search I'd like to share. I'd rather not yell, though. May I come in?"

Cooper growled again. This time I heeded my dog's warning. "Can you come back in a few hours when my son is here to unlock the door? I'm not supposed to be up and around."

Then I thought about what I'd said and wanted to kick myself. That told him I was alone. His face disappeared from the window, and I heard him walk around the side of the house. Grabbing my phone, I sent a text to Dave.

SOS. Doyle is here. Wants in. Cooper in full protection mode.

Dave replied immediately. **On other side of county. Fifteen minutes. Keep him out however you must.**

Cooper turned, following the officer's progress with his ears. He went to the front door and barked in words I couldn't understand, but as soon as he was done, I heard the yipping of coyotes in full throat, moving from the front, around the side, and to the back. Even inside the house, it was nearly deafening.

Cooper ran to the deck door just as I heard a pane of glass break. Ignoring my ankle (again), I stood, grabbed the gun, and put it to my shoulder as Grandpa had taught me, spreading my legs to balance against the recoil. I wasn't sure I'd hit whatever I aimed at – I was shaking like a leaf.

Ranger Doyle's hand reached through the broken pane, turned the deadbolt, and withdrew. With startling clarity, I noticed he scraped his thumb on a jutting shard, and as soon as the line of red blood appeared, it disappeared. A moment later, he opened the door and walked in.

"I offer no violence," he said, holding his hands up. "You can lower your weapon."

"Stay, Coop," I admonished my dog when he prepared to lunge. I turned my attention to the man standing in my breakfast area.

"We're going to disagree on your statement," I told him. "You just broke into my house. If you value your life, you'll turn right back around and leave."

"You won't shoot me," he said with a smile. "You're shaking. All I want is your dog. He's been trouble."

Not that I believed him, but *that* statement galvanized me more than anything else. "You don't get him or anyone else."

I took a deep breath and held it as I was taught, aimed, and squeezed the trigger. As I'd feared, my shot went wide, shattering the window behind Ranger Doyle's head.

Cooper barked one more time and lunged for the ranger. At the same time, coyotes poured through the open door. Canine bodies pounced as one, for a moment overwhelming the man…vampire as I now thought him to be.

A white streak flew from the bedroom into the fray, and I saw a couple of foxes come in the door, too. But in a split second, canine and feline bodies went flying. Ranger Doyle threw them off with the same ease as I shrugged myself out of a coat. He stood, and my suspicion was immediately confirmed. His face was the color of good quality pearls, his eyes had taken on a reddish hue, and his eye teeth were on full display.

And like my dog, he growled. He reached for the nearest ruff and picked up one coyote out of the pile.

"Drop it," I screamed, aiming my gun once again. He just smiled as he bit into the animal, who howled in pain. His eyes never left mine, and I saw him smile through a mouthful of fur and skin.

I heard my grandfather whispering in my ear, "Both eyes open, take a deep breath, and hold it. Don't pull but squeeze the trigger. And don't hesitate."

Praying as I'd never prayed before to any god listening, I aimed at his face and squeezed the trigger again. This time I hit him in the shoulder. He dropped the coyote in surprise and turned his attention to me.

"Cooper, you and the rest get the hell out of here," I said as I aimed once again.

The coyotes ran out the door, supporting their friend who'd been bitten, the foxes on their heels. I hoped the animal would heal. My dog and cat, however, did not run. They stood to one side, hackles and fur raised, watching.

"Well, well," the vampire said, blood dripping down the sides of his jaw onto his uniform. "The lady has some spunk. That generally means the blood is tastier. I'm going to enjoy you, sweetheart." I took a moment to notice the gaping hole in his shoulder showed only a small amount of blood. One of the legends was true: they healed quickly. I'd have to aim better.

I pulled the trigger yet a third time, aiming for his face. And hit my target. I'm not sure where the bullet went in, but he no longer had a forehead, and much of the top of his head was missing. His eyes widened as his body slowly sank into a heap. As soon as what was left of his head was at Cooper's level, my dog jumped on him, and with one snap of his powerful jaws, bit the rest of his face off. A second snap took out most of his neck. Coop stood on the heap, ready to attack again if necessary.

I stood motionless for a moment, trying to take in what had just happened. Then I heard heavy boots rushing up the deck stairs. Deputy Sorenson, the one who'd been with Doc Martin when Coop got hurt, filled the door, service weapon at the ready.

He took in the sight of me standing with a rifle aimed at the heap, and the body – or what was left of it – at his feet.

"Ma'am? Ms. Mackay? You can lower your weapon now."

It took a few moments for me to register what he'd said. "Is it dead?" I asked.

"I think so," came the reply. "It's not moving, and I don't think it can do any more damage without a mouth."

I shakily lowered the rifle to my side but didn't let go. "Cooper," I called. "Let the officer take charge."

Cooper looked first at Deputy Sorenson then at me. "*I will protect*," was all he said before returning his vigil to the faceless heap underneath him.

"You've done your job," I replied. "Did he hurt you or Patches?"

"*I am unharmed*," my cat told me.

Cooper reluctantly moved over to my side. "*I'm sore but not bad*," he said.

Deputy Sorenson moved with my dog and gently took the rifle from my hand. "You need to sit," he said as turned me toward my chair. "Dave is on his way and will take charge when he gets here. Can I get you some water?"

I made my way to my chair, telling him a glass of water would be nice. While he rummaged in the cabinet for a glass, I turned back to the breakfast area and took in the scene. There wasn't as much blood as I'd thought there would be, but gray goo, which I assumed were brains, and chunks of an ivory-colored substance covered the windows out to the deck. What windows were left. I'd shot out most of them.

"Can you call Doc Martin?" I asked the deputy. "That thing tried to eat a coyote. I don't know how bad it's hurt, but if he can help it, I'd like him to."

"Sure," he said, setting the glass of water on the table next to me. "Do you know where it is?"

I had no idea where they'd gone. "Coop? Do you know where the hurt coyote went?"

Cooper barked twice, and I heard a yipping reply come from the front of the house. Another bark and another yip, then, *"They're back under the front. They want to know if it's safe to come out."*

"They're all under the front porch," I told the deputy. Looking at Cooper, I said, "I think it's safe. Would you tell them I'm going to ask the same human that helped you to help the one that was bitten, if he can?"

Cooper barked again. A lower bark replied, and this one I understood. *"That one was too badly hurt. It has gone into the woods to die."*

Tears filled my eyes. It had tried to help me and paid the ultimate price for doing so. I told the deputy what Cooper had said. He just nodded sympathetically.

I rose, grabbed my crutches, and headed to the front porch. The deputy was right on my heels. "Where are you going?"

"To talk directly with the coyotes," I said. "Stay here."

It's hard to find and turn a deadbolt when your eyes are swimming, but I finally managed to get myself out the front door and down off the porch. I crouched so I could see underneath.

"I don't know the words," I began, my face wet with tears. "But I want you to know I appreciate what you did to try to help me a few minutes ago, and I am so sorry about your friend.

"I think we killed it, though, so you should be able to go back to your normal lives. Is there anything else I can do?"

A higher voice, female by the sound of it, said, "*We will be fine. Fighting and dying is normal to us. We thank you for the shelter and water. Humans do not normally help creatures such as we.*"

One by one, eleven coyotes of varying ages came out from under the porch. As they passed me, each licked my face once. It only took a few seconds for them to melt into the woods at the southern edge of my property. In the distance, I heard a police siren screaming, then cut off.

I was just mounting the steps back into the house when a patrol car with light bar flashing flew up the driveway and scattered gravel when brakes were slammed. Dave got out of the car before the wheels had even finished skidding on the rocks.

I found myself enveloped in strong arms. "Are you okay?" he asked.

Deputy Sorenson appeared in the front door. "I'd say she's going to be fine," he said with a grin. "Come see the mess she made of her house."

Dave helped me back into the house and to my chair, noting the gore on the back windows and the body slumped on the breakfast area floor. "Jesus Christ, El. How are you still standing?"

I plopped down. "I'm not. Not now. I don't think the adrenaline's quite left my system, though."

Right on cue, I started shaking.

"You're going into shock," Dave said. "Call the coroner to come get this thing," he told the deputy as he headed into my bedroom.

A moment later, I felt a blanket being tucked around me. Dave's presence left me, and I heard the sound of running water, then the microwave being started, and the sound of cupboard doors and kitchen drawers being opened and closed. A minute and a half later, a mug of hot water with a teabag in it appeared on the table next to me.

"Drink that as soon as it's steeped," he admonished. "It's probably too sweet for your palate, but the sugar will help.

"I don't know if you can understand me, but Cooper? I need you and Patches to snuggle up to El. She needs your warmth."

Cooper hauled his large body into my lap and curled up as best he could, leaning his head on my shoulder. "You understood him?" I asked through chattering teeth.

"*I understand snuggle. And you are cold.*" A minute later, Patches wormed her way between me and the chair's armrest.

Because of Coop's bulk, I couldn't see anything that was happening around me. I heard Dave on the phone talking to someone about the body. I heard the word "vampire" in there, too.

Slowly, the warmth of the blanket and the animals seeped in, and the shaking started to subside. Dave sat in the chair opposite and eyed me.

"Drink the tea," he said. I took the mug off the table and, transferring it to my other hand and holding it to the side to get around Cooper's head, dutifully sipped at it.

I made a face when all that sugar hit my tongue. "Ugh. I'm from the Midwest. We don't do sugar water with a bit of tea flavoring."

"You can go back to your midwestern un-sweet tea after this."

I heard another car pull into the driveway. Dave stood and looked out the window, then headed for the front door. Footsteps pounded on the stairs and porch floor.

"Hey," Dave said to the unseen person. "Sheriff, I'd like to introduce you to the heroine of the hour, Ellen Mackay. El, this is Sheriff Tyler Danforth."

Cooper hadn't moved, but I felt him stiffen. Peering around his bulk, I saw a man probably in his forties. Not quite as tall as Dave, he had brown hair with just a few strands of gray at the temples, and serious brown eyes. He appeared to be a bodybuilder, if the taut fit of his shirt and jacket were any indication.

Cooper stiffened even further, and I wrapped an arm around his middle to calm him. "It's okay, Coop," I said as I held out my other hand to be shaken. "Pleased to meet you," I said to the sheriff.

A warm hand enveloped mine and shook it firmly. "It's honestly a pleasure," he replied. "Between you and Dave here, I've had an eye-opening week. Do you feel up to telling us what happened here today?"

"Coop, I think I'm okay now. Will you get down, please, so I can see who I'm talking with?"

"*You are still shaking. We will stay,*" Patches announced. Cooper just settled himself more firmly against me.

"My apologies, but it looks like my friends aren't going to let me properly see you," I said. "Please sit. I'll tell you what I can."

Before he sat, Sheriff Danforth went to look at the body, which Deputy Sorenson was watching with a keen eye in case it should come to life again. "What a mess" was all he said. Then I heard him quietly speak to the deputy before returning to the living room.

"El, before you start, can I make some coffee?" Dave asked. I nodded. The sheriff sat on the sofa while I heard Dave putter in the kitchen. A moment later, the coffeepot started gurgling, and I inhaled the aroma of brewing coffee. Dave sat in the chair opposite and motioned for me to talk.

"How much has Dave told you?" I asked Sheriff Danforth.

"I know everything up until this afternoon," he replied. "Not that I really believed it all, but I'm starting to change my opinion on some things."

"Okay, then," I started, then had a thought. "Jason! He won't know what's happened here and is going to panic when he sees all the cop cars in the drive!"

"He knows, El," Dave said quietly. "I texted him as soon as I got you settled. He was already on his way back from Woodstock and was north of Jasper. I told him you were okay, I was here, and not to break any speed limits to get home."

"You know my son's phone number?" I was indignant.

"We exchanged numbers the day I took him to the range. Just in case. So he won't panic. Tell us your story."

I took a deep breath. "Dave told you about the weird visit I had from Ranger Doyle back in January, right?" The sheriff nodded. "He also told you I can talk with animals like dogs and cats, too?" He nodded again.

"Okay." I took another deep breath. "When Ranger Doyle was here in January, Cooper didn't like him. He said he smelled wrong. At the time, I didn't think much of it.

"Then, sometime this afternoon…What time is it, anyways?" I realized I had no idea when I'd been woken or how long it had been since then. I looked over Cooper to the phone on my side table. It was almost five o'clock.

"So maybe a little after four? I was awakened from a nap by a knock at the front door. Cooper didn't like what he smelled. He said he'd smelled it before but couldn't remember when. Dogs don't have the best memories, you understand.

"Then Ranger Doyle looked through the front window. He wanted to come in. He said he had something to share about the vampire search but didn't want to yell through the door.

"I made the mistake of showing him my cast and asking him to come back in a couple of hours when my son would be here. He left the porch and walked around to the deck, where he broke the window on the door and let himself in.

"I told him he'd just broken into my house and to leave. He basically laughed at me, so I fired the gun. The shot went wide.

"Then Cooper, Patches, and a bunch of coyotes that had been sheltering under my front porch, and a couple of foxes, I think, attacked him. He shook them off like they were flies on a horse, picked up one of the coyotes, and bit down. I fired again, hitting him in the opposite shoulder. He at least dropped the animal but didn't slow down.

"He said I had spunk and he was going to 'enjoy me.' So I fired again, taking off the top of his head. Cooper pounced and did the rest on his face and neck. Then Deputy Sorenson arrived."

"Three shots only? Not bad for someone who doesn't like guns," Dave said approvingly.

"It has those fancy bullets in it, doesn't it? They probably helped. And I said I didn't *like* guns, not that I couldn't shoot one."

"Fancy bullets?" Sheriff Danforth asked Dave.

"Armor-piercing with a heavy load to do more damage," Dave replied. "I made them up when you wouldn't approve a departmental purchase."

"We'll talk about that later. Is that all, Ms. Mackay?"

"That's all I can think of right now. Is that coffee done? I could use some."

Dave got up to fix coffee for everyone. The sheriff eyed me. "He didn't hurt you, did he?"

"He didn't get anywhere near me. I'm told the coyote he bit went off to die. Cooper is bruised but otherwise okay."

"Coyotes coming to the aid of a human. What next?" the sheriff muttered.

I pushed at Cooper. His weight was putting my legs to sleep. "Please get down, Coop. I'm okay."

He looked at me dubiously. *"Are you sure? You're still shaking every now and then."*

"I'm sure. I really would like to be able to feel my legs."

Cooper turned and slid over the chair arm, sitting next to my ottoman, and laid his head in my lap. Patches didn't move a muscle. I took a deep breath and rubbed my legs to get the feeling back.

"That's an awesome dog you have," Sheriff Danforth said.

"I think so, too," Dave said, handing me a mug of blessed elixir before giving one to the sheriff and sitting down with his own.

My son barreled through the front door and ran over to me, leaning over to take me in his arms. "Are you okay, Mom? Dave said you were, but are you?"

I hugged him. "I'm fine, kiddo. Really. Still in a little shock, but that will wear off."

Jason had left the door wide open in his haste, and another man politely knocked before walking in. "I'm told there's a stiff for me," he said to Dave. Seeing me as I looked over Jay's shoulder, he added, "Oh. I'm sorry. I didn't know there were civilians here. I need to pick up a body?"

Dave pointed. "Over there. What's left of it, anyways. Have fun trying to figure out how to report it!"

He left, and a moment later, he and the Deputy Coroner who'd been here…was it just a little over a week ago?…came in, wheeling a gurney between them. Everyone was quiet as they lifted the body into a black bag, zipped it shut, thumped it on the gurney bed, and wheeled it back out again, closing the front door behind them.

Jason left me long enough to pour himself a cup of coffee before sitting on the floor next to my dog, his arm resting on Cooper's back.

"I've heard and seen enough to know this was a pure case of self-defense," Sheriff Danforth announced as he rose. "Now I need to get with the county commissioners to figure out what sort of spin to put on it. We need to tell the public the 'vampire murders' have been solved without pointing a finger at a LEO."

"May I ask one question before you leave?" It had been on my mind all day.

"If I can answer, I will." The sheriff smiled at me.

"What happened to the officers who were supposed to park their cars in my driveway and walk into the woods from here?

Dave said they were redeployed. To where? They might have been changing shifts when all this went down, and I might have had some help."

Sheriff Danforth grimaced. "We had what was purported to be a credible threat along the trail about two miles south of here. It came from the Forestry Service. After Dave called me, I asked *who* had made the report. Turns out it was the…man…you killed.

"If I'm putting the timeline together properly, he arrived here right after his shift ended. So he wanted everything to appear normal, and the redeployment ensured there would be no officers around when he got here.

"He wanted to ensure you'd be alone. But we had no notion this…thing…was one of our own. We do tend to think of ourselves as upright citizens when some of us may not be. For that, I am deeply sorry."

He sighed. "I'll try to keep your name out of it, Ms. Mackay, but I can't guarantee it. The commissioners will need to know, for sure, but hopefully, the media can be kept in the dark.

"Thank you for what you've done here today," he said as he shook my hand once again. Then he left.

Dave stood. "Can you eat, El? It's getting to be dinnertime, and I'll go get something if you can."

I nodded my head over my shoulder. "If it's all the same to you, I'd rather eat out. I'm not sure I'm ready to tackle the mess behind me, nor do I want to look at it or smell it while I'm eating." In the intervening hour or so, a noxious aroma had started permeating the house. I'd never been in a morgue, but I associated what I was smelling with fictional accounts of autopsies. It wasn't pleasant.

Jason stood, too. "We need to stop at the hardware store to get plywood to board the windows up until they can be replaced. And probably some deep-cleaning solution to get all that crap off the window frames, walls, and floor."

Dave eyed me. "Tell you what. Jason, you go get what you think you need at the store. I'm calling Jack and ordering a mess of wings and French fries. You can pick them up before you come home. In the meantime, I'll start cleaning up with whatever supplies are here. I've seen shit like this before, so my stomach is probably more used to it than you two.

"Who installed the windows? We'll need to get them back out here."

"All the house paperwork is in the file cabinet in the office," I said to no one in particular. "Is this covered by insurance?"

"It's not, Mom." The sorrow in Jason's voice was evident. "You fired the gun yourself." He held up his hand. "Yeah, I know it was in self defense of what we'll call an intruder, but nonetheless, you still did it. I'll pull the window company's info out of the file and call them in the morning. I know exactly which windows need replacing and can tell them the blueprint info."

I sighed. First the front yard, now my windows. My idyllic life in the woods had turned into anything but.

"I can help clean," I sighed as I rose to my feet. "I've changed too many infant diapers to be fazed by some brain goo and blood."

"You're supposed to stay off your ankle!" both men yelled in unison.

"It's fine. I've been standing on it a lot today, and it's not bothering me at all. Besides, Dave, you're taller. You can get the walls and windows, and I'll be on the floor. No weight on the ankle at all."

"Okay." Dave was dubious. "But if it starts hurting again, you stop and sit."

Dave grabbed his phone and called the Whistle Stop, asking for Jack in particular. As much food as we'd ordered from them in the last week, Dave must get a "frequent-eater" discount. Jason quickly measured the windows and left in my car.

I pulled my cleaning supplies from under the kitchen sink and ran a bucket of warm water. When it was nearly full, I poured two cups of vinegar into it.

Dave wrinkled his nose. "The house is going to smell like pickles."

I laughed. Most men truly had no clue about cleaning. "No, it won't. It'll evaporate. But this will at least get the blood off the floor and walls. I'm not sure how it'll work on brain goo, but it's a start. Would you kindly open the house windows? I'd like the smell of a morgue to dissipate sooner rather than later."

"*Can I go out my door now?*" Cooper padded over to my side. "*Or do you have to watch me still?*"

I'd totally forgotten about the doggie door. "I *think* it's safe enough," I said as I hobbled over to his door and unlocked it.

"But until we know for sure that was the vampire killing people, please don't go beyond the clearing."

"*I won't. I need to stay close to protect you,*" he said as he nosed his way out, Patches right behind him.

Dave and I worked in companionable silence. It only took about five minutes for the water to be gross enough to need changing. Dave dumped the filthy water down the toilet then refilled the bucket per my instructions.

As I'd noted before, there wasn't as much blood as I thought there would be. Recalling my high school biology class, the human body had around a gallon of blood. I cleaned perhaps only two pints off the floor. I started giggling.

"What's so funny?" Dave asked, squeezing his sponge out, looking at the water, and grabbing the bucket handle to empty it again.

"A thought. If vampires have less blood circulating than the average live human – this one apparently did – and they drink blood, where does it go? Do they pee or defecate it out like we do our food after we've absorbed the nutrients?"

"What a question! If I ever meet another vampire, I'll ask. At least we know their brains are still like ours." He chuckled, too, as he walked down the hall to the bathroom.

An hour later, we'd cleaned as best we could…brain and bone chunks were gone, and the tiled floor was white again. There were still streaks of gray on the window frames and walls, but those would have to wait for a stronger cleaning solution than vinegar. We'd just collapsed back into the chairs when Jason pulled into the garage.

A moment later, he came into the house with a pile of Styrofoam containers and a paper bag. "I am the mighty hunter," he said in what I supposed to be a caveman voice. "I bring food."

"At least you're not dragging me by my hair into the cave to cook it," I quipped.

"Me not drag you anywhere," Jason said in the same voice. "Me not like getting shot by independent woman."

We all chuckled and ate the wings and fries Jason had brought home. The aroma of chicken had brought both Cooper and Patches in, and they sat on the floor at my side, looking expectantly between the three of us. I'll admit they got their more-than-fair-share of chicken.

The conversation was purposely lighthearted in an attempt to not think about the day's events for a while. Dave and Jason traded horrible jokes, each trying to top the other in groan-worthiness. I smiled as a I watched them. Jason was more relaxed in Dave's company than he'd ever been in his father's.

Dave was cleaning up after dinner and Jason was hauling plywood and screws in from the garage when we heard a sharp rap at the front door. Cooper and Patches both went on alert. We three looked at each other in confusion, and it only took Dave a moment to transform from regular guy to law enforcement officer.

"Sit," he said in a commanding voice to me and Jason. Because he'd made a beeline to my place from wherever he was, he was still in uniform, complete with sidearm. He drew that now, and I heard the safety click as he walked to the front door.

Service automatic held down by his thigh, he opened the door. "Yes? May I help you?" he said to someone standing beyond my sight.

"My name is Priscilla, and I have business with the lady who lives here," said a woman's voice in a rich contralto. The voice was smooth and a little smoky, like what I'd been told a good scotch would taste like. That I had to take others' word for.

"She's not receiving visitors right now," Dave countered. "I'll be happy to pass along a message, though."

A long arm with a pale hand shoved Dave back from the door, and she strode into the house. She was so strong he stumbled but quickly recovered. In the blink of an eye, he had his gun trained on her back and said in a firm voice, "Stop right there, or I'll shoot."

"Your weapon is not necessary," she said. "I will cause no harm." Her eyes landed on me, but she came no farther than the entryway.

"Priscilla" was *gorgeous*. Nearly Dave's height in her four-inch heels, she could have been a model with her perfect curves – of which I was envious. The planes of her face appeared to be carved by a sculptor, and her honey-blonde hair looked silky and shiny in its upswept do. She wore what I was certain was a custom-tailored skirt suit in midnight blue slubbed silk. The only thing marring her perfection was her cold, blue eyes. They hadn't a trace of warmth – or humanity – in them. I saw a pearl sheen in the skin on her hands and legs (her makeup was flawless) and would have bet the house that if provoked, she had fangs. Real ones.

I swallowed audibly. "This is my house, so I assume it's me you want to talk to."

"I want to first apologize, and then thank you," she started.

"For?"

"The man who was killed here today was one of mine."

"One of yours?" Dave said as he cautiously walked around her to come stand by my side. Jason had already positioned himself at the back of my chair. Dave still had his gun pointed at her, and although I couldn't see behind me, I knew my son well enough to know the rifle was back in his hand.

Priscilla still hadn't moved a muscle. As a matter of fact, I don't think she had even blinked.

"Yes. How much do you know about vampires?"

"Only the stories. And what I saw here today with my own eyes," I told her.

She sighed. "So much misinformation. May I sit? This will take longer than the five minutes I had thought, and it will be easier on your neck than looking up at me the whole time."

I looked to Dave for guidance. He shrugged. "Go ahead. Just know both guns trained on you have the same rounds that killed *your man* this afternoon."

"Understood. As I said, I offer no violence here," she said as she smoothly lowered herself to the sofa opposite me with all the grace of a queen.

"First, a bit of history. Vampires have been around nearly as long as humans. In the Dark Ages, it was easy to feed because there was brutality and war everywhere. What we did was simply wait for the humans to stop fighting and feed on the wounded and freshly dead.

"When Man started to become civilized, we had to adapt or be found out and killed. Since the weapon of choice in those days was a sword, lopping off our head was fairly easy for those strong enough to do it. We civilized right along with the humans, developing clans and a code of honor. Without the constant human warring and our ability to govern ourselves, we became fairy tales to most. With our code to guide us, we could live and feed among humans with no one hunting us to extinction.

"Outside times of war, our code demands we only drink from humans *with their consent*." At my raised eyebrows, she chuckled. "Believe me, we do not lack for food sources. Our saliva is much like a narcotic in its effect, so it's a mutual satisfaction. The one you killed today was mentally unstable. I did not know this when I made him."

"Care to tell us about him?" Dave interjected.

"I am an opera singer, and believe it or not, Mister Law Enforcement, your colleague liked opera. We met about six months ago when I was in a production of *Falstaff* in Chattanooga. Caleb somehow managed to get backstage after the performance. I thought he was cute, and we started a relationship. I told him what I was, and it didn't seem to bother him.

"Two months later, he asked me to turn him. After explaining the code to him and with his agreement to it, I did. I spent another month teaching him to live alongside humans, to feed without killing, and how to avoid detection.

"It was time for me to move onto my next role, this time in Memphis. I felt confident Caleb would be okay on his own after that month, and we parted with his assurance that he would come see me perform as soon as he could get some time off work. We kept in touch via email and text with an occasional phone call, and he seemed to be doing all right.

"A week ago, word came to me that someone had gone rogue in this area and that bodies were piling up. I asked Caleb about it in one of our phone conversations, and he said he didn't know who it was, but that he was asking around the locals if they had any clues. I took him at his word."

"Wait," Dave said. "There are other vampires here?"

She chuckled. "Of course! We are *everywhere*. I do not know the exact population in this little town of yours, but I know of at least three – well, now two. There are probably more, but not many. Even your tourist population cannot support more than a half dozen or so.

"After your problem aired on CNN, my sire contacted me. He knew, of course, that Caleb was mine, and asked if he was the one causing the problem. When I told him I'd had assurances from Caleb that he was not, my sire contacted the head of the clan in this area of the country to find out more. Rogue vampires are publicity we do not need. Any of us.

"Yesterday, my sire called again. After investigation, the elders determined that Caleb had lied and he was, indeed, the rogue. I was told to take care of my problem. I arrived in Atlanta this morning, checked into a hotel, then drove up here to find my wayward child.

"He was a crafty one, much more familiar with these woods than I. He evaded me with ease, I am ashamed to admit. I was finally able to track him down just a moment before he entered this house. I was about to come in after him when I heard the animals and the gunshots. A quick look through the window showed me he had been taken down. I left just before the first police car pulled up.

"I was relieved to know the problem had been solved. I was going to return to my hotel in Atlanta, then thought perhaps I should explain what had happened to the courageous human woman who killed a vampire. I waited until I was certain the house was quiet before returning."

She smiled at me. "You have guts, lady. I admired the stance you took against a creature who could have easily overpowered you. We are *at least* three times as strong as a human, and as small as you are, in your slightly incapacitated state…" She pointedly looked at the cast on my ankle. "…it wouldn't have been a problem at all for him to kill you, too. But you didn't hesitate. At all.

"So, I come now to apologize for the havoc my child wreaked, and to thank you for taking care of the problem that was mine."

"I have a question," I said.

She cocked an eyebrow. "Ask."

"I can tell *you're* a vampire. Your makeup covers your face and neck, but the rest of your skin and your eyes give you away. Why could I not tell Caleb was one when he first visited me?"

She thought a moment. "He must have just fed. For about three hours after feeding, our skin looks human. Then, as the blood works its way through our system, our skin pales again. It's been about eight hours since I fed, so that is why my skin looks the way it does.

"My eyes, though? What gives those away?"

I hesitated. "I don't mean to insult you…"

"You won't."

"Your eyes lack warmth. There's no…light, for a better word, in them." I wasn't about to tell her they lacked humanity.

"Ah. I believe that is age. Caleb is newly-made. I am over three hundred years old. If you had seen what I've seen over the years, my dear, your eyes would probably lack warmth as well.

"I have said what I came to say – and more," she said as she rose.

She looked at Dave. "Yes, human, creepies live among you. But know that it is rare for one of us to cause trouble. Like you, we just want to live peaceful lives."

She looked over my head at Jason. "And you, young human. Your mother, and yes, you smell very similar so I know she gave birth to you, is someone you should look up to and try to emulate. If you have any siblings, you should tell them, too. She has what the Greeks call *Thrasos*, who was actually a god embodying boldness, but they also use the word occasionally for courage. I think they used it in a movie back in the 80s. But not blind courage. She thought before she acted."

"I've learned that over the past several days," Jason said from behind me. "But it really isn't all that newsworthy. I always knew she had it in her."

Finally, she looked at Cooper, who was still sitting at attention by my side, keeping an eagle eye on the vampire. "And you, pooch. I can still smell the gore on you. Good job."

Without another word, she let herself out the door. All three of us rushed to the front window to see her walking down the driveway in her stiletto heels, not even bothered by the uneven surface of the gravel. As she walked around the bend in the drive, she seemed to melt into the night.

I plopped back down in my chair, Dave and Jason following suit on the sofa. "*That* was…weird," I said.

"Definitely," Jason agreed, rifle still in his hand.

"I've had more of an education in the last week than I had in fourteen years of school," Dave said, leaning back to holster his gun. "Who knew fairy tales and horror stories were true?"

"Would someone pour me a straight shot of the good rum, with two ice cubes, please?" I asked. "I need something stronger than water."

Jason rose, leaning the rifle against the sofa. "What's the good rum?"

"Centenario. It's way in the back of the cabinet. I'm savoring it slowly it because I don't know when I'll get back to Costa Rica to get another bottle."

Jason turned to Dave. "You?"

"Her regular rum and Coke will be fine for me."

Jason played bartender, returning with a rocks glass full to the brim (but only two ice cubes) for me and a tall glass for Dave. He went back to the kitchen and returned with a rocks glass in his hand. Before I could yell at him for drinking my special rum, he saluted me with his glass.

"Whiskey," he said. "I'm not a rum drinker anyway, but I know better than to drink your special stuff."

"So, that's the end of it?" I asked after I'd swallowed almost half my glass in one gulp.

"Probably," Dave said. "She pretty much confirmed it was Caleb doing all the killing. I'll call Tyler in a bit to tell him what she said."

"Leave her name out of it, though," I told him. "She can easily be traced with what she told us of herself. She came here in good faith. I don't think we should out her."

"I agree," Jason said. "If they're peaceful, and only take blood with consent, why upset the applecart? It's no worse than, um, prostitution, which..." He interrupted himself before Dave could speak. "...I know is illegal but it's mutual consent so it shouldn't be."

"I agree with you both," Dave said. "And yes, Jay, I know prostitution is illegal, but I don't think it should be. I don't enforce that law unless they're really blatant about it or we find a human trafficking ring."

"*She said I did a good job*," Cooper piped up from his spot next to my chair. "*What's a pooch? But if I was good, do I get a treat?*"

I laughed and ruffled his fur. "My brave dog. 'Pooch' is an affectionate human word for a dog. And yes, you'll get a treat tonight. Patches, too," I said as she trotted in from my bedroom. "You *both* did good things today."

Dave yawned and stood. "It's been a long day, and I'm going home to my own bed. I'm glad everything turned out okay in the end." He put his glass in the dishwasher, kissed me on the cheek, thumped Jason on the top of the head, and left.

I looked at my son. "I have a question."

He raised an eyebrow. "Yes?"

"You seem more at ease with Dave than you ever did your father. Why?"

He thought a moment. "I'm honestly not sure. But he's not as uptight as Dad was. You know, Dad's coldness because of the empathic thing? Dave is…at ease with himself and who he is. He's one of those 'what you see is what you get' kind of people. It's honestly rather refreshing. I don't have to interpret the vibes I get. Why?"

"It's odd to me to see you be so friendly with someone you basically just met. Usually, you're a lot more reserved. And I don't *ever* recall you trading jokes with Dad."

"Did Dad ever tell a joke? I don't remember it."

I thought a moment myself. "Not that I can remember either. He was always really serious, even when it was just the two of us relaxing in the evening."

"My point."

I yawned, too. "We need to get the windows boarded up before I fall asleep. Come on."

I pointed Jason in the direction of my drill and its screwdriver bits. Fifteen minutes later, I had been teased once again about my pink tools, but the windows were boarded up. I put the next morning's coffee together while Jason fed the dog and cat early (with the requisite treats) then crawled into bed. I was just about to fall asleep when I felt both animals curl up next to me. With the threat of the vampire apparently gone, I easily dropped off and slept soundly.

I woke with the sun the next morning, feeling refreshed. Coop and Patches had already left the bed, so I didn't have to extricate myself from them *and* sheets. I walked out to the kitchen for coffee and stopped dead in my tracks at the end of the hall.

The breakfast area looked just as it had when I moved in. The plywood was gone, and in its place were sparkling new windows. All the gray streaks awaiting an application of TSP to get them off were gone.

I couldn't help but stare. *What the hell?* I thought.

Cooper nosed his way through the doggie door and sat in front of me. There was a piece of paper in his mouth which I took from him. The ink on the note was smeared from his saliva, but it was still quite legible and carried the faint scent of lilacs. In beautiful calligraphy was the message:

"*We thank you for ridding the world of a nasty creature. Your efforts to help the animals have not gone unnoticed, either. Fixing your house is the least we could do.*"

I looked at Coop. "Who did this? Who gave you this note?"

He gave me the doggie equivalent of a shrug. "*Little people with wings. And magic. Six of them came while you were still sleeping. I don't know what they did, but I saw something like that glitter stuff you complain about floating around, then it looked like it does now. I found this paper outside.*"

Jason barreled into my back, almost knocking me over. "What the hell?" he said as he looked at the back wall.

I showed him the note. "Your reaction is identical to mine. Cooper said 'little people with wings' did this. I'm assuming they were fairies."

"Wow. I think I need coffee," he said, going around me to the kitchen. He grabbed two mugs from the cupboard and filled them. He turned to hand me one and froze.

"Uh, Mom? Where's your cast?"

I looked down. I hadn't noticed until he pointed it out, but the cast was gone. I lifted my leg and inspected my ankle. It looked *fine*. It should have looked dry and scaly, and maybe even a little yellow, green, and blue at this point. But it didn't. I wiggled my foot. Nothing hurt. I looked up at my son.

"I feel fine. It doesn't hurt!"

Then I looked at my dog. "These little people with wings. Did they go in my bedroom, too?"

"*One or two might have…*"

"And you just let them?"

"*The big one said they were going to fix you. I did watch them. And besides, if they had hurt you, I could have eaten them.*"

"If you could catch them," I retorted.

"*They were no faster than birds. I would have eaten them,*" Patches announced as she came out from Jason's bedroom.

Jason looked from me to the animals and back again. "Well? What did they say?"

I translated, and he chuckled at Patches' statement.

I walked to the back door, opened it wide, and shouted at the top of my lungs, "Thank you!"

A wren, I thought, flew toward me, but before I could even duck, slowed and landed softly on my shoulder. (I really needed to get a bird book so I could tell them apart.)

"*It is we who should thank you,*" he said in a child-like voice that sounded very much like the one I'd rescued from the screen all those months ago. "*We have no power to help you, but we know those who do. We asked. They answered.*" He flew off.

I returned to the kitchen and took my coffee from my son. "It should be much later in the day so I could doctor this," I said as I made my way to my chair. Naturally, I tripped over the crutch I'd left lying on the floor next to it.

"Geez, Mom. They just fixed you. Take it easy!" Jay said as he brought a towel to mop up the spilled coffee, taking the crutch away with him. He returned with the pot to refill my mug – after I'd sat in the chair.

"What did the wren say?" he asked when he'd sat down with his own mug. I told him.

"Seems you've made some friends," he observed.

"I think so, too. But it's all so *weird*."

"It took me several years to become completely accustomed to my gift," Jay said. "You've only had yours for what? Six months? Give it time."

I turned on the television and he opened his laptop. Within minutes, he was cussing under his breath.

"What's wrong?" I asked. Jason didn't normally swear. At least where I could hear him.

"A client. There's an email from a contractor saying there's an unauthorized change order. I need to get my butt up to Delaware."

His fingers flew over the keys. "There's a flight leaving in three hours. Another one in four and a half. Which one should I take?"

I looked at my phone for the time. "You need to turn in the rental car and get through security. You can't do that in three hours from here in Atlanta traffic, even with just a carryon. Better take the later one."

He typed some more then powered his computer down. Taking a huge gulp of his coffee, he dashed into his room, then the bathroom. Fifteen minutes later, he was out of the shower, dressed, and emerged with his bags in hand.

While he stuffed his computer into its bag, he asked, "Do you have a travel mug you don't mind losing?" he asked. "I need more than a half cup of coffee."

"Take the silver one with the handle," I said. "It was a freebie from the car dealership, but I never use it."

He filled the designated mug and set it on the table next to his chair. He came over to me and knelt in front.

"I hate to leave you on such short notice," he started.

I patted his shoulder. "It's okay, kiddo. I'm fine. Finer than I was yesterday. And you need to pay attention to your job."

"This will only take me a couple of hours to resolve. If I need to come back, I can be here late tonight."

I gave him a playful shove. "Go home, Jason. You know I love having you here, but I can take care of myself. And you have a life to get back to. Besides, I'll talk to you and Sam tonight."

It was Tuesday – our regular chat night. "I can fill you in on any further happenings then."

"Okay." The expression on his face said he wasn't pleased. He rose, gave me a long hug, then kissed me. "You're an awesome mom, you know that? I love you."

I hugged and kissed him back. "Love you, too. Now go, so you don't miss the later flight, too!"

He stood, taking his bags in one hand and the travel mug in the other. I stood, too. He couldn't open doors with both hands full. I walked him outside to the car, Cooper and Patches right behind me.

"*Is he leaving?*" Patches asked. She twined around his ankles. "*I like having him here.*"

Jason laughed, picked Patches up, and gave her a kiss on her nose, then put her down and scratched Cooper on his neck.

"I'll miss you two, too!" he said as he climbed in the driver's door. "Talk to you tonight!"

We retreated to the porch and watched him leave. As I walked back in the house, I translated what he'd said for the animals' benefit. Then said he'd be back at some point.

"You haven't met my daughter, yet, Patches," I said. "She's a lot like her brother. You'll like her, too."

"They both play," Cooper added. *"And they both give treats when this one isn't looking. You'll like her."*

"I will reserve judgement," Patches sniffed. *"Now that the danger has passed, is it permissible to chase birds and squirrels again?"*

"Squirrels? Yes! I would like to chase squirrels!" Cooper agreed.

I laughed. Order was slowly being restored. "I think you may, yes. Just…no messes on the deck or porch, please."

Both of them raced through the doggie door, pleased to have life back to normal. I sat in my chair and watched the news while sipping my coffee. Then remembered I still had some thinking to do. I had to find *something* to fill my time. But first, I had to get back out to the garden.

Once I felt awake enough, I changed into outside clothes and made my way to the garden. I was pleasantly surprised to see the gnomes had kept their word, and the bed walls had been expertly repaired – I couldn't tell where they'd been damaged, even though I knew exactly where it had been. Then I noticed the damaged wall was even neater than I'd originally made it, and there was no mortar visible between the stones. I inspected all four beds…they looked like they'd been built by expert stone masons rather than an inexpert gardener. They'd completely rebuilt the beds!

I spent the entire day clearing the beds of their unwanted grasses and putting the shrubs Jason had purchased into the ground around the foundation. Cooper and Patches both supervised but made no move to help. I made plans to get seeds and seedlings for the garden beds the next day. I fell into my chair in late afternoon, happy to be working in the dirt again.

I was drinking my fourth glass of water to rehydrate when my phone rang. It was Anne.

"Oh my god, El," she said when I answered. "I just got back and caught up on the local news. Did any of that shit happen around you?"

I sighed. "Yes. Most of it, actually." I proceeded to tell her all the gory details. I could hear a wine cork pop in the background.

"I'll have you know this has caused me to drink before five," she chided. "That's *awful!* But you're okay, right?"

"More than, I think." I told her about the fairies, then Dave.

She laughed. "Fairies, huh? Can you get them to come spruce up my RV? Kidding. And it's not fair, you know. I've never met Mister Right, and you get two of 'em. You'll have to introduce me sometime…and ask if he has a friend. One who's as tolerant of weird as he is."

"Since the Whistle Stop seems to be one of his favorite restaurants, we'll meet for dinner some night. You'll like him," I told her.

"Okay. I need to finish up a couple chores before seven, so I'm going to let you go. I'm back for the foreseeable future, so we're going to have a girls' night soon. *Then* you can introduce me to Sergeant Handsome."

I laughed and agreed to both before we hung up. I'd just hit the 'disconnect' button when my phone pinged with a text from Dave.

Everything still okay there?

Fine. J had to go to DE for work. Spent the day outside. Delayed chicken and potatoes for dinner?

Deal. See you in an hour?

I sent him a thumbs-up emoji, then decided if I was having company, I'd better get myself cleaned up. I quickly showered then put chicken legs and potatoes in the oven to bake. I had just pulled the cork on a bottle of wine when Dave pulled up.

He gave me a peck on the cheek when I let him into the house. Then stopped dead in his tracks as he saw the back wall.

"You got a glazier here that quickly?" he asked in astonishment.

"Nope." I lifted my left leg. "Didn't fix myself, either. Look," I held out the note Cooper had brought me that morning, which I'd put in my pocket, knowing I'd have to show it to him almost immediately.

He read it, his jaw dropping. "Fairies?"

I nodded. "I think so. Cooper said they were 'little people with wings' and that a couple of them went into my bedroom last night. Then a wren told me they had no power to help me, but they knew who did and asked.

"And you should see the garden beds. The gnomes didn't fix them; they rebuilt them. When, I don't know because I haven't been out there in a couple of days, but it must have been at night. And they didn't make a sound. The workmanship is *gorgeous*!"

"I am in *awe*," he said. "Is there booze?"

I laughed. "I wanted to doctor my coffee this morning. I've held off until now. Wine's uncorked and just needs pouring."

I poured two glasses, and we sat in the living room. Dave took his service belt off and put it on the table next to the door, then returned to the chair opposite mine. He was obviously trying to process all that had happened in a little over twenty-four hours. Or at least, that's what I thought he was thinking of.

"The DNA on Doyle was rushed through. It's a match on every murder. So, that case is closed. Tyler and the commissioners still haven't figured how what spin to put on the blood loss, but they did release a statement saying the serial murderer had been caught and killed in a shootout with our office. That was to keep your name out of it.

"They released his name and position with the Forestry Service who, in turn, issued their own statement expressing regret they'd not cottoned onto Caleb's 'mental instability.'

"So, in theory, life should be back to normal. Now that I think I won't have to rush off to another murder scene anytime soon, I'd like to take you on a real date this Friday. One with candles, and wine, and maybe some soft music. Do you like Italian?"

I nodded. "Yes, I like Italian, and yes, I'll go out with you Friday night. It would be nice to have a conversation that didn't revolve around gnomes, and vampires, and other things that go bump in the night."

"I'll pick you up at four-thirty, then. The restaurant I have in mind is on the square in Marietta. If you don't mind driving that far."

My eyes lit up. "I know the one you're thinking of. It has the *best* eggplant parmesan for miles! I don't mind driving for that at all."

We talked of little things while dinner finished cooking. After we ate, he helped me clean up the kitchen, and we retreated back to the living room with more wine.

"I do have one question for a law enforcement officer," I said after we'd sat.

"Yes?"

"Jay, naturally, left the rifle here. I don't like guns, but I think I ought to keep it, just in case a vampire starts rampaging again. How do I get it in my name?"

He cleared his throat. "Um. About that. It's already in your name."

"What?"

"I had planned on convincing you to keep it after all this shit was over then taking you to the range to get you comfortable with it. Jay agreed with me, so we put your name on it."

I arched an eyebrow. "And no one thought to ask my opinion?"

"Well, I thought I could persuade you, and Jay would have lent his voice. Sorry?"

"It's done. Water under the bridge. You both were right in the long run. So, okay."

My phone alarm went off. "It's time for the weekly chat with the kids," I said.

Dave stood. "I'll leave then."

"No need," I assured him. "You can get in on it, too, if you want. Jay really likes you. Come, sit over here with me so they can see you, too."

I grabbed my laptop and wine and moved over to the sofa. Dave sat next to me. I started Skype and opened the group chat. Moments later, both my kids' faces appeared in their little boxes.

"Hi, Mom! Hi…Dave?" Sam said.

Jason just waved. "Yep. That's Dave, Sis."

"Hello," Dave was hesitant.

I just grinned. "He was here, so I invited him in. You should probably get to know him because I think he's going to be around for a while."

"Cool beans!" my daughter said. "What's been happening?"

While Jason and Dave listened in, I filled Sam in on the week. There was no way I could have been honest with her without telling her of our family's gift, so I had to tell her about that, too. Dave knew this was difficult for me and put his arm around my shoulders in silent support.

Before she could say a word, Jason chimed in. "I have something to tell you, too, Sis, so shut up a minute while I get this out." Then he proceeded to tell her about the abilities he'd inherited from his father.

When he'd finished, Sam was quiet. The she looked directly at the screen. "Anything special about you, Dave?"

"Nope. I'm plain-vanilla human."

"Good. I'm going to get off now, because I have a lot of processing to do. Mom, Jay, I'll text you tomorrow." Her little box went black.

"Well. That went well," Jason said.

"You think she'll be okay with all this?" I asked.

"Sam's the most resilient of all of us," he replied. "It'll take her a while to wrap her head around it, but yeah. She'll be fine. We probably won't hear from her tomorrow, though. Probably not until Sunday. She'll need some downtime from work and a lot of wine first."

I sighed. "I didn't want to dump it all on her, but there was no way to tell her what happened this week without it. Why'd you tell her about you?"

Dave squeezed my shoulder. "Because it's better to get it all out in the open. Otherwise, she'd eventually figure out someone was holding something back and feel resentful."

"What he said," my son opined. "She'll be okay, Mom. Really. I'm going to get off, too. You two enjoy the rest of your evening…together. Alone. Without me there." He winked, and his box went black, too.

I signed off, too, and closed the lid on my laptop. I took a huge swig of my wine, which emptied the glass. Dave retrieved the bottle from the island counter and refilled it before sitting next to me again, putting his arm back around my shoulders.

"You okay?" he asked.

"I think so. I really didn't want to tell Sam, but on the other hand, there was no way not to."

"She'll figure it out. If she's like your son, she'll eventually accept it as an *is*, and things will be back to normal between you two in no time."

"Oh, I know. Jay was right – she really is the most resilient of us all. It's just…I don't know."

"I know Jay said for us to enjoy the rest of the evening, but I do need to go. Tomorrow's a work day."

I made a quick decision and snuggled deeper into him. "You could stay here tonight."

He sat up and gave me an incredulous look. "You're sure? I mean, we've only known each other less than two weeks. And your husband hasn't been gone a year. I haven't even given you a proper kiss yet. Not that I haven't wanted to, mind you."

I took matters into my own hands – and lips. We parted, a little breathlessly, a minute later. "It feels right. I'm sure."

I rose and pulled him up from the sofa. We walked in silence, and when we got to the bedroom, I found the bed already occupied. "Out," I said. "No audience."

Cooper nudged Patches with his nose before hopping off the bed. "*Come on. They're going to make babies.*"

She followed him off the bed. "*They are? They need the bed to do that?*"

I chuckled as I closed the door. At Dave's questioning look, I told him what they'd said. He got a concerned look on his face.

"Is that still a possibility? I, uh, haven't carried a condom in my wallet for years."

I kissed him again. "No. I had my tubes tied after Sam. We're good." I started unbuttoning his shirt.

Time stopped. It could have been an hour, a day, or a week. I only knew the bliss of being loved and giving love.

I was nestled in his arms, toying with the hair on his chest, basking in the afterglow. It had been, well, never, since I had actually "made love" instead of just "having sex."

"You didn't bat an eye when Jason told Sam of his abilities," I said into his chest.

"I knew," he murmured into my hair. "He told me the day we went to the range. It was a warning, he said. He wanted me to know he could almost literally read me like a book and that there would be hell to pay if he felt I was being false with you."

"Good kid," I said.

There was a scratching at the bedroom door. I looked over Dave's chest at the bedside clock. "Duty calls," I announced. "It's feeding time."

I reluctantly rose from the warmth of his arms and opened the door. Cooper and Patches looked up at me expectantly. "*We're hungry,*" they said in unison.

"I know," I said as I went into the kitchen. Dave followed, and while I fed the animals, he put the morning coffee together.

"Do you mind if I change the time it's set to go off?" he asked. "I'll have to go home to shower and change before my shift."

"No. Change it to whenever you need. I can set the alarm for you, too."

"That I don't need. I am, sadly, usually awake before the sun rises. Unless I've been exhausted from the day – or night – before." This last was said with a sidelong glance at me.

"I'll set the alarm," I replied with a grin.

I woke with the alarm the next morning, still curled up next to Dave. I'd left the bedroom door open, and my queen-sized bed was almost overflowing between two humans, a large dog, and a smaller cat.

"Good morning," Dave said after he'd slapped the top of the alarm clock several times to stop it beeping. He kissed me gently. "How did you sleep?"

"Like a baby," I said after I'd kissed him back. "You don't snore, and you don't move much. I only woke up when Patches tried to worm between us. How'd you sleep?"

He laughed. "Soundly. I, uh, got quite a bit of exercise last night. And I do snore, but Amy said it was really quiet. Obviously, it wasn't loud enough to bother you."

We rose. I put on my bathrobe; Dave pulled his pants on. I admired the view as I followed him to the kitchen. He didn't have an athletic body, *per se*, and was slightly soft around the middle, but his shoulders, arms, and butt were still tight.

We drank the first cup of coffee standing on the front porch, watching the sun rise above the trees.

"It's going to be a lovely day," he said. "What are you going to do?"

"Go get my seeds and seedlings and get them into the garden. I'm about a week behind schedule. I also have to stop at the pet store to get a carrier for Patches. I'm taking both in tomorrow – Cooper to get his stitches out, and she needs a checkup."

"After that?"

"I don't know. Read? Think? I still haven't figured out what I want to be when I grow up."

He kissed the top of my head. "Whatever you decide to do to fill your time, you'll be brilliant at it. I'm certain. I have to finish dressing and go if I want to be on time for my shift."

He went back in the house and returned a few minutes later, dressed like the law enforcement officer he was. With the donning of his uniform, his demeanor changed slightly, to that of someone in authority.

"I'll call you tonight, okay?" he said after he'd kissed me thoroughly.

I nodded and watched as he got in his truck and after turning around, disappeared down the drive.

"*He is a nice man*," Cooper said from the bottom of the steps. "*He likes you better than your other mate, too.*"

"What do you mean he likes me better? And *other* mate?"

"*He is…softer? Toward you. And yes, mate. You smell right when you are together, as mates should. More right than the other.*"

I didn't want relationship advice from my dog, but as I watched the news then showered, I thought about what he'd said. I couldn't argue with the fact that being around Dave felt *right*, as Cooper had put it. However, it was still early. I'd revisit the *rightness* a few months down the road.

Three weeks later…

Dave and I were having a leisurely morning, sitting on the deck in our robes (he'd bought one to leave at my house), talking about the garden and my plans to put a multi-level fountain in the middle as drinking water for the wild critters, when we heard a car pull into the drive. He immediately went into 'cop mode,' motioning me to stay where I was while he answered the door.

A moment later, I heard him say, loud enough for me to hear, "Tyler, what are you doing here?"

I heard a murmur, then the men moved into the kitchen where I heard a cupboard door open and the sounds of a cup of coffee being poured. Then both men appeared on the deck.

Dave sat next to me on the glider, and Sheriff Danforth put his mug on a side table before sitting on one of the chairs, pulling it around to face me.

"Hi, Sheriff," I said. "What brings you here?"

"A proposition," he said, looking sidelong at Dave.

"Yes?"

"After the events of a month ago, I've been talking with friends in the surrounding departments and even a couple of folks in the GBI. We're all concerned about, um, paranormal activity. Especially activity we can't see with our own eyes.

"Although that was the first time anyone was hurt or killed, there *have* been incidents we couldn't explain. Of course, no one wanted to talk about them because it'd make us look like idiots, right? But once all that shit, excuse me, went down, we all started talking. At least, to each other.

"We decided we needed someone who could see stuff we couldn't. So we all looked at our budgets and came up with a couple of dollars to pay an independent consultant when we need one.

"You're the only person I know who can see what I can't. No one else knew anyone. I told them I knew someone…*without* mentioning your name, but they were all on board. There's a consulting job for you if you want it."

"Doing what?" I asked.

"Going to wherever something weird happens in north Georgia and telling us what you see or can find out. If plain humans can handle it, we will. If we can't, we'll rely on you to tell us what to do."

"She's not doing this alone," Dave interjected. "It wouldn't be fair to put her into a LEO situation without any training. It could be dangerous."

"I'm aware of that," the sheriff replied. "Which is why you'll be detailed to her if she's needed. You're the only one I know who's been up close and personal with other beings besides her. I can do without a watch commander at times. I can't do without someone like her. The weird stuff seems to be increasing in frequency. We need to be able to respond, which we can't right now, because we don't know what, who, or how."

"What sort of weird stuff are we talking about? I presume it's not bloodless bodies," I said.

"Weird, as in theft or vandalism where security cameras don't seem to pick up anything, or a couple of security guards falling asleep when five minutes earlier, they said they were wide awake. That's most of it, at least right now."

"My dog has to come with me," I stated. "He's helped a lot, and his nose is much better than mine."

Sheriff Danforth gave me a curious look. "Would you be willing to undergo K-9 training?"

"My knees aren't in good enough shape to go traipsing through the woods on search and rescue, if that's what you're thinking. But if that's what would be needed to be able to take him with me, then I suppose so."

"I wasn't thinking about search and rescue, although we can always use more help there. Technically, it's a two-year course, and the dog is usually younger than I think yours is. But I can pick and choose the courses you'd take to get you at least partially certified in just a few months. After that, I can get him an official vest."

"Can I think about it?" I asked.

"Of course! This is a request, not an order."

"How far would I have to drive?"

"Right now, it's only four counties…Towns, Union, Fannin, and Gilmer. So, less than an hour most times, unless someone screws up on the road between Blairsville and Hiawassee, which does happen with alarming frequency. We're hoping to find other people like you who can help in other counties," he paused. "You haven't asked about the money."

"And I'm not going to," I replied. "That doesn't concern me. I know budgets are stretched thin and it won't be much. I just want to think about it, to see if I'm interested."

"Understood." Sheriff Danforth rose, draining his coffee mug. "You know how to get hold of me when you decide. *Or* Dave can just tell me." He looked between us, noting, probably not for the first time, that Dave was in a bathrobe. He chuckled. "It'll probably be the latter."

"It won't," Dave asserted. "She'll make her decision and let both of us know." He got up, too, presumably to walk the sheriff to the door.

"One more thing," Sheriff Danforth said, turning toward me. "Call me Tyler. Everyone else does." He smiled and walked into the house.

I heard more quiet conversation before the front door opened and closed and a car started up. Dave returned to the deck with the coffeepot, refilling both our cups.

He sat next to me again and put his arm around my shoulders, moving the glider back and forth with his foot. "So, what do you think? Does it sound interesting? There's no shame in saying no if it's not."

"I have no idea," I replied truthfully. "I'm still getting used to this *gift*. Oh, sure, it's cool to be able to converse with my dog, especially when I want him to do something he isn't interested in. Or convincing Patches to go in the carrier without a fight.

"But the rest? I mean, come on. Vampires? Gnomes? *Fairies?* It's still really weird."

"And it isn't for me?" he squeezed my shoulder. "While I'll admit I saw some strange stuff in Atlanta, this is really the first time I've been up close and personal with it. Now, I'm listening to one side of a conversation and seeing garden gnomes come to life.

"Not that that's a bad thing, mind you," he said hastily. "I don't love you *only* for the oddities you've exposed me to."

I snuggled into him. "It's been a whirlwind month, hasn't it? But if it weren't for that crazy vampire, we might never have met. I'd thank him if I could."

My phone rang. When I looked to see who it was, the screen indicated it was a Facetime call from my daughter. I'd not heard a peep from her in three weeks, not since that Skype call where my son and I had clued her into our family's oddities. Nor had she joined us on our weekly chat. I had been worried but at the same time, trying to give her space. I looked at Dave before I answered.

"Hi Sweetie!" I said, trying to keep the trepidation out of my voice.

"I owe you an apology," she said without preamble. "I should have called or texted or something long before this."

"You had a lot to take in," I said gently. "I didn't mean to dump it all on you, but I had to. Otherwise, the rest of the story would have made no sense. I didn't know Jay was going to tell you about himself, either."

"I know," she sighed. "It's not that I don't believe in that stuff. I've seen enough on the internet to know it exists. I just didn't think it'd be right in my own family, you know?"

"Is that Dave's shoulder I see? He's there?"

Dave took the phone from me and looked at it. "Yes. It's me. Get used to my presence."

He handed the phone back so Sam was looking at me again. "Dave. You're okay with Mom being…whatever she is? And Jay, too?"

He chuckled, and although she couldn't see him, her face relaxed a bit. "If I wasn't, would I be here, sitting on your Mom's deck in a bathrobe?"

I blushed. "TMI," I said under my breath. Or at least I thought I'd said it quietly. Apparently not.

"Oh, Mom," Sam chided, her eyes twinkling. "You think we don't know what's going on? I had a long conversation with my brother last night. Like, two hours long. He filled me in on your *beau* and the fact that he approved of him. *And* that you were probably getting properly laid for the first time in your life."

I blushed again. "Samantha Ann Mackay!" I blustered. "These are things parents and children shouldn't discuss. At least this parent and her children. What's been happening in New York?"

Changing the subject was my best defense. I felt Dave shaking with laughter next to me. I elbowed him and listened as Sam detailed what she's been doing with clients and girlfriends. She'd had a second date with Jim, the guy she'd met at the gym, and decided two was enough. The guy was *boring*, she said.

Twenty minutes later, we hung up. She promised to be on the Skype call on Tuesday. I was relieved she was back to her perky self.

"Resilient, Jay said," Dave hugged me closer. "She certainly is that.

"So what are we going to do today?"

"I have no idea," I replied. "Right now, sitting here with you, drinking coffee, and looking out at the garden and woods is enough."

Just as I'd finished my sentence, Cooper came bounding out of the woods and barreled onto the deck. "*Come quick,*" he called.

I stood, concerned at his urgency. "What's wrong, Coop?"

"*A fox and a raccoon are arguing about who gets to use a den. If someone doesn't stop them, it's going to get ugly fast.*"

"That's not something I should intervene in."

Dave stood, too. "What's going on?"

I told him what Cooper had told me.

Dave looked at my dog. "She's right. The fox and raccoon have to sort it out themselves. Just because she *can* speak to animals doesn't mean she *should.*"

I reiterated what he'd said for Cooper's benefit.

"*But they'll hurt each other! You don't want anyone to get hurt!*"

"Calm down, Coop," I admonished. "I will not interfere in the natural order of things, which is what this spat is all about. I doubt it'll go beyond arguing, though. Most foxes don't care where their den is. She'll go somewhere else, probably before I could get dressed and get out there."

I had done some reading about wild animals and their habits when so many of them convened under my house, wanting to know what I might possibly face. I had been grateful they'd called a truce. Otherwise, it would have been a literal bloodbath, with no neat vampire eating.

Cooper plopped on the deck with a huff, looking up at me with his puppy dog eyes. "*You interfere when Patches and I disagree.*"

"That's different," I told him. "If I didn't, you two would make a mess of each other and my house."

"*If you say so*," he grudged.

We both sat back on the glider. Dave chuckled. "It seems your dog has appointed you as a wild critter arbiter."

"Not happening," I said, picking up my coffee cup again. "I'll help where I can, like when that raccoon got caught in plastic, but refereeing a dispute? Not my job."

"Speaking of," Dave said. "We need to talk about Tyler's proposition. I'm not in favor – it could be dangerous, even with me or Sorenson there."

"You don't get to decide. I do," I retorted. "And I'm seriously considering trying it *once* just to see if I like it. I need to fill some time, Dave. I don't want a regular job, but I do want to feel productive at something other than having a nice garden to play in.

"I think I've proven I can handle weird situations," I continued. "As long as I have someone bigger than me and with a badge as backup, it might be interesting on occasion."

Dave cleared his throat. "You'll likely have your own badge, probably from my department since Tyler is spearheading this. It's the only way other agencies will give you any respect. And up here? You'll need every bit of authority Tyler can give you. Female LEOs are rare as hen's teeth in the mountain counties, and it truly is a 'good ol' boy network.'"

"*Are* there any female officers?" I asked, now a little wary of getting into any arguments about women's abilities.

"Only two patrol officers that I know of, down in Dahlonega. There are several female dispatchers, though."

"Hmmm," I mused. I thought about it for a bit. Except for the gnomes and their misogynistic ways, the men I'd met thus far (with the exception, of course, of Ranger Doyle) had treated me with respect. On the other hand, I'd heard too many stories of the opposite. While I disliked being treated as less than a man, it might be an interesting way to show some 'good ol' boys' that women are good for more than cooking, cleaning, and having babies. Especially since I had an ability most of them didn't.

"Cooper," I looked at my dog. "What would you think about helping officers like Dave catch bad guys…like the gnomes and such?"

His ears perked up. *"Like last year, when you asked me to follow that trail of blood?"*

I laughed. Dogs' sense of time always amused me. "That, or maybe stand on a gnome like you did so I could tie him up."

He lowered his ears at the mention of the gnome. *"But I might get hurt again. You might get hurt. That would not be good."*

"I won't lie to you. That is a possibility. But sometimes doing the right thing means going into danger. We won't be alone, though. Dave or someone else like him would be with us."

"If you think it would be a good thing to do, then I will help," Cooper said.

I made up my mind. "I'm going to try it," I announced. "At least once. Maybe I won't be able to help at all. Or maybe I won't like it. But it's not painting or making jewelry, which I don't think I'm cut out to do."

Dave threw back his head and let out a deep belly laugh. "I never saw you as an artist, no offense. But you just *had* to pick the oddest job I've ever heard of."

"Ellen Mackay, Paranormal Criminal Hunter has an interesting ring to it, don't you think?" I snuggled into his side.

He laughed again, then handed me his phone. "Tyler's number two on speed dial."

"Dave?" Tyler said when he answered.

"No, it's Ellen Mackay," I took a breath and dove off the deep end. "I'd like to take you up on your offer."

ACKNOWLEDGEMENTS

My thanks to Rachel Thompson for Cooper's name. I haven't owned a dog in more decades than I care to count and she was a pug cross, smaller, even, than a couple of our cats. I hit a wall trying to come up with a name for a dog more than five times Puggins' size and Rachel saved the day.

After you've looked at a manuscript probably hundreds of times, you fail to see the trees for the forest. As always, Laura Perry, editor extraordinaire, saved my bacon writing-wise.

Profound thanks to my three Ks and an R: Karla, Kate, Keith, and Rowan, those brave souls who read an unedited draft. Their constructive criticism made this a better book.

Last but not least, thanks and love to my husband, Pete. He lets me do this odd thing called writing without complaint – even when dinner is late because of it.

AUTHOR'S NOTES

While I have changed the restaurant name (mostly because those change so often, anyway), every place mentioned in this book exists. Blue Ridge, Georgia, is a *lovely* small town, surrounded by *gorgeous* mountain scenery. If you have the chance, I highly recommend visiting at some point.

The odd house existed, too. It was one of the first houses we looked at when we decided to move to the mountains. Unfortunately, we didn't have Ellen's resources to make it not-so-weird – I loved the property. Thanks to the miracle of fiction, I could remodel the house to suit me!

And a request: I'm an indie author. The best way to get word out about my books is through *you*, the reader. If you like this book (or any other author's, for that matter), please leave a review wherever you bought it, on Goodreads, or on social media. It helps. Thank you!

ALSO BY DEBORAH J. "DJ" MARTIN

<u>Nonfiction</u>
Herbs: Medicinal, Magical, Marvelous!
A Green Witch's Formulary
Baneful! 95 of the World's Worst Herbs
A Green Witch's Cupboard

<u>Fiction</u>
Ogre's Assistant Series:
Stressed!
Upheaval!
Transformation!
Immortal Spirit

ABOUT THE AUTHOR

A semi-retired accountant, Master Herbalist, author, and witch, Deborah J. "DJ" Martin abandoned frozen Minnesota many moons ago and now lives in the woods of the southern Appalachian Mountains with her husband, four cats, and numerous woodland creatures. If you can't find DJ in the garden or visiting her grandchildren, check Facebook http://www.facebook.com/authordjmartin, Twitter @authordjmartin, or her website http://www.authordjmartin.com.